Born in Tasmania and now living in Sydney, Susan Geason is a freelance writer and books editor of the *Sun-Herald* newspaper. Educated in Australia and Canada, where she did an MA in political theory, she has been a researcher, journalist and government policy adviser. This is her fourth novel.

WILDFIRE

Susan Geason

An Arrow Book
published by
Random House Australia Pty Ltd
20 Alfred Street, Milsons Point, NSW 2061

Sydney   New York   Toronto
London   Auckland   Johannesburg
and agencies throughout the world

First published in 1995

National Library of Australia
Cataloguing-in-Publication Data

Geason, Susan, 1946– .
Wildfire.
ISBN 0 09 183216 0.
I.Title.
A823.3

Typeset by Midland Typesetters, Maryborough
Printed by Griffin Paperbacks, Adelaide
Production by Vantage Graphics, Sydney

'Throw Your Arms Around Me' written by Hunters & Collectors
(Human Frailty Pty Ltd/Mushroom Music)

This book is dedicated to the memory of all the girls and women who didn't make it home.

The author wishes to thank Detective Sergeant Peter Scott for his help with police matters; Patrick Geason, Grace Ditton, Susan Marshall, Susan Woods Giordano and Cate Jones for critical readings; and Ron Clarke for his consistent encouragement. And, of course, Jane Palfreyman and Julia Stiles from Random House for backing this book and Carl Harrison-Ford for the fine detail.

The Good Samaritan

It is the middle of December, and life in Sydney has slowed to a crawl. Anyone who can afford a package deal, a holiday house or even a tent in a camping area, has fled north or south. Pale-skinned Europeans and Asians flood in to take their place in the sun. Some people have to work, though.

Lisa Broderick steps off the train, her pretty face glowing. That pale, fine redhead's skin, and the wine at dinner have brought a high colour to her cheeks and a sparkle to the dark blue eyes. She's spent most of the trip standing up near the door of the noisy old red rattler, desperate for a breath of air.

Cooled by harbour breezes, the city was bearable, but out here at the end of the line the air is as thick as treacle. Peeling her damp cotton dress away from her thighs, she scans the platform and the parking lot. No white station wagon, no father.

The sound of a squabble attracts her attention. Down the platform, a young woman is struggling with a drunken man. Mistaking it for an attack, Lisa starts forward, but when the girl shouts 'Give me the keys, Garry! You're drunk!', realises it's a lovers' quarrel. It has frightened her, though, and she discovers that her fists are clenched.

The boyfriend wins the argument by breaking away and sprinting to the car park, where he fumbles with the keys in the door of a dusty blue four-wheel drive, wrenches open the door, clambers in and starts the wagon. The girl follows reluctantly, and the youth revs the engine. Sullenly, she climbs in and slams the door, and they drive off with a screech of tyres. Engrossed in their private drama, they haven't even registered Lisa Broderick's existence.

She begins to pace, then gives up and sets out for the nearest phone box—the family car must have broken down again. If worse comes to worst, she can always walk: her parents' house is only fifteen minutes away. Avoiding the shadow-ridden car park, she keeps to the main street. The town centre is as quiet as a country graveyard. She isn't frightened yet, but when she hears a car approaching from behind, tenses instinctively and looks around for support. Not a soul. She keeps walking, staring rigidly ahead. Her heart thuds.

When the car slows to a crawl beside her, the adrenalin surges and she gets ready to run. But when the driver winds down his window and says: 'Lost?' she breathes again: she knows the voice.

She looks directly at him for the first time: 'I'm waiting for my father. Something must have happened to him.'

'Want a lift?'

A long-standing uneasiness around this man, something skewed about him, makes her hesitate. It is this instinctive revulsion that has made her so unfailingly nice to him in the past. Guilt.

'But he might be on his way,' she says. 'He'll worry if I'm not here.'

'You can direct me. That way we'll run into him.'

She cannot fault the logic. It isn't just the fear of hanging about the desolate streets at the mercy of cars full of drunks that sways her; it is also the prospect of hurting this Good Samaritan's feelings. Sensing his advantage, he forces the issue by opening the passenger door. An enticing blast of cold air gushes out. Taking one last look around for her father's battered old Ford, she gets into the car.

Arriving five minutes later, upset and angry at all machines that let people down, particularly cars,

Graham Gallagher drives into the station car park. The platform is deserted. He rolls down the windows to catch even the hint of a breeze, and hunkers down to wait. There is no-one to ask if the train had come in, as the Government has decided it's too expensive to staff stations after peak hour. After half an hour, he admits defeat. The 12.05 was the last train, and it's unlikely to be this late.

She's missed it, he prays.

Just in case, he searches the car park, checks the phone box and every doorway and alley in the shopping centre. On the way home he drives slowly, half expecting to see Lisa, hot and irritable, hiking the suburban mile. He imagines himself blowing the horn, his daughter looking up, frowning, then breaking into her big smile.

Before he wakes her mother, he rings the hospital where Lisa works, and all the friends who might have put her up for the night, even though it would be unlike her not to call. Nothing. It is only after talking to his sleepy, then alarmed ex-son-in-law, that he begins to fear the worst. At 2 a.m. he wakes his wife and calls the police. The nightmare has begun.

The Devil You Know

Something warm had reached out from him and curled around Rachel Addison like smoke the very first time she saw Michael Ross. Something had snapped her head around, although he was as quiet as a cat, the moment he walked in. She knew what it was, but tucked it away, like an unread love letter, in a place she might visit later.

What she saw was a slender, dark young man of about thirty with closely cropped black hair, high cheekbones and intelligent, glittering black eyes. There should have been a gold ring in his ear.

A pirate, she thought. Or an ancient Egyptian.

He seemed enigmatic, self-contained as an egg, radiating the seductive aroma of self-confidence. Rachel smiled briefly and bent over her work. Looking was as far as she went these days.

Standing in the doorway, not as certain at this

moment as Rachel thought, Mike Ross saw the woman's head lift even though she could not have heard him over the racket in the room. The bright green eyes flashed as she took him in, but were quickly veiled by the long dark lashes. Only then he noticed the white skin, the chiselled features, the short, straight nose and the kinky hair escaping in springy tendrils from a knot at the back of her neck. Afterwards he had trouble recalling anything but her eyes; that bright green look burned out his memory circuits like a lightning strike.

He asked for directions and left. Rachel felt the absence and her shoulders relaxed. Nobody in the room had noticed, but they seldom saw anything in her face but an entirely appropriate level of interest or concern.

Behind her back, her colleagues speculated about her sex life, about frigidity and lesbianism. There were no photographs of men, babies or pets on her desk—she usually had flowers, though: gardenias, violets, freesias, very occasionally daphne—and the only personal messages had been from an aunt. Even that had stopped months ago. Rachel had later taken a couple of days compassionate leave, and a rumour about a stroke sped through the office.

Rachel Addison had been seen working out at a gym and someone said she practised a strenuous type of yoga. They suspected she could do things

6

with her body they couldn't even imagine, though they occasionally tried.

Quickly realising she was getting a reputation for aloofness, Rachel had expanded her store of small talk into queries about their families and weekends, but she preferred to discuss business. And she was very good at business. Even though most of them had opposed the decision to include a psychologist in the homicide team, they now had to agree she was a valuable addition. She had a way of reading people, absorbing their fears and insecurities, their weaknesses, through her pores; all without formal interrogation, without raising her voice, without threats. When suspects or witnesses bridled, she gentled them like spooked horses. People wanted to tell her things, to please her. Only the very hard cases recognised the danger and shut down, excluding her.

Occasionally they wondered whether the technique was simply something she'd learned from a psychology textbook, or if there was more to it—some weird Eastern philosophy, maybe.

Detective Constable First Class Rachel Addison and Detective Sergeant Mike Ross, both members of the Homicide Squad of Major Crimes in the North-West Region, were assigned to the Lisa Broderick murder investigation. Positions on the team had been hotly contested: this was going to be a high-profile investigation, an opportunity to shine. There was talk of codenaming the investigation Redhead, until Rachel pointed out that this might distress the victim's parents. It was now named Task Force Nightingale, the significance of which had to be explained to some of the younger members. Privately, Rachel thought Florence Nightingale would have had her work cut out whipping some of these lads into shape.

Mike Ross was already in the command room, clutching a coffee and catching up on scuttlebutt, when Rachel entered. By this time they'd been introduced and she knew he'd been transferred from Special Branch. She nodded to the others, then to him, and sat down, crossing her legs. The soft, insinuating hiss of the nylon hose sent a shiver up his spine.

The assembled police officers soon exhausted their sketchy knowledge of the Broderick case and turned to gossip, some of it about the unsolved murders of several backpackers in a national park over a three-year period. Everybody had their theories. Some believed two men must have been involved; others held to the lone killer thesis. Though nobody sought her opinion, Rachel thought that one man with a gun could easily have controlled the victims this serial killer had chosen. They were middle-class kids, brought up to believe the best of people. If they'd suspected their driver was a bit strange, they wouldn't have known how to extricate themselves without making a fuss and maybe hurting his feelings. Then, suddenly, it would have been too late.

The babble of comment was interrupted by the entry of Chief Inspector Bob McDonald, who was leading the investigation. He quickly got down to brass tacks, assuming they'd all heard the morning news and knew that the body of Lisa Broderick, a young nurse, had been found by a man walking his dog at dawn in a paddock on the western outskirts of the city. The woman had probably been abducted from a nearby railway station after arriving on the last train. The media were baying for blood.

Photos of the crime scene were passed around. Even Lisa Broderick's own mother would have trouble recognising the girl in these pictures. She'd been brutally beaten about the face and body; her eyes were swollen and cut, and her face and chest were black and blue. Her breasts and abdomen had been stabbed repeatedly, with frenzied force. The post-mortem was scheduled to take place later that day, so they had little forensic evidence to go on, but it was safe to assume the victim had been raped.

Rachel surveyed the photos with her usual mixture of rage, pity and disgust. She must have been unconscious when he stabbed her, she thought. It was a prayer.

Mike Ross watched Rachel covertly as she stared at a photograph. What was she thinking? The victim was about her age...

Rachel's face was unreadable, but then she touched the photograph with her finger (it was a stab wound on the girl's left breast, over her heart), and the back of his neck prickled.

The Chief told them Lisa Broderick was twenty-six, divorced—so they'd have to check out the ex-husband—and had moved home to live with her parents recently when her female flatmate had gone overseas.

'They're taking it hard,' he said. 'They blame themselves for not picking her up at the station in time.'

'Why didn't they?' asked Dick Kellett, an old-style, hard-man copper with the soul of a hanging judge.

'The car wouldn't start. Her father got there about ten minutes late.'

Ten minutes, thought Rachel. All those years of love and care thrown away in ten minutes.

Someone suggested she might have set out to walk home and been abducted on the way. The Chief shrugged: 'We don't know. Nobody's come forward with a sighting so far.'

'Would she have hitch-hiked rather than wait around?' asked Mike Ross.

'Her parents say not. Her mother says she'd

made her promise years ago she'd never hitch-hike.'

'Girls promise their parents all sorts of things,' said Kellett, voicing their thoughts.

'What if it was a gang rape that got out of control?' asked Ray Larsen.

'Let's hope so,' said Kellett. 'If it was a bunch of drunks, one of them will eventually crack and spill his guts to his girlfriend; then she'll tell her girlfriend, and eventually someone will tell us. In the meantime, we'll just have to wait for the results of the post-mortem.'

'Maybe she got a lift from someone she knew,' suggested Rachel.

They turned to look at her: they could still be surprised by a female voice in a crime conference. 'It's more often the devil you know… ' she added.

It was a criminological truism, as well as one of the great paradoxes of human nature, that lovers and friends were a greater threat to women than strangers.

The paddock where Lisa Broderick's body had been found was part of a stud farm, one of the last original rural properties left in the area. It was doubly isolated from housing estates by a council reserve. The murderer had chosen well. Not only were the owner's family and two employees the only people to use the road to the farm regularly, but on the night of the murder the two stable-hands had left for home before 6 p.m., and the farmer and his family had been tucked up in bed by ten.

By the time the Nightingale team arrived in convoy to inspect the crime scene, the body had been taken to the morgue, but scientists were still working in a roped-off area where it had been found. A line of uniformed police were scouring the paddock for clues, watched by a couple of skittish horses in a nearby field. Occasionally something would spook the handsome animals, and they would thunder around the adjoining field, providing a soundtrack to the searchers' grim task and adding a surreal note to the situation.

The Chief of Detectives from Crossley, nose severely out of joint because the investigation had been turned over to regional headquarters, briefed the team. He wasn't encouraging. When they'd reconstructed the crime, they'd found the place where the killer had dragged Lisa Broderick across the barbed wire, leaving behind a tiny piece of fabric from her sundress. They had also discovered tyre marks and an oil leak in the gravel on the side of the road—though they could have come from another vehicle—but so far they had no clues to his identity. There were drag marks in the long grass, but because the weather was so hot and dry and the ground hard as iron, no footprints had turned up.

Trying to concentrate on this discouraging litany, Rachel fought a sense of unreality. In the middle of the morning, under a cloudless blue sky, with the sun beating down, birds clamouring from gum trees, the sound of pounding horses' hoofs, and the smell of eucalyptus, dry grass and the faintest tang of manure, it was almost impossible to imagine the savage scene that had been played out here. At night, the field would have been deadly quiet and sinister. She tried to put herself into Lisa Broderick's shoes, to imagine her state of mind when she realised what was going to happen to her.

Mike Ross, who didn't miss much, saw Rachel shudder and realised what she was doing. He hoped she wasn't too sensitive to atmosphere. A certain amount of imagination was invaluable in a copper, but too much usually led to a crack-up or a career change.

When the duties were handed out, Mike and Rachel were assigned the hospital where Lisa Broderick had worked. Their eyes met briefly, then veered away. The rest of the men were relieved. They wouldn't know how to behave with this one: she was too well educated, and too cool. Pleasant enough, but you never knew what she was thinking. And you'd have to watch everything you said:

Rachel Addison wouldn't put up with the sexual banter and off-colour jokes reluctantly tolerated by the other female officers.

Rachel knew all this, but it didn't worry her. She didn't care if she struck them dumb; anything was better than listening to their opinions about politics and women. Mike Ross was an unknown quantity, but she already knew he was no chatterbox.

Mike Ross wondered what he was in for, and what it would be like partnering a smart and confident woman. The female political staffers he'd worked with in Parliament House on his last assignment had opened his eyes. They were all intelligent, savvy, tough, attuned to political realities. Some treated him like a fellow professional, a few with careless contempt. None had showed any desire to socialise with a policeman. The experience had taught him his true place in the social order, and it had been a tough lesson. But it had also made him a much better cop.

'It could be anybody,' he remarked, as they walked to the car park.

'Let's hope it was a rejected lover,' said Rachel. 'Otherwise we've got a mad dog with a taste for blood and a million and a half suspects.'

3

This Close to Chaos

The hospital, in an inner-city suburb thick with coffee shops catering to an arty crowd, was famous for its high-tech medicine, especially advanced heart surgery techniques; but more recently it had become a centre for AIDS research and treatment. Leaving their car outside the new wing, the police found the reception desk and were pointed at the Director's office.

The man himself was big, handsome, imposing, inclined to condescend. Rachel chose not to take it personally. Except for a few Catholic institutions, hospitals were still strict hierarchies controlled by male doctors, so Dr Hardwick and his ilk expected to be flattered and obeyed. From the staleness of the air and the lack of ashtrays, Rachel deduced the doctor was also a closet smoker.

'You don't mind if I call in our Public Affairs Manager, do you?' he said. It wasn't a question.

'He's the one who'll be handling all our dealings with the media on this unfortunate business.'

Unfortunate business, thought Rachel. Evidently the hospital regarded the murder more as a public relations problem than a human tragedy.

Summoned on the intercom, a smooth, thirtyish man in an expensive, understated suit entered and was introduced as Greg Jones. Jones's sympathetic manner had been honed by years of dealing with tricky life-and-death issues, distraught relatives, ethics committees, rich donors and determined lawyers. Rachel thought him a fake.

His face a serious concerned mask, the media man shook hands with both of them.

Not bad, thought Rachel. Didn't miss a beat. Some men got confused when a woman proffered her hand.

Jones rapidly reverted to type, however, automatically addressing himself to the male officer.

Hardwick, who'd been acting as if Lisa Broderick had gone and got herself killed just to interrupt his busy schedule, had calmed down considerably when the professional minder arrived. Protected now, he was prepared to talk about the unfortunate business. Though it was clear he knew absolutely nothing about a lowly registered nurse, he nevertheless expected a superhuman police effort to clear up the case. Finally, he turned them over to the PR man, who had organised interviews with Lisa Broder-ick's colleagues.

'Pompous sod,' muttered Mike as Greg Jones escorted them through corridors that smelled of floor wax, disinfectant, a whiff of mould that turned out—on upward glance—to belong to a bubble of damp in the ceiling, medicines, illness and, unless Rachel missed her guess, the faint, astringent smell of marigolds on someone's bedside table. A nurse in starched white cotton wafted past trailing a wake of White Linen.

As they charged down the hallways in an authoritative phalanx, Jones told them he'd been unable to reach three staff members who'd gone on leave or could not be contacted by phone for some reason.

'They'll keep,' said Mike.

Perhaps aware of the impression his boss had made, the PR man took pains to convey his distress about the murder.

It will certainly make his life harder, thought Rachel. They'll have a recruitment crisis on their hands if we don't catch the killer.

When they reached the conference room where the interviews were to take place, Jones handed Mike a schedule, then took out a key-ring. Growing increasingly agitated, he tried key after key. Waiting in silence, Rachel absorbed the hospital's special atmosphere, compounded of equal parts despair and frightful optimism.

'Jesus Christ,' muttered Mike irritably. It occurred to Rachel that the PR man was unused to menial labour like unlocking offices, and she pondered, not for the first time, the almost feudal nature of hospitals.

Bowing to the inevitable, Greg Jones confessed that the conference room key did not appear to be on this key-ring. Rachel was almost certain she heard Mike groan.

'So how do we get the right key?' asked Mike, with exaggerated patience, and Jones—who had been secretly hoping the police would find it all too hard and take themselves off and do something useful like arresting unemployed drug addicts—sighed, pushed past them, hurried down the hall and knocked on a door.

The door opened and a heavy-set, dark man peered out into the light like a suspicious mole. Jones said something and he disappeared, emerging with a huge ring of keys, like some medieval turnkey. Apparently deciding the PR man was too inept to be allowed to drive the key-ring unassisted, the janitor shambled up the corridor. Fighting impatience, Rachel stepped back as the man pushed past her. Then came the terrifying sensation of falling into a well.

Jerked into consciousness by an acrid whiff of

smelling salts, she found herself lying on a bed in what appeared to be a hospital room. 'Ah, you're back,' said a voice. 'How are you feeling?'

She didn't know yet. Then she registered the concerned faces of a young doctor and a nurse hanging over her, and it came back: 'I fainted?'

'It seems so,' said the doctor. 'Do you make a habit of fainting, or is it just hospitals?'

Rachel was affronted. 'I've never fainted before in my life!'

Having decided she was going to live, the doctor told her she could get up as soon as she felt fit enough, advised her to have a check-up if it happened again, folded up his stethoscope and rushed away to someone who really needed him.

'You aren't...?' asked the nurse, when he'd gone.

'No,' she said. 'I'm not pregnant. I've got no idea what came over me. It was like falling into a black hole.'

'It's probably just the heat, dear,' said the motherly nurse with such compassion that Rachel had to quell a surge of self-pity. 'But you should look after yourself. You girls don't eat properly. You probably aren't getting enough iron...'

Catching Rachel's expression, she trailed off. 'Are you well enough to talk to that gorgeous hunk out there?'

Gorgeous hunk, thought Rachel bleakly. He must think I'm a dead loss.

She nodded. 'Thanks for everything.'

'Are you up to this?' asked Mike, whose initial concern had turned to irritation now that he knew it was just a fainting fit. He couldn't decide what had bothered him more—the real fear he'd felt when she collapsed, or the poor impression the police had made. They probably all thought she had a bun in the oven.

As they strode towards the conference room, he asked Rachel if she had bad memories of hospitals. She was about to say she'd never been in a hospital as a patient when she saw, unreeling like an old black and white movie, footage of herself as a small child being carried into a hospital room. She was in a man's arms, looking back. But was it a memory, a film she'd seen, or an old nightmare?

'Not that I know of,' she said.

It was an odd response, but Mike wasn't diverted: 'But what triggered it?'

I don't know, damn you, she thought. Get off my back!

But she had to admit he was a good cop; he stuck to the point like a burr. She tried to reconstruct the moment. Up until they'd reached the conference room, she'd felt fine, but after the janitor had arrived with the keys, everything was a blank.

Rachel shrugged, the sudden movement setting off a small explosion at the corner of her left eye.

'Excuse me for a minute, will you?' she said, and ran along the hall till she found a washroom, stumbled in and vomited into a lavatory bowl.

What's happening to me? she thought, rinsing her mouth and washing her face. I'm coming unglued. It must be the smell of the hospital.

Rachel's keen sense of smell had given her trouble all her life. Before menstruation and during the migraine headaches she'd suffered for years, her sense of smell became preternaturally acute. The smell of people's bodies, their perfume, car exhausts, cigarette smoke, assaulted her senses like blows—she'd once astonished a suspect by ordering him to go into another room and spit out the Juicy Fruit—but she'd never fainted before. The loss of control terrified her. Her fear was her own affair, though, and by the time she rejoined Mike she had pulled herself together.

Her partner wasn't fooled for a minute; her skin had a greenish tinge, and her eyes were almost black. He'd seen enough victims in his job to know something had shaken this self-contained, secretive woman. Given time, he'd find out what it was.

The interviews were not without their own drama.

Many of the young women who'd worked with Lisa Broderick broke down under questioning and sobbed out their sympathy for their friend, their guilt at being spared, and the fear they might be next. Rachel and Mike worked well as a team, with Mike opening the batting to win the women's confidence, and Rachel moving in with sympathy when a witness became distressed.

By all accounts, Lisa Broderick had been above reproach, a nice girl from a good family. Her first marriage had broken down, but there appeared to be no ongoing acrimony; no-one here could remember her mentioning problems with her ex-husband. She had dated several men since the divorce, but didn't seem to have a steady boyfriend.

Gratefully sipping bitter, scalding hospital tea at the end of the interrogations, Rachel and Mike compared notes.

Mike thought it had been a waste of time. 'No faults, no enemies, no boyfriend, still friends with the ex. Too perfect by half. Why her?'

Why any woman? thought Rachel. Until she knew Mike better, she would have to assume he shared many of their colleagues' casual contempt for women, so she kept her feelings to herself. Her position was tenuous: if she came across as a pro-selytising feminist, the men on the team would close ranks and she'd learn nothing. Fortunately silence came easily to Rachel. Guarding her tongue was second nature, though she'd long forgotten why.

She said: 'What I kept hearing was how nice she was to everybody, how she went out of her way for anybody who needed help or comfort. Maybe she was nice to the wrong person.'

'You mean she did a good deed for a perfect stranger and he returned the favour by hacking her to pieces?' he asked. That meant a real psychopath, a much more difficult proposition than your run-of-the-mill jealous lover. He hoped she was wrong.

'Not necessarily,' said Rachel, thinking it through while she spoke. 'What if she knew this guy, who just happens to be a killer, always on the lookout for his next victim, and something she did made her the target.'

'Like what?'

'She might have simply been polite when nobody else acknowledged his existence. Some men interpret a kind word as a come-on, especially if the woman is attractive. Lisa Broderick wasn't just attractive, she was beautiful. Sometimes these losers get obsessed and turn into stalkers, and some stalkers end up assaulting or murdering their victims. Women do it too, of course—get fixated on someone who throws them a bone and pursue them to the ends of the earth—but they don't usually kill them.'

'Thank God for small mercies,' said Mike.

Rachel wasn't listening. 'From his point of view, it would have been as if Lisa were volunteering,' she said.

Slightly stunned, Mike didn't reply. He'd wondered what it would be like partnering a psychologist, and now he was getting a taste. As they walked to the car, he said: 'Do you think you should see a doctor about that fainting?'

Rachel flushed. She'd been hoping he'd leave it alone. 'Do you?'

'It would be nice to know it was stomach flu rather than an emotional reaction to this murder,' he said, staring ahead, not wanting to embarrass her further. 'That could hamper the investigation, don't you think?'

Rachel recognised a threat when she heard one. He'd keep his mouth shut about her little episode if she could convince him it wasn't connected with Lisa Broderick's death. If she was unfit for the job—in any way—she could hold him back or let him down in a crisis. Rachel knew he was right, but it stung. The rapport they'd established in the interviews suddenly seemed illusory, normal professional teamwork: he was just a cop doing his job. Keeping the resentment out of her voice, she said: 'I'll see a doctor.'

As they were getting into the car, he sneaked a look at her face. She'd shut down on him. He discovered he didn't like it. On the drive back to police headquarters, trying to re-establish contact, he asked Rachel why she'd joined the police force.

People often asked her this. Her university friends and colleagues were highly ambivalent about the police. Several of her former teachers, who'd opposed the war in Vietnam and remembered agents provocateurs and cracked heads, were overtly hostile; to them, she was joining the enemy. Others couldn't understand why an educated, liberated woman would let herself in for the sort of sexual discrimination that had largely gone underground in professional circles in the outside world. So Rachel had given the decision long and careful thought. She tried to answer Mike honestly, but she wasn't sure she completely understood her own motives.

'I think I needed to understand evil,' she told him. 'If I understood it, I might be able to control it. It was order I wanted, I think. All my life I've had this feeling that I was this close'—she held up her hand, fingers curved like a pincer—'this close to chaos.'

Pre-empting him, she said 'Don't ask me why. Apart from losing my parents, I've led a very orderly, ordinary life. Sheltered, even. But I expect chaos. I keep waiting for things to fall apart. I don't expect the centre to hold.'

His silence was a goad: he'd be a good interrogator. 'It's not rational, it's just what I feel.'

He wanted to know more, of course, but they had arrived.

Rachel rang Katrina Westwood at home. Kate had been Rachel's doctor since her days as a shy, nervous psych student suffering from loneliness and alienation in a big city university. The doctor had been working part-time in student health and bringing up a couple of children: now she was a partner in an all-female practice, and her boys were at university.

'Can I come and see you tomorrow, Kate? It'll have to be very early, I'm afraid; I'm on the Lisa Broderick murder.'

'That poor little girl,' said the doctor, echoing every mother in the country. 'How early?'

'Seven-thirty?'

Kate groaned. She knew she needed the occasional early start to catch up on the literature and paperwork, but preferably not tomorrow. 'You don't want to come over tonight?'

'It's not that urgent,' said Rachel. 'I don't think.'

Something about the tone, and the afterthought, brought Katrina Westwood to full attention. After she'd put down the phone, she turned to her husband and said: 'Remember Rachel, the psychologist, the one who was so brilliant, the one

26

who drove the department mad because she went into the police instead of doing her PhD and teaching?'

They'd considered Rachel a defector. Kate, herself a veteran of protest marches in the sixties and no fan of the police who'd opposed them, had been appalled at first, but had come to believe that Rachel's career choice was the result of some deep-seated need for security. And having faced similar peer-group disapproval for choosing family practice over medical research, she sympathised with her friend. Like Rachel, Kate had chosen live people and real problems over abstractions.

Alec Westwood, a professor of medicine who unofficially consulted on the occasional difficult case for his wife, nodded vaguely. He recalled that Kate had been intrigued by the young Rachel Addison, convinced volcanic emotions bubbled under the disciplined exterior. He'd tended to agree with Kate's theory that the insomnia, the anxiety attacks and the nervous eczema Rachel had experienced as a teenager were a reaction to psychological trauma.

The only clue in Rachel's life story, when it emerged, was the early death of her parents in a road accident, and Kate had concluded that she was suffering from grief and a sense of abandonment. But once, when Rachel had broken up with a boyfriend who'd become violent, the doctor had caught sight of real fear in the girl. Despite their closeness, however, she'd been unable to find the key to Rachel's estrangement from the world. Perhaps now the time was right.

'Something's happened,' Kate said to her husband. 'Maybe this is it.'

Accustomed to her Delphic statements, the professor grunted and went back to his journal. He'd hear it all eventually.

That night Rachel paced the house, restless as a caged tiger, unable to settle to a book. She put on some music, but its only effect was to agitate her further. She tried television, then a mindless video, but it was all din and confusion.

This is mad, she thought, and switched off the television set.

Finally she put herself through an hour of yoga, ending with thirty minutes of breathing exercises. The activity and the discipline took the edge off the manic energy, but there was no prospect of drugless sleep when she was in this mood. She knew her insomnia was caused by anxiety: she knew she was afraid to sleep, but didn't know what it was she feared.

Unlike many doctors who'd become cautious or moralistic about hypnotics, Kate Westwood continued to prescribe sleeping pills for Rachel, reasoning that lack of sleep might tip her over the edge. Over the years the two had tried every new sleeping drug that came on the market, and were experts. Rachel was now using a brand favoured by junkies hanging out for the next fix: the irony amused her.

Even with the help of the drug, she tossed and turned for what seemed like hours. When she did sleep, fragments of the colour photographs of Lisa Broderick's body, the events at the hospital and Mike's suspicious face whirled through her dreams.

The alarm woke her at six, and as usual she was grateful for daylight. However bad the days might be, even on the homicide squad, they were never as bad as the nightmares she'd suffered all her life. At night, with the subconscious rampaging, there was no control: it was like clinging to a runaway horse. Reality was never as frightening as her imagination.

'There's absolutely nothing wrong with you, from what I can see,' pronounced Kate Westwood after a full physical examination the next morning. 'You're in excellent shape. Of course I could have further tests done if you think you might have something exotic like a brain tumour.'

Buttoning her shirt, Rachel sat down on the couch beside her doctor (Kate regarded desks as a male control mechanism, and never used them).

'We both know I haven't got a brain tumour,'

said Rachel. 'What ails me can't be cut out or zapped with chemicals. I've got something wrong with my mind, not my brain, Kate. I feel as if I'm sitting on the lid of a basket of snakes. I've always felt like that. That's what pushed me into psychology. I thought I might be able to heal myself. And I thought I had it licked. I'd decided my problem was your common or garden post-traumatic stress disorder caused by the death of my parents. There's masses of documentation. I had lots of the symptoms as a kid. But I should have grown out of it. Now I'm wondering if that diagnosis didn't mask something else, something deeper.'

Kate Westwood had been waiting for this for a very long time: 'Like what?'

Rachel shrugged. 'That's the problem. I don't know. If there is something, I can't, or won't remember it. I suspect it's something that happened before I went to live with Louise.'

'You've never mentioned this before.'

'I don't think I knew it, not consciously. But I always knew I was afraid of something, that something must have made me so desperate for order.' She paused. 'I thought I was coping…But I'm not coping any more, am I, having a fit of the vapours in front of my colleagues?'

'You think the fainting and throwing up are that significant?'

Rachel paled at the memory. 'You said yourself there's nothing physically wrong with me. So they've got to be some kind of warning that I'm getting too close...'

Rachel's posture was rigid and her eyes huge. Kate was afraid to push any harder: 'What do you want to do?'

'I have to find out what scared me so much I forgot it. I can't treat myself any more: I need professional help.'

For a woman who prized self-control highly, this was a costly admission. But they both knew the risks involved in therapy. 'Are you absolutely sure?' asked Kate. 'You're an insider, you know all the horror stories.'

When Rachel nodded, Katrina Westwood ran her mind over the psychologists and psychiatrists she knew, personally or by reputation. There were the Freudians, the Jungians, the eclectics. There were the power trippers who danced on the heads of their victims, the seducers, the crazies who needed the company of the worse off, and there were a few good and honest people doing their best.

'Persia Lawrence,' she decided.

What a wonderful name, thought Rachel. 'Tell me about her.'

'Sixtyish, got her medical degree at Sydney University, studied psychiatry in the US and Europe

31

and came back to Sydney. Super bright, humane. The Persia part of it comes from her father, who was a leading light in some explorers' society in the dim, distant past. She's tough, but trustworthy. I don't know much about her private life, except that she's single. I've never seen her with a man, or a woman for that matter. I think she's dedicated her life to science.'

'Psychiatry's hardly a science,' interrupted Rachel.

'Art, then, if it makes you happier,' replied Katrina, before returning to Persia Lawrence. 'It was a pity, really. She was a marvellous looking woman.'

'Kate! You're like those bloody policemen who say what a waste, when they see a good-looking female corpse. Every dead woman is a lost opportunity to score.'

Katrina laughed. 'You haven't changed. How do those coppers handle you when you're in your militant mode?'

'They never see me like this. My self-control is legendary. Or at least it used to be.' She stood up. 'Can you plead an emergency and get me in soon? If I blow it again, they'll drum me out of the corps as psychologically unsuitable.'

'It's as good as done,' promised the doctor, rising to show Rachel out.

When she was paying at the reception desk,

Rachel asked after Kate's boys. The doctor wrinkled her nose. 'The house reeks of testosterone, but with any luck a couple of lust-crazed women will take them off my hands before too long. Then I'll never cook another Sunday dinner as long as I live.'

They laughed and hugged and Rachel left, watched from the doorway by Kate Westwood, much more concerned than she'd let on. It was like letting a friend go over a cliff without a rope.

4

More Like a Vision
Than a Memory

In the Nightingale incident room, they were huddled over the day's tabloid headlines—'NO PROGRESS IN BRODERICK SLAYING'.

'Police baffled,' commented the task force wit, and a couple of officers laughed sourly.

'What's new?' asked Mike.

'Bugger all,' began Kellett, but he was prevented from elaborating by the ceremonial entrance of the Police Commissioner flanked by his closest advisers. All came to attention, every back stiffened with what they would have called respect, but the respect was tinged with fear, as everyone knew the big man's studied good nature could turn into lacerating sarcasm with terrifying speed. They feared his tongue the way convicts feared the lash.

'Bugger all is right,' said the Commissioner, glaring from under bushy grey eyebrows. 'It seems a maniac is loose. Vicious sex crime, nice girl, no suspects. The media are eating us for breakfast, gentlemen.'

It wasn't Lisa Broderick he cared about: the force was under attack in Parliament for corruption. They badly needed some runs on the board.

His pale wintry gaze raked them, then came to rest on Rachel. 'And lady, of course.'

The flatterers sniggered. Rachel's expression remained carefully neutral. This man could whisk her off the investigation with a word.

He let his message sink in, then said: 'You know what you have to do. Go out and do it.' With that, he turned on his heel and left, his retinue falling in behind.

Talk broke out as soon as he was safely out of earshot. The Chief Inspector let it go for a few minutes, then called the meeting to order. 'Let's get on with it.'

Kellett opened with a report on his interview with Lisa Broderick's ex-husband: a sales rep for a medical supplier, he'd been in Sydney, alone, on the night of the crime. Absolutely no alibi. 'He's got to be our best bet at the moment,' he concluded.

'Our only one, you mean,' said someone.

The forensic evidence was not promising, either. The pathologist had found sperm from only one man in Lisa Broderick's vagina, ruling out the possibility of a gang rape. The perpetrator was a secretor, but was blood type O positive like almost half the population. Some blue denim fibres had been collected at the scene, but three-quarters of the males under fifty in Sydney owned at least one pair of jeans.

At the back of the room, Rachel stole a glance at the front page of a newspaper on a desk and flinched at the sight of Tony Broderick's desolate face. He still loved his wife. Why wouldn't he? Even the old, grainy newspaper photograph of Lisa Broderick in a ball gown couldn't dampen her glow or dim the wide, trusting smile. But loving her didn't necessarily mean he hadn't killed her.

She looked up and caught Mike Ross watching her, flushed, and returned her attention to the briefing. Larsen was saying that anyone who'd dated Lisa Broderick over the past year had been grilled. So far none was a serious suspect.

'Think any of them could have done it?' asked the Chief.

'Not unless they're good actors,' replied Larsen. 'They were all pretty cut up. I think most of them were still carrying a torch. She seemed to have that effect on men.'

Rachel's attention wandered again. She was uncomfortably aware of her partner's scrutiny, and on a deeper level, the fiasco at the hospital nagged incessantly. Losing consciousness in public was unforgivable; even worse was not knowing why. Even more disturbing was the knowledge that her reaction was downright dangerous. Fainting in the face of a threat was like baring your neck to the executioner's knife.

And Rachel was embarrassed. Cool rationality was her style. She could only remember crying once—at her parents' funeral when she was four. This inability to show emotion wasn't something she broadcast, however: an innate sense of self-preservation told her some people—especially her psychologist friends and colleagues—would find it interesting. She had a horror of being discussed at dinner parties.

Mike Ross was preoccupied, too. With one ear on the proceedings, he replayed the scene in the hospital. Although he didn't know Rachel Addison well enough yet to predict how she'd act in every situation, her reaction seemed wildly out of character. What could have spooked her? It had all been so ordinary. Almost unconsciously he kept an eye on her, afraid it might happen again. But the woman who'd passed out for no apparent reason in a hospital corridor remained outwardly unmoved by the forensic evidence and a graphic reconstruction of a brutal murder. It just didn't make sense.

I'm overreacting, he thought. It was probably premenstrual tension or a hangover. It was unlikely she'd confide in him in either case.

So Mike was caught daydreaming when his turn came. Recovering quickly, he nodded to Rachel as a courtesy, and launched into a report on their conclusions about the hospital interviews.

Rachel's stomach plummeted: if he were going to expose her, it would be now. But he simply reported that Lisa Broderick seemed to have been unspoiled, despite her good looks, was kind to strays—human and animal—and as a result was universally loved.

'Not quite universally,' murmured Kellett, and a couple of his cronies snickered. Rachel was probably the only person in the room to notice the flush move up Mike's neck, marvelling, in passing, how vulnerable were the backs of men's necks, how eminently touchable...

Is he embarrassed or angry? she wondered. She didn't know him well enough to judge.

The Chief ignored the remark. It was gratuitous but fair, and besides, Kellett was a valuable police officer with excellent political connections, a bad man to cross.

'Any witnesses at Crossley?' asked the Chief.

'A young couple thought they might have seen her at Town Hall where they boarded the train, but can't remember seeing her get off anywhere,' said Steve Midgely. 'They were having a row about him being pissed and wanting to drive home, so they didn't see where she went.'

'Did he drive?' asked Larsen.

'Of course not,' said Midgely, po-faced. 'He told me so.'

'Book 'im, Danno,' said the comedian, and a roar of laughter relieved the tension.

By now they were aware this would be a tough and thankless case. The media knew the value of a vicious sex slaying (their words) of a pretty, irreproachable girl, and had quickly dubbed the murderer a monster. They were bound to keep the case alive as long as possible with an endless supply of heart-rending interviews with family and friends and the occasional detail leaked in a pub by a tired, venal or big-mouthed police officer.

There would be heavy political pressure, too. Law and order had become a sure-fire vote-winner over the last decade, and the government would be leaning on the Police Minister for quick results. Those with an axe to grind—in and out of the Minister's party—would make capital out of any police mistakes, some would even hope for failure. It would be one more strike against a police force already reeling from a series of political setbacks.

For their part, the public were frightened and affronted by the brutality and daring of the crime, and Lisa Broderick's parents had made it clear they wouldn't rest until the murderer or murderers were found. Ordinary, good folk who obviously worshipped their only child, the Gallaghers had made an indelible impression on the public and the police. The Broderick case had all the ingredients of a public relations nightmare.

With no more concrete evidence to go on, the conference slid into speculation, and Rachel ceased to listen. Surreptitiously reading the newspaper, she marvelled at the change in public morality over one generation. In Selena Gallagher's day, a woman with a sexual history like her daughter's would have been viewed as promiscuous, and therefore more deserving of a violent end than any virgin or safely married woman. Recently, though, there had even been an outcry when a Law Society spokesman expressed the opinion that the rape of a prostitute was a lesser crime than, say, the rape of a nun.

Rachel was jolted out of her reverie by the sound of her name. They wanted her assessment of the murderer's character. She told them it was far too early for anything but informed guesses, but they urged her on.

'If it's not one of her boyfriends getting even, we're dealing with someone operating under a compulsion, someone who can't stop himself,' she told them. 'But that doesn't mean he can't appear normal under superficial scrutiny. He's probably a loner, an isolate, a loser. But that doesn't mean we should underestimate him. So far he's acted quickly, quietly and totally effectively.

'If we're dealing with a sex murderer, either he was trawling for victims, ready to strike, and Lisa Broderick just happened to be in the wrong place at the wrong time; or he had her staked out and waited for an opportunity. He could have been stalking her for weeks waiting for an empty car park, a badly lit street, or even an open window.

'If the murder was opportunistic, random, he could be anyone in Sydney. But if he chose her, he knows her, and that makes it easier for us. Not easy, easier, because she worked in a hospital and met hundreds of men every year, and because he's cool and cunning and very fast. For all the evidence we've got, Lisa Broderick could have been plucked off Crossley station by Martians—if she ever got there. In fact, there were probably more sightings of UFOs that night than sightings of our killer.'

Silence fell as the team digested this. Stranger murders were as unpredictable as lightning strikes and notoriously difficult to solve. A new serial killer was everyone's worst fear, but so far nobody had voiced it, in case it came true.

Rachel wasn't superstitious, however, and it was time they faced facts. 'We shouldn't rule out the possibility that he's done this before and might do it again.'

'You've presented the options, Addison,' said the Chief. 'What's your opinion?'

'There's absolutely no way of knowing, Chief,' Rachel replied. 'Speculation might just send us off in the wrong direction.'

When the meeting wound down, the Chief Inspector caught Rachel's attention: 'In my office, Addison.'

Rachel's heart sank—maybe Mike Ross had shopped her after all—but she forced herself to calm down and brazen it out.

The Chief was ensconced behind a huge polished desk littered with files. Command centre. Lights flashed on and off on his phone, but he ignored them, letting someone field his calls outside. He nodded towards a chair and Rachel sat down.

Good-looking woman, he thought. And smart with it, if the rumours are true.

He would have loved to know what a woman with her education was doing in the police force, but refrained from quizzing her: in these tricky times it could be misconstrued. Motioning her into a chair, he said: 'I need a favour.'

Persia Lawrence had her office in a rather regal terrace house in a wide, tree-lined street in Woollahra, an elegant precinct in the eastern suburbs. Rachel identified it from a discreet but well-polished brass plaque. While she hesitated at the gate, a woman, with traces of tears on her face, passed her on the way out.

Inside, a friendly, middle-aged receptionist greeted Rachel and gave her a questionnaire to fill out, after which she sat fighting nerves and leafing through a copy of *World of Interiors* in the waiting room.

At some hidden signal, Rachel was ushered into the presence. Persia Lawrence was tall and slender, with good bones, deep-set, piercing blue eyes and well-cut, straight grey hair falling to her shoulders. She wore tailored pants and a crisp white shirt: a silky-soft pale blue suede jacket was draped over her chair. Apart from pearl studs in her ears, she wore no jewellery, not even a watch.

The room was painted eau-de-Nil, with polished floors and a pale Chinese rug. A very good landscape by a venerable painter (in his late, almost blind, Turner period) hung on one wall, and there were yellow roses in an ivory porcelain vase, probably Japanese, on an antique sideboard which had been buffed to a high gloss by some loving hand. A cleaner's, no doubt.

Rachel looked back from her survey to find the psychiatrist scrutinising her.

'You like the room,' said the doctor. After thirty years observing people's reactions, she could read volumes into the twitch of an eyebrow.

'I like the, uh, simplicity,' Rachel replied, knowing how much this sort of austerity cost.

Persia Lawrence decided she was going to like this young woman.

Then, all business, she consulted Rachel's questionnaire—Master's degree in psychology, two years with the Family Court, then the Police Academy followed by a year on the beat and promotion to the Homicide Squad. An unusual career trajectory for a female psychologist. The client had attended an expensive, all-girls school that prided itself on its academic reputation, turning out professional women, most of whom married well and sent their daughters to their alma mater. The school paraded its commitment to equal opportunity, but Rachel's decision to join the police force must have tested their rhetoric, the doctor thought, and the notion amused her.

Whatever ailed Rachel Addison was bound to be more exciting than lawyers with mid-life angst and the victims of divorce, the doctor decided. Though Kate Westwood had already briefed her about Rachel's crisis, Persia Lawrence wanted to hear her client's version. 'Would you like to tell me why you're here, Rachel?'

'I'm with the police, a psychologist attached to the Homicide Squad,' began Rachel. 'I love my job, ghoulish as that may sound, and I think I'm in danger of blowing it.'

She stopped, waiting for a prompt, received an inquiring look, and went on. 'Yesterday, I went to

44

St Bartholomew's to interview friends of Lisa Broderick's—you know, the girl who was raped and murdered at Crossley—and I fell apart, fainted. That's never happened to me before.'

'Before we get into the reasons for that, I think we should get to know each other better, don't you, Rachel,' said the doctor. 'Would you like to tell me a little more about yourself?'

It was one of those impossible questions, but the answer—what Rachel thought important, what she left out—would speak volumes to a trained listener. As a psychologist, Rachel knew this, and considered her reply carefully.

'I'm twenty-eight years old and single. I've got an MA in psychology. I own my own house.' She stopped and looked expectantly at the doctor, like a candidate at an oral exam.

The doctor homed in on the omissions. 'What about family, lovers, friends?'

Rachel coloured, feeling reproved and knowing that was irrational. 'I'm an orphan; my aunt raised me, my mother's sister, Louise. I have a few friends, but I don't get to see them very often. You know what it's like when people get married and have kids, you almost have to make an appointment with them. Plus I work pretty strange hours.'

She paused. 'I have no lover.'

'What about a best friend?'

'I suppose not, not now anyway. I had a very close friend at school. Her name was Holly. We went on to university together, but she had a breakdown in first term and her parents whisked her off somewhere and cut off all communication. Someone told me she went to India eventually. I haven't seen her in, oh, ten years.'

'You haven't tried to contact her?'

Rachel hadn't, and felt guilty about it. But it seemed too complicated. They'd been so young, and it had all been so long ago. She felt like a different person now. Would she and Holly have anything in common if they did meet?

'No. I wasn't sure she'd want to see me. When she started to get depressed, I tried to help her, but I wasn't up to it...Let's face it, I wasn't handling university myself: it was all I could do to get out of bed some days. But Holly wasn't sleeping or eating, and she was running around with a wild crowd. I was afraid she'd kill herself and it would be my fault for not doing anything, so I called her parents in. I'm not sure she could ever forgive me for that.'

'You feel guilty for saving her from herself?' asked the doctor.

'Yes, but it could have been me I was really trying to protect. I was terrified of losing her, and I knew I would never get rid of the guilt if I did nothing.'

She shrugged. 'I lost her anyway, but at least she's alive.'

'What about Kate Westwood? You two seem close.'

'Kate's a good friend. She dragged me through an emotional smash-up in my final year, and we've kept in touch.'

'What sort of smash-up?'

'A failed love affair.'

The tension in Rachel's face told her it wasn't the whole story. 'Do you want to talk about that?'

'No.'

The doctor waited but Rachel didn't change her mind. 'This business about being terrified Holly would die, do you think it might have had anything to do with your parents' death?'

'I never thought of it that way,' said Rachel. 'But I suppose it fits.'

'What happened to your parents, Rachel?'

'They were killed in a head-on collision in the Riverina, where we used to live.' There was no emotion in Rachel's voice. This was something known, rather than felt. It wasn't as if she could remember them.

'You weren't in the car with them?'

'No.'

The silence lengthened. 'I don't know where I was,' said Rachel finally.

'You can't remember?'

'I was only four. It's a blank. I don't remember much of my life before I went to live with Louise. But I don't suppose many people would.'

The doctor wasn't so sure. Some people insisted they remembered their mother's face looking down at them in their crib: others had few memories before the age of four or five. 'Have you asked your aunt about it?'

Rachel wondered how best to explain the fragile, complex relationship between herself and Louise, the contract of silence, the unspoken agreement that no-one would bring up the subject of Claire Addison's life and death.

'Louise made it impossible for me to ask,' she said. 'But she dropped hints from time to time that it was my father's fault, that he was drunk. She didn't approve of the marriage.'

'Have you ever asked her where you were at the time?'

'No.'

'Why not?'

'I knew she wouldn't tell me.'

'Or you were afraid she might?'

Rachel was uncomfortable, but she eased her way out of it. 'That's what I'm here to find out, doctor.'

'You're speaking about your aunt in the past tense…'

'She had a stroke last Christmas. I took some

time off to look after her, but she didn't improve. Then she had a second stroke. That was in January. It will be the first anniversary of her death soon.'

'Do you want to look at that?'

Rachel shook her head. 'I don't think it's connected to whatever is bothering me at the moment.'

Persia Lawrence doubted that, but it would keep. 'So now you'll never be able to ask her.'

'No.'

This was fertile ground, but the doctor decided she'd pushed Rachel far enough in that direction for the time being. It was time to get back to the event which had forced Rachel out into the open.

'Do you want to tell me what happened to you at the hospital yesterday, Rachel?'

'I don't know exactly what happened. I mean, I know I fainted, then threw up after they'd revived me, but I don't know why.'

'Was it the hospital? Some people are frightened by them.'

'Maybe. I've given it a lot of thought. At first I thought it couldn't have been, because I'd never been in a hospital before, except to be born, of course, but then I had a sort of flashback and saw myself in one.'

'Can you describe it more clearly?'

'It was strange, more like a vision than a memory, as if it were happening to someone else.

I could see this child being carried away by someone in a white coat. She was very frightened, but she wasn't howling or crying. She seemed stunned. There were two grown-ups present. They were very distressed, the man particularly.'

'What do you think it means?'

'The child must have been me, and the adults must have been my parents, though I can't really remember their faces. If I try to take it any further, I seize up.'

'Do you remember having any illnesses as a child? Or an accident?'

'No. My aunt says I was as healthy as a horse, but if my parents were present, it must have happened before I went to live with her.'

It seemed to the doctor that the incident in the hospital could be a doorway into Rachel's past, and she felt Rachel knew it. Could they open that door wider? Perhaps: it depended on how much Rachel really wanted to know.

'What made you come to me about this, Rachel?'

Rachel reddened. 'My partner told me to find out what was wrong, or he'd take action. Report the incident to our superiors, he meant. He doesn't want to be at the mercy of some fruit loop in a dangerous situation.'

'You're angry at him?'

'I suppose I am. Let's face it, it's human nature

to be angry at someone who sees you fail. It's not his fault, though. He just happened to be there.'

The psychiatrist was intrigued at the way Rachel used her psychological training to erect a smoke-screen, turning an intensely personal reaction into a generality, distancing herself from the normal human emotions. 'Tell me more about this partner of yours.'

Rachel started to speak, stopped, then laughed. 'You've got good instincts, doctor. Yes, I am a little bit attracted to him. And, of course, it upsets me that he was the one to see me make a fool of myself on the job. But it's me I'm angry with, really. I feel as if I've betrayed myself, or as if my unconscious betrayed me. That scares me. What else is in there, and when is it going to rear up and threaten me?'

'So you really want to know what's happening? It's not just a tactic to get your partner off your back?'

The silence stretched as Rachel thought about the doctor's challenge. Did she really want to stir up the past? She was getting by, wasn't she? Or had been until her lapse in the hospital. She raised her eyes and looked at Persia Lawrence. 'I think so.'

Persia Lawrence scrutinised the troubled young woman. So many secrets, so much doubt, so much unknowing. All those years spent studying psy-chology, trying to get the measure of the enemy, arming herself against her own mind. It would be a challenge to work with Rachel Addison. And a pleasure, too, she decided.

It was getting dim in the room. The older woman pulled aside the curtains, letting in the twilight. Brought back to the everyday, Rachel started and blinked.

'I think we've probably done enough today, Rachel. How about another talk a few days from now?'

Rachel hesitated. 'All right.' Then realising it sounded half-hearted, 'Yes.' She rose. 'Thank you, Doctor.'

'Persia,' said the psychiatrist. They shook hands, and Rachel left by the side exit. It had cooled down while she was inside and the street lights had come on.

It's started, and I'm still alive, she thought. I'm scared, but I'm handling it.

Strangely light-hearted, she strode to her car, warmed by the memory of yellow roses glowing in the dusk.

If anything could alleviate the anxiety of baring her soul to a perfect stranger it would be a hard physical workout, Rachel decided, and set off for the gym. Tired of fashionable health clubs and their narcissistic clientele, she had looked for an old-fashioned, serious gymnasium and had found it in the back streets of an industrial suburb. As well as the usual martial arts types—accountants with fantasies, women learning self-defence, kids inspired by karate movies—there were footballers keeping fit and a few older ex-cons maintaining their jail muscle.

To escape from her work and its associations, Rachel had avoided any place where the police hung out. This gym was her secret. She relished its sweaty egalitarianism, and guarded her anonymity. In fact, nobody had ever evinced the slightest interest in her life outside, and she returned the courtesy. And although the sexual revolution had largely bypassed the sorts of men who hung out here—they called her love and bullied her into greater effort if she seemed to be slacking—it didn't matter. She was accepted, an old hand.

The thump of bodies hitting the mat and the grunts of men, women and kids in a martial arts class greeted her at the door, music to her ears. A couple of acquaintances from past classes saluted her briefly: otherwise her arrival went unnoticed. Rachel relaxed.

In the change room, she was joined by a small, fragile-looking lobbyist for a social justice group, and agreed to a practice bout of karate with the woman, who displayed the same attractive mixture of toughness, tenacity and compassion on the mat as she did in the political arena.

While the two women towelled off, they gossiped. The lobbyist told Rachel she was off to a branch meeting to fight for Lally Regan, a popular female Member of Parliament and a personal friend. Asked what the fight was about, she said the party was trying to edge Regan out of the seat in favour of one of its golden boys.

Rachel knew of the man. An adviser to the Treasurer, he was young and nakedly ambitious, though not conspicuously intelligent, and if he'd been behind some of the financial fiascos the state had suffered over the past three years, he should be unemployable. 'What are you going to do?' she asked.

'Fight dirty, be disloyal, all that stuff the men do as a matter of course. Honour makes losers in this game. We'll run a media blitz, and if that fails, try to make sure it doesn't happen again.'

'How do you stand it?' asked Rachel.

'The same way you stand the police force, I suppose. If you want it enough, you find ways of dealing with the shit until you can change it. And to be honest, I love it. I couldn't imagine doing anything else, whatever the cost.'

'Neither could I,' said Rachel, and the two young women smiled at each other in complete understanding, in perfect complicity.

God, if only there was one other woman in Homicide, thought Rachel.

Afterwards, Rachel took herself to the gym's old indoor swimming pool, dived into the chlorine-scented water and swam a few laps, alone except for the sound of her own breathing. While she was lolling in the cool water in the dim, cavernous, echoing room, her mind blissfully empty, the door opened and a man stepped into the room and stood there, silhouetted by the light, watching her. It was impossible to see his face in the gloom, but his shape didn't look familiar. Rachel tensed, feeling dangerously exposed, like a goldfish in a bowl.

The man soon left, but Rachel's mood was shattered. She climbed out, took a shower, grabbed her gear and left. Outside, she kept her eyes peeled, but saw nothing unusual, nothing that aroused her suspicion. Reassured, she drove home.

5

Free Will is a Complex Notion

Three more hospital employees were located and presented themselves for interview. Nothing much came of it. The last hope, a close friend of Lisa Broderick's, had managed to break her leg the day of the murder, forcing Mike and Rachel to drive out to her parents' house to talk to her.

The episode in the hospital and Mike's ultimatum had put a strain on their relationship. Rachel was embarrassed and a little angry; Mike was concerned but exasperated by the complication. The case was going to be difficult enough without worrying about his partner's reliability. They spoke little, and the atmosphere in the police car was cool. Outside, it was unbearably hot, and tempers were frayed. Mike, who was driving, was happy to keep his mind on the road, as the highway to the south-western suburb was fast, and the drivers aggressive. Traffic cops were conspicuous by their absence, lying low after revelations of traffic-fine quotas in some jurisdictions. Motorists, who fiercely defended their right to drive dangerously, had been incensed.

Denise Young's mother, Marian, greeted them at the door of a small suburban bungalow surrounded by native trees. Somebody in the house was a keen gardener.

'She's in a terrible state,' the woman whispered. 'First the accident, then hearing about poor little Lisa. I don't know what the world's coming to any more.'

'We'll try not to upset her,' Rachel soothed. 'I'm sure she'd want to do all she could to help us find Lisa's killer.'

When the woman led them into the living room, Rachel understood the garden: it was an escape hatch. The room was poky and crowded with furniture, including a piano, which displayed silver-framed photographs of the Young children in graduation gowns. Pale and exhausted-looking, Denise Young was slumped in front of an electric fan, plastered leg resting on a stool. Marian Young fussed about for a bit, then disappeared into the kitchen to make iced tea.

'We're sorry we have to put you through this,' said Mike, 'but as a close friend of Lisa's, we thought you might know if she was worried about anything, or anybody, before the...before it happened.'

'No, not that I know of...,' the woman began, then burst into tears. The police waited till she regained her composure. She blew her nose and said: 'I feel terrible. I split up with my boyfriend a couple of weeks ago...I wasn't really paying much attention to Lisa's life.'

'She didn't mention anything out of the ordinary happening, someone following her, or watching her?' asked Mike.

'No. Even I would have registered that.'

'Ms Young, did any of your colleagues have a crush on Lisa?' asked Rachel.

The girl smiled for the first time: 'All of them, I think. She was nice to everybody. Never talked about anybody behind their back, never complained about people not pulling their weight. God, it's not fair. When you think of some of the rotten bitches you know...'

Mike interrupted, forestalling tears: 'Why did she break up with her husband?'

'It was about kids. Tony decided he didn't want any. His brother's kid was born with some genetic disorder that turned out to be from the Broderick side, and he wasn't prepared to take the risk. Lisa desperately wanted to have a family. But there wasn't any hostility. Tony respected her decision to leave.'

She faltered, suddenly realising she'd given Tony Broderick a motive. 'At least he said he did.'

Our first motive, thought Rachel. 'Who are the hospital creeps?' she asked. 'You know, the ones you wouldn't want to be caught in the car park with?'

It didn't take Denise Young long to decide. 'One of the couriers is a druggie, I think. Speed, by the look of his eyes. I'm not all that keen on him, but I don't see him as a murderer. And one of the male nurses was fired last year for molesting a patient under anaesthetic, although it was hushed up.'

Rachel shuddered. Until recently, when there had been a spate of sexual abuse claims against doctors and psychiatrists, sexual exploitation had been a taboo subject in the medical and paramedical fields. When she'd been working with clients, Rachel had tried to reduce the risk by referring women to female practitioners.

Mike looked at Rachel and made a small grimace of distaste: 'Do you remember his name?'

'Joel something...Sorry, you'll have to ask at the hospital.'

'Anything else, Denise?' asked Rachel.

'Not really. The rest of them seem pretty inoffensive. Statistically there must be a few alcoholics and wife-beaters among them, but they keep it under wraps.'

Marian Young interrupted with cold drinks and home-made cake that made Mike's eyes light up.

Before they left, Rachel asked mother and daughter for their honest impressions of Lisa Broderick. 'I don't want to sound like a cynic, but Lisa Broderick seems almost too good to be true,' she said. 'What was behind all that niceness?'

'I always thought it was lack of self-confidence,' remarked the older woman. 'I know people thought Lisa had everything, but I don't think she ever trusted it. She was a tall child, apparently, and that's always a problem for girls. I got the impression she didn't grow into her looks till quite late. Maybe the niceness came from the days when she was trying to compensate for being gawky and plain.'

'Really, Mum, where do you get these weird ideas!' scolded her daughter, but Marian Young just shrugged and smiled.

Mike Ross began to revise his opinion of Rachel's professionalism. She had an uncanny knack of asking the right people the right questions, and by refusing to take anything at face value, was uncovering a side of Lisa Broderick that he hadn't suspected. Did she think Lisa Broderick's character was the key to the crime?

On the way back into the city, Rachel was preoccupied, mulling over what Mrs Young had said.

'What's the verdict?' asked Mike, startling her. She relaxed a little: maybe he was beginning to thaw.

'I have a feeling that was important.'

'Why?'

'Marian Young saw a side of Lisa Broderick most people missed because they couldn't get past the good looks and niceness. If it's true, it could be the key to the abduction.'

'Whoa, slow down,' said Mike. 'You've lost me.'

'It's sexual politics, Mike. Nobody talks about it any more, but it's still there. One of the first things attractive women have to learn is how to fend off sexual advances without making men angry. Most of the time it doesn't matter, of course, but some men get violent when they're knocked back. It's about power. Men think beautiful women have all this power, and some of them resent it. If Lisa Broderick was a late bloomer, she mightn't have learned how to handle the power, how to cut the geeks off. Somebody might have mistaken good manners for a come on.'

It rang true to Mike. 'You think someone might have killed her because he thought she'd led him on then wouldn't come across?'

'Maybe. On the other hand, he might have decided to kill someone, and chose Lisa because she was naive. Why try to kidnap a woman off the streets if you could talk one into your car?'

'So you think she could have gone with him

of her own free will?' asked Mike.

Rachel shrugged. 'Free will is a complex notion. Someone once said it was easier sometimes to die than make a scene. Maybe Lisa Broderick died because she was afraid to make a scene.'

It was incomprehensible to Mike Ross that a woman like Lisa Broderick would get into a car with a murderer rather than hurt his feelings. He'd never analysed his feelings about beautiful women, though he knew they were complicated. If he were to be honest, he probably thought good-looking women understood and exploited their power over men. Working with Rachel Addison was turning into quite an eye-opener. He reminded himself to keep his mouth shut in case she started analysing him.

'But she could have been dragged screaming off the street into a car by a perfect stranger,' he said. 'There was nobody around to hear.'

Rachel realised she'd been squelched, but decided it was a knee-jerk male response and chose to ignore it. 'That bothers me, too. It was a Saturday night and that was the last train. How come there were no witnesses?'

The police had door-knocked the area and put out appeals for witnesses through the media, but so far nobody had come forward. 'Yeah, there's something wrong, there. Somebody must have seen something.'

'I'm going to suggest we do a re-enactment of the train ride,' said Rachel.

They were silent for the rest of the journey, thinking their own thoughts. As they pulled into the Police HQ parking lot, Rachel said: 'About what happened the other day in the hospital. I'm doing something about it.'

He almost asked what, but catching sight of her closed face, he changed his mind. The prospect of losing Rachel Addison as a partner and spending countless hours in the company of Kellett or Midgely, with their tasteless jokes and predictable responses, had little appeal.

'Good,' he said. 'I was worried.'

That afternoon, Rachel slipped away and drove to a television studio in one of the northern suburbs. She had never been in front of a television camera before, and was nervous, though she had been exhaustively briefed by the Chief Inspector and the Police Commissioner's public relations staff and had the benefit of a carefully prepared statement. The human face of the police force, the Chief had called her. Rachel was fully aware that using their token female officer to reassure the public and to soften the aggressively masculine image of the police service was blatant sexism, but she was in no position to refuse. It had been a long struggle to get any woman on to a high-profile murder inquiry, and besides, it might just help them find Lisa Broderick's killer.

In the nightmare she was hiding in a confined space, too terrified to speak, almost too frightened to breathe. Somebody—almost certainly, a man—was looking for her. She was being hunted down. She knew he would kill her if he found her, but she was helpless as a baby, rooted to the spot. Her mind raced, her heart pounded, but still she couldn't move. Then the hunter was almost upon her. Silhouetted against the light, he was monstrous. A giant.

Surveying the dark circles under her eyes in the mirror next morning, Rachel re-ran the dream. Why was she so affected by this particular murder, she wondered. How had Lisa Broderick's murderer invaded her subconscious?

At noon the next day, the Nightingale Task Force incident room was abuzz.

'What's going on?' asked Mike.

'The Lisa Broderick Story,' said Midgely. 'Channel 9's done some sort of documentary—the Chief Inspector was interviewed a couple of days ago—and Lisa Broderick's parents are going to be on.'

'The secret weapons,' said Kellett, who, as senior investigative officer on the case, had interviewed them.

Though devastated by their daughter's death, Selena and Graham Gallagher were so dignified in the face of intrusive and often prurient media attention that even the most cynical police had been impressed. This increased the pressure on the team: not only was Lisa Broderick being transformed into a paragon of young womanhood in the public's mind, but her parents' well-articulated grief had provoked media commentators into a frenzy of blame.

After an enterprising newspaper reporter documented five assaults on the Crossley line in the twelve months before Lisa's murder, a scathing editorial had appeared demanding to know why there had been no guard on the station late at night. An attempt by the Director of State Rail to justify the decision on economic grounds had led to a front-page attack headlined 'What Price Our Daughters' Lives?' and it was generally accepted that the bureaucrat's career had been derailed.

The Police Commissioner, a tough, taciturn survivor, had already given one press conference promising swift and effective action, and the pressure from his office was intense. One of his policy advisers, a savvy troubleshooter who would have been a worthy aide to Hitler, had been appointed to liaise with the Nightingale team. His high-handed manner and general obnoxiousness had precipitated a number of screaming matches—all behind his back, of course.

Rachel and Mike stayed to watch the show. The babble died down as a portentous voice recapped the murder over flashbacks of Lisa Gallagher as a stunning, big-eyed baby, then a gap-toothed schoolgirl. One of her primary school teachers came forward to say she'd been bright and helpful, and had always wanted to be a nurse. This was followed by home-movie footage of an adolescent with acne and a self-conscious stoop who couldn't meet the camera's eye. Then, as if by magic, time transformed the ugly duckling into a beaming swan in white chiffon and a deep-blue sash proclaiming her Miss Nursing 1988. Her fiancé, Tony Broderick, looking suitably proud and possessive, was visible in the background.

'Good looker,' remarked Kellett. 'She was wasted on sick people.'

He was shushed for the Gallagher–Broderick white wedding, a small but lavish affair in the Gallaghers' local church, complete with bridesmaids in emerald-green taffeta and proud parents from both sides. When the camera panned to Tony Broderick's handsome, self-satisfied face, Kellett said: 'Why would a lovely girl like that marry a prick like Broderick?'

'You've answered your own question,' said Midgely, and the men laughed.

There was a stunned and not entirely friendly silence when Rachel's face appeared on the screen. Heads turned to see how Rachel was responding, and to compare the real person with the screen image. As soon as Rachel was out of earshot, the men would discuss it at length, wanting to know why a rookie like her had been chosen to represent the force. They would come up with all sorts of conspiracy theories, mostly to do with her looks, but the bottom line was that the Chief Inspector had made the decision, and they had no choice but to accept it. It wasn't going to win her any friends among her colleagues, but that wasn't management's problem: it was hers.

Mike Ross, watching the men watching Rachel, doubted the wisdom of exposing Rachel to such sensational publicity. They were, after all, dealing with a very dangerous man who'd already murdered one young, good-looking woman.

Surely they haven't got some lunatic notion of using her as a decoy, he thought, then dismissed it. They weren't that Machiavellian. It was more likely one of those bright ideas dreamed up by some ambitious political minder to enhance the image of the force and win a pat on the back from the Minister. It probably hadn't occurred to them that they were recklessly endangering one of their officers.

Then the faces of Lisa Broderick's parents filled

the screen, deflecting attention from a grateful Rachel. Graham and Selena Gallagher were ordinary people who believed in God, tolerance, social justice, civic duty. They spoke of their daughter with pride and said they were thankful to have had her as long as they did. They refrained from railing against the killer or demanding justice or vengeance, but begged viewers to come forward if they had any information to help the police find their girl's murderer. They were a knockout. The pressure would really be on now.

'Not a dry eye in the house,' said Kellett sourly as the credits rolled.

'You interviewed Tony Broderick, didn't you Dick?' asked Rachel. She'd read the transcript of Kellett's interrogation, but he didn't need to know that.

'Yeah. Fat lot of good it did me. He's a smooth bugger. Too arrogant for his own good, specially for someone without an alibi. It would give me great pleasure to put that one away.'

'You can't arrest people for being shits,' interrupted Midgely. 'More's the pity.'

'The jails wouldn't hold them all,' said Kellett.

Interrupting the laughter, Rachel said: 'Tell me a bit more about him, Dick. Could he have done it?'

'I'd say so. He's angry. Part of that's probably hurt pride from being known as Lisa Broderick's discarded husband, but it's more than that. I reckon he never forgave her for walking out on him. He's a cold little shit.'

Rachel longed to talk to Tony Broderick, but protocol forbade it. Though many of the men disliked Kellett and his bullying ways, he was their senior and one of them, an old cop: she was a woman and a latecomer. It would be a gross breach of etiquette, and a poor career move, to question Kellett's abilities, even implicitly.

The unsuspecting Kellett was flattered by Rachel's interest. Mike, who'd been checking his phone messages and catching up on gossip, caught the tail end of this exchange and grinned to himself. As a new recruit to the team, Mike was low in the informal pecking order, and had to tread carefully. If he occasionally thought someone had bungled a job and that he could have done it better, he held his tongue. But if push came to shove and the investigation stalled, they'd be forced to abandon some of the professional niceties. He wondered how long it would take Rachel Addison to find a way of interrogating Lisa Broderick's husband.

At four o'clock Sheree and some of the other support staff cleared a couple of tables and laid out cold cuts, cheese, fruit and assorted junk food and had the men carry in several plastic garbage cans filled with ice, beer and soft drinks. At this time of year every office in Australia was holding its Christmas party, and the Task Force was no exception. It was refreshingly normal, a relief to get away from matters of life and death and talk and laugh and drink. The murderer himself could well have been sinking a few beers at a Christmas party somewhere in Sydney at that very minute.

Sipping on a lite ale, Rachel had to put up with a certain amount of flak about her new-found fame. She chose to see most of it as good-natured teasing, but Kellett's insistence on calling her our little TV star began to grate after a while. She'd put up with bigger horses' arses than Kellett in her time to get what she wanted, though. With her colleagues relaxed and garrulous after an infusion of alcohol, this was too valuable an opportunity to ruin with a show of temper.

Rachel eventually cornered Brett Marcantonio, the young constable who'd interviewed Joel Breen that morning, and shouting above the noise, asked him how it had gone.

'Jeez, I couldn't believe it,' said Brett. 'They reckon this bastard was caught feeling up some unconscious woman. You'd have to be desperate, wouldn't you?'

'Why?' interjected Kellett, who'd been eavesdropping. 'You couldn't tell the difference with some birds.'

Brett Marcantonio blinked and glanced nervously at Rachel, expecting her to bite.

Kellett will keep, she thought, and ignored him. 'Does this Breen character have an alibi?' she asked Brett, wondering how long it would be before this innocent became as cynical as the rest of the men.

'Yeah. He said he went to an AA meeting, then started work at 11 p.m.'

'Can anyone vouch for him after eleven?'

'Yes. An old man died around midnight, and he called in a doctor and the ambulance.'

Rachel was alarmed. 'Where is Breen working, Brett?'

'Um, at an old people's home.'

There was a horrified hush, then Kellett's voice broke in. 'Not after today, he won't be.'

At about seven, Mike suggested that the stayers move to a local pub. Kellett, Midgely and Brett Marcantonio took up the invitation. Rachel wanted to go home, but noticing that the alcohol had lowered Kellett's guard, decided to go along. You never knew what you'd learn in a pub.

The reek of stale beer, cigarettes and disinfectant assaulted them as they entered the Royal George, a run-down Victorian-era cops' hangout with the regulation dingy, puce carpet, jukebox and cigarette machine lit up like spaceships, and a row of old stagers who spent hours eavesdropping on police gossip, watching sport on the television and boring the barman with tales of their exploits in

71

the war. Most of them lived alone in rooms in nearby boarding houses, and they were tolerated mainly out of superstition and a vestigial compassion.

'Ah,' said Kellett, breathing deeply. 'Home at last.'

They ordered beers and began obsessively to post-mortem the case.

'That bloody television show is going to up the ante,' complained Kellett. 'Those Gallaghers are dynamite.'

'But they didn't have a go at us,' said the constable. 'I thought they were nice.'

'Too bloody nice, young Brett,' growled Kellett. 'They've got the whole country sobbing into their Kleenex. The Premier's wife will be whispering in his ear in bed tonight about poor little Lisa Broderick, and he'll be on the blower first thing tomorrow morning screaming at the Minister. Mark my words.'

'You nasty old cynic, Kellett,' boomed a voice. It was Len Cooper, the Police Commissioner's press secretary.

Kellett introduced him around, and he looked hard at Rachel. 'Ah, the thin end of the wedge in person,' he remarked. 'I'd heard about the feminist plant in Homicide. Until I saw you on TV, I figured you probably had muscles and a moustache.'

'And I'd heard you were a lady-killer, Len. Where were you on the night of December the 17th?'

Cooper blinked, and the table erupted in laughter.

Game, set, match, Rachel Addison, thought Mike Ross.

'Watch her, she's good,' said Midgely, closing ranks. If anyone was going to insult Rachel and get away with it, it would be a fellow police officer, not some fat-arsed, deskbound public servant.

'Anything happening that I should know about?' asked Cooper, retreating.

'The husband's the only real suspect we've got so far,' said Kellett. 'Motive, opportunity and no alibi, but unless he breaks down and confesses, we've got bugger-all.'

'If this is a maniac, we're in deep shit,' said Cooper. 'There are a hell of a lot of women out there, and they've all got a vote.' He paused for effect, staring directly at Rachel. 'Unfortunately.'

Unmoved, Rachel stared back.

'She was seeing a couple of men,' said Mike, marvelling at Rachel's self-control.

'Seeing?' said Cooper, with a leer.

'Screwing one of them, I reckon,' said Kellett, 'Roger Blair. Not that he'll admit it. He's out of the running, anyway: the killer's blood type is O, and he's B.'

'Why would he lie about it?' asked Mike.

'Probably a Catholic,' said Midgely.

'Nothing that highfalutin,' said Kellett. 'He's her ex-husband's best friend.'

Rachel was sure that Kellett's report of the interview hadn't mentioned anything about Roger Blair being Lisa Broderick's lover. Because the man was the wrong blood type, Kellett had written him off. But if it were true, Lisa might have confided in Blair. She wondered how she could get to talk to the man without upsetting Kellett.

The old cop hadn't finished, though. 'One of her admirers is blood type O, but he was at a political fund-raiser and went home with a politician,' he said.

'Which one?' asked Len Cooper, for whom every tidbit of gossip was a potential bargaining chip.

'Wouldn't you like to know?'

'Male or female?'

'Female.'

'Which party?'

Kellett told him.

'Married or single?'

'Married.'

'That narrows it down to three,' said Cooper, commenting unwittingly on the paucity of women in political office in the state. 'Cough it up, Dick.'

'It'll cost you,' said Kellett, and after Cooper

had bought him a double Scotch of a venerable age and esteemed brand, gave the press secretary the name.

Rachel was appalled at Kellett's lack of discretion, although she knew why he was currying favour with Len Cooper. A cop who operated as close to the line as Kellett always needed credit in the Commissioner's office, and Cooper, a hardened political warrior, could protect him. But Rachel also suspected that Kellett was testing her, finding out if she'd rush to the politician's defence. If she had fallen for it, he'd have told his cabal she was a lesbian feminist.

Mike saw immediately what was going on. Rachel was poker-faced, but her knuckles were white around her glass. He noticed Len Cooper monitoring her reactions closely, too. Feeling the scrutiny, Rachel looked up and gave Cooper a cool stare. He was the first to look away.

Round two, Rachel Addison, thought Mike, and grinned.

Cooper shot him a sour look, and said to Kellett: 'So, did Lisa Broderick know her killer or not?'

'I reckon it was random. She was probably just in the wrong place at the wrong time.'

Kellett gestured towards Rachel with his glass. 'But our lady psychologist here reckons it was probably the devil she knew.'

'The statistics back that up,' said Brett Marcantonio, who'd listened, watched and kept his mouth shut till now. Rachel favoured him with a smile.

Cooper signalled for another round. 'What makes you think that, Addison?' he asked, feigning intense interest.

'Women's intuition,' scoffed Kellett.

Rachel wasn't going to be provoked. 'I think there was something about Lisa Broderick that made people project on to her. So if there was a sexually disturbed male at the hospital, she'd be the one he'd get obsessed with. Men are still obsessed with her, even though she's dead.'

'What do you mean?' asked Brett.

'Look at the media coverage. Lisa Broderick isn't the only young woman who got murdered in Sydney this year—I can personally recall five others—but they got a few paragraphs on page three and nothing much until the killer was caught, if he ever was. But when Lisa Broderick gets killed, there's a massive hue and cry.'

'It's because she's a nice girl,' said Mike. 'If she'd been a prostitute, half the population would have thought she had it coming.'

'Well, she would have, wouldn't she?' said Kellett.

There was a silence. Recently, a judge who'd voiced a similar opinion, had been pilloried. Mike and Rachel exchanged a look.

Into the hiatus, in one of those sudden lulls in the pub racket, the young constable said: 'It's her smile.' Everyone turned to look at him, and he blushed.

'Go home and have a cold shower, Brett,' said Kellett, and the men laughed.

No, he's right, thought Rachel, conjuring up the ubiquitous photograph of Lisa Broderick wearing her beauty queen's sash and her shy, lovely smile. The smile was sexy and vulnerable at the same time.

Everybody wants to take her home and look after her, she thought. Or go to bed with her, or both. That's why they're so angry at her killer. He betrayed her trust.

With one ear on the conversation, Mike Ross was watching Rachel. She was miles away. He was intensely curious about what was going on in her head, but this wasn't the place to ask. Anyway, it had been a long day.

'I'm off,' he said.

Rachel said she'd go, too, and Midgely rose. The young constable followed suit, unwilling to be left alone with two hard men like Kellett and Cooper, who were well away by now.

'Nobody going to rock on?' asked the press secretary, disappointed. He was a famed drinker, always the last to leave any gathering. He'd traded his private life for power years before.

'I'll stay,' said Kellett.

They left the two old comrades in arms ensconced at the bar. Between them, they knew where most of the bodies were buried. Cooper was paid to do the Commissioner's dirty work, and Kellett was the sort of cop he'd choose to do hush-hush jobs, especially those involving politicians. Mike wondered whose downfall they'd plot after they left, and hoped it wasn't his. Or Rachel Addison's.

'What's with Kellett and women?' Rachel asked Mike as he walked her to her car. As a female, she was shut out of most of the men's personal gossip.

Mike hesitated, then said: 'His wife left him for their marriage counsellor.'

They looked at each other po-faced, then burst into laughter.

'So much for professional ethics,' said Rachel. 'Though I have noticed ethics aren't Kellett's strong suit.'

Mike decided to leave that alone. 'It wasn't funny for the boyfriend. Dick got him struck off and hounded him out of Sydney. He's making mud bricks in hippie country up near the Queensland border, apparently.'

'What about Kellett's wife?'

'She went with him.'

Though Kellett and Cooper were two of the

most unpleasant specimens Rachel had encountered outside a correctional facility, she decided the evening hadn't been a complete loss. She knew why Kellett hated women, and she knew Mike Ross had started to trust her. And she might have found Lisa Broderick's lover.

6

Really An Orphan Now

It was the night before Christmas Eve, the date of the re-enactment of Lisa Broderick's last night on earth. Rachel had helped choose Helen Winning, a young police officer about the same height and build as the victim, and had gone looking for clothes and shoes similar to the ones Lisa had worn. She'd obtained an exact copy of the almost new yellow sundress from the manufacturer in Melbourne, but it had been impossible to match the sandals, which Lisa had bought in Florence the year before on a holiday. But then, who looked at a pretty girl's feet?

Watching a make-up artist transform Helen Winning into Lisa Broderick, Rachel had last-minute misgivings. What if the killer liked what he saw and transferred his malign attention to Lisa Broderick's stand-in? Though they'd kept her identity from the reporters who'd been invited along to cover the proceedings, Helen Winning was growing apprehensive, too, as the hour approached.

At 11.50 p.m., Central Station was crammed with home-bound teenagers and a few older movie-goers, but the usual late-night catcalling and horseplay ceased when the Lisa Broderick circus hove into view. Silence fell as the crowd digested the scene, craning their necks to get a better view, then the chatter began anew. But the presence of the police was inhibiting, and the atmosphere remained subdued.

Plain-clothes police were strategically placed to monitor the crowd, with Rachel close by in case Helen Winning became agitated. The commuters gave this phantasm a wide berth, and when the train pulled in, let her board first. Though the train was crowded, the seat beside her remained vacant. Against a low rumble of rumour and speculation, Lisa's ghost pretended to read a copy of the paperback crime novel found spilled out of the victim's bag in the killing field. From her shaking hands, Rachel knew Helen wasn't taking in a word.

We should have looked for someone with less imagination, she thought, angry at her lack of foresight. But where in Sydney—in the world— could they have found a woman who didn't identify with the murdered girl, who couldn't imagine herself walking in Lisa Broderick's shoes?

It was a long way to Crossley. State Rail had agreed to run one of the old red trains on the route again, so it was noisy, uncomfortable and hot. Sweaty and sticking to her seat, Rachel envied the kids hanging out near the doors catching the breeze. Aware they were under surveillance, they were on their best behaviour: on the night Lisa Broderick had been travelling towards her fate, they would have been noisy and obnoxious. Some of the males might even have harassed her.

By the time it reached Crossley, the train was almost empty. Apart from Rachel and Helen Winning, there were no women travelling alone. Lisa Broderick's murder had jolted the railways out of their complacency, but the new safety measures they'd instituted had come too late. Late-night trains had become one more no-go area for females and taxis were enjoying a boom.

The television crews picked them up again at Crossley, but kept their distance as they'd been commanded. Following the police reconstruction of Lisa Broderick's last hours, Helen Winning waited on the station for ten minutes, crossed the car park to the street and set off in the direction of the Gallaghers' house. At the edge of the shopping centre, she stopped: if Lisa had been still on the road at this point, Graham Gallagher would have seen her. It was over. Rachel's shoulders relaxed, and she realised how tense she'd been.

Mike Ross was there waiting, and picked up the two women.

'God, can you imagine turning up here and finding nobody waiting for you,' Helen Winning said, visibly shaken. 'It's so dark. What do you think was going through her mind?'

'She was probably hoping that her father would turn up, but I think she would have started to walk home, rather than hanging around here,' said Rachel. 'I know I would have.'

She was interrupted by the roar of a car full of drunk teenagers careening around the corner. When the kids saw the police cars, the media vans and all the activity in the street, they threw a U-turn and tried to make a run for it. They were too slow: a police car turned on its siren, gave chase and quickly flagged down the miscreants.

'Another quiet night in the burbs,' said Mike.

The three police officers drove in silence for a while, then Helen said: 'Is this going to do any good?'

Mike and Rachel exchanged a glance. 'I don't know,' said Rachel. 'I really don't know.'

As they dropped the young woman off at home, Rachel handed her a card. 'Helen, we've all been upset by this. If you need to talk...'

The girl nodded and dashed inside. Rachel imagined her staring at Lisa Broderick in the mirror, then tearing off the dead girl's clothes and trying to get back inside her own skin. Her own young, alive, skin.

A sense of anticlimax settled on Rachel like a fog. 'Does this sort of stunt ever work?'

'Probably not,' said Mike. 'But it makes it look as if we're doing something.'

That night she pretended to watch a film on video, but found her thoughts turning to her aunt and their last Christmas together. Louise had always gone to enormous trouble to make the holiday festive, with stuffed turkey and home-made plum pudding and too many presents. And because there were only the two of them, she'd usually invited a couple of waifs and strays along for Christmas dinner. Rachel grinned as she remembered the occasional disaster when her aunt's deserving cases got into the sherry and let down their hair.

I'm really an orphan now, she thought. Absolutely alone in the world.

She wondered if she'd ever manage to marry and have a family of her own. From this vantage point it looked impossible. She tried to imagine herself presiding over a Christmas dinner, but the husband and children in the picture remained shadows, refused to come to life. Discouraged and dispirited, she worked her way through half a bottle of expensive Chardonnay.

Watching the re-enactment of the fatal train journey on the late news, Rachel was amazed at the ease with which the camera lied. Helen Winning's face showed no sign of emotional turmoil as she acted out Lisa Broderick's last public appearance: she seemed calm, impassive even. But the cameras did catch a glimpse of the truth about Rachel. Captured for a few seconds in the background at Central Station, her face was so pale it seemed lit from within. Compared with all the tanned, healthy young animals enjoying their Friday night out, she looked sad and drawn.

Like a ghost, Rachel thought.

Sleep proved elusive. As soon as she closed her eyes, the details of the case began to swirl in her mind, fractured, like fragments in a kaleidoscope. She knew she wouldn't get any real rest until the pieces fell into a pattern.

But sleep finally came, bringing with it the familiar sense of being hunted. The paralysed terror was the same, but the scene was becoming clearer. She was in some kind of hallway or corridor, crouched on the floor behind something. The hunter began to move towards her, and despite the dread, she didn't wake up, stayed locked into the dream. The fear loosened her bladder. She could distinctly feel the scalding urine cascading down her bare legs.

Rachel woke. It hadn't all been a dream: the

gush of urine was real. Standing under a hot shower, trying to scrub off the shame and confusion, she relived the humiliation she'd suffered as a child. When she'd first come to Sydney, she'd begun wetting the bed, and though her aunt had been tactful, the indignity had been almost too much for a fastidious little girl to bear. It was even more distressing twenty-four years on.

Her mind jumping, Rachel pulled the bed apart and threw the sheets in the washing machine, made herself a cup of coffee and sat in the kitchen watching Christmas Day dawn. It was as if a dam had broken inside her, and the flood was sweeping her along willy-nilly. But why now?

Lisa Broderick's murder was the only new element in the disciplined, safe life she'd constructed, but it wasn't as if she'd never faced a vicious murder before. Only a year ago she'd been assigned to a case where an outwardly ordinary, quiet railway worker had taken a woman home from a pub, raped her and run his car over her repeatedly. Everything about the murder had saddened and horrified her, but she'd kept her head, acquitted herself professionally. What was it about Lisa Broderick's murder that was making her subconscious riot?

The prospect of telling another soul about her loss of physical control was almost unbearable. Rachel's aunt had been the only person in the world who knew about the bed-wetting; now she'd have to spill her secret to a psychiatrist. First a fainting fit, then paranoid dreams and bed-wetting. Was she having a nervous breakdown, or re-experiencing something real? Either alternative was terrifying. Fighting the desire to put her head down on the kitchen table and howl, Rachel made herself a substantial breakfast and got ready to face the day. It was Christmas after all, the season to be jolly.

'Fa, la, la, la, la la,' she said, staring at her wan face in the mirror. It was the first Christmas after her aunt's death. In a few hours she'd be safe in the bosom of the Westwood family, but somehow she had to live through the day. So far, work was the best substitute for living she'd found, longer-lasting than drugs and more reliable than sex. She decided to go into the office. It would be blissfully quiet there; everybody else would be opening presents with children, having neighbours in for drinks, preparing food for Christmas dinner. Even Lisa Broderick's murderer was no match for Santa Claus.

At headquarters Rachel hit the computer and spent hours sifting through some of the thousands of tips that had flooded in from the public.

If the Chief came in now, he'd think I was dedicated, she thought. But right now I need Lisa more than she needs me.

As usual, dozens of women had informed on husbands and boyfriends. Not for the first time, Rachel wondered how women could continue living with men they thought capable of brutal, cold-blooded violence against another woman. Maybe it turned them on. And how would these men react if they found out what their women were saying about them?

At the Westwoods', a flushed Kate greeted Rachel at the front door, which was adorned with a huge wreath of Australian wildflowers.

'A republican household, I see,' said Rachel, handing Kate a bottle of champagne.

Laughing, Kate said: 'The boys made me do it. They think holly is unpatriotic.'

With its comfortable, dowdy, well-used air, Kate and Alec's house was the polar opposite of Rachel's. Books threatened to colonise every flat surface, the sofas were threadbare, and some of the furniture still bore the scars of children and long-departed cats. After a visit to Kate's, Rachel invariably became discontented with her own house, finding it too lifeless and conventional.

Tonight Kate's living room looked like a set from *A Christmas Carol*, with a huge pine tree decked with tinsel and coloured lights and a rather bedraggled angel teetering on its pinnacle. Rachel's mood lifted as she greeted Alec and added her gifts to the pile under the tree.

Kate's sons Oliver and Gabriel were there, Oliver with Lucy, a university friend whose parents were in the diplomatic corps in Rome. Lucy, a dark-haired beauty dressed in the sort of exotic tat that Rachel had admired but had never been brave enough to wear when she was a teenager, was bright and enviably self-assured.

Rachel was quickly gathered in and given a glass of champagne, and before long, Kate was beckoning her into the kitchen for a gossip. All the time stirring, tasting, seasoning and adjusting gas flames, Kate filled her in on Oliver's new girlfriend. Apparently Lucy had got tired of being dragged from country to country by her peripatetic parents, and dug in, refusing to leave Australia.

'When I look at some of these young women, I'm glad I've got sons,' Kate said. 'Lucy's been living in a communal house with a bunch of other teenagers since she was sixteen. It's not right: kids need guidance.'

She bent down, opened the oven, peered at the turkey and said: 'I don't know how her mother can sleep at night.'

A lot more soundly than you, I'll bet, thought Rachel. Privately, she believed that Kate, like too many guilt-ridden middle-class mothers, coddled her boys to the point where they were totally useless. She doubted they'd ever picked up a sock or a wet towel or knew how to do more in the kitchen than make toast, and pitied the women they married.

But she only said: 'I think girls are more self-sufficient than boys, and Lucy seems pretty well-adjusted.'

'So was Lisa…' began Kate, then stopped, realising Lucy had slipped into the kitchen unnoticed.

Embarrassed, Kate changed the subject. Lucy gave no indication she'd overheard the two women discussing her, but as they left the kitchen in a procession, bearing heaped plates of food, the girl caught Rachel's eye and slipped her a wink. In their absence, the Westwood males, proving Rachel wrong, had set the table, and judging by the noise level, had made short work of the champagne. Alec Westwood said grace over the groaning board, and the feast began.

Heaping her plate with turkey with chestnut stuffing, baked potatoes and pumpkin, fresh peas, and rich dark gravy, Rachel found herself envying Kate Westwood, wishing she were the sort of woman who could juggle a tough job and a family and still find the time to whip up tasty meals for dozens of blow-ins on Sunday evenings without batting an eyelid.

In the midst of the hilarity and good-natured teasing, Rachel quietly observed Kate's children, marvelling at how they'd changed in the ten years since she'd first seen them. Hogging the limelight as usual was Oliver, an impossibly perfect young man with dark gold hair and loads of charm. The product of a benevolent gene pool, excellent nutrition, expensive orthodontic work and thousands of hours of parental care, he wanted to be an actor. Aghast, his practical parents had managed to talk him into getting a degree before he started his training at the National Institute for Dramatic Art.

The other Westwood son, Gabriel, was Alec all over again, a gawky, gangling science student and computer whiz who was terrified of girls and soap and water. Kate was hoping he'd blossom late, but he seemed blissfully unaware of his drawbacks and was as friendly and foolish as a floppy dog.

Inevitably the conversation turned to Lisa Broderick, and Oliver began quizzing Rachel about progress in the case.

'Why are you asking Rachel?' asked Lucy.

'Because she's a cop, dopey,' said Gabriel through a mouthful of food.

'Rachel's on the task force investigating Lisa Broderick's murder, Lucy,' said Kate, a warning note in her voice. 'She might not want to talk about it over Christmas dinner.'

'It's all right, Kate,' said Rachel, and gave them a run-down on the case, leaving out the confidential bits and skating over the gut-wrenching physical details of the murder. Even the blasé Lucy was agog.

'So you've got no idea who did it?' asked Oliver.

'Not so far. We've worked our way through most of the men she knew, but we don't believe any of them had anything to do with it.'

'I saw that creepy re-enactment on television last night,' said Lucy with a shudder. 'Were you there?'

Rachel nodded.

'Aren't you afraid this jerk will come after you?' the girl asked.

'No, why should he?' said Rachel, noting Kate's alarmed expression.

'Well, you're gorgeous and you've been on TV. He might get the hots for you.'

'Lucy!' said Kate.

Peace-keeping as usual, Alec Westwood cut in. 'Relax, Katrina. Rachel can take care of herself.'

I wonder, thought Rachel.

Gabriel chimed in: 'Was Lisa Broderick really a paragon of virtue, or is it just a media beat-up?'

'I've got bad news for you, Gabe,' said Rachel. 'She seems to have been a perfectly nice girl. She should have remarried, had babies and grandchildren and died of old age in her own bed. She was good at her job, loved her parents and had a reputation for being kind to losers.'

'Like you, Gabe,' jeered Oliver.

Before his brother could retaliate, a young man

burst into the dining room. A handsome youth with flashing dark eyes and long, unruly brown hair, he was wearing tattered jeans, boots, a faded checked shirt and an earring. He was angry and upset.

Obviously surprised, Kate rose and went to the boy. 'Jonathan! Rachel, this is Jonathan, my brother's boy.'

Rachel murmured hello, and the young man nodded vaguely in her direction, not really seeing her. Alec pulled up another chair, but Jonathan refused to sit down; instead he grabbed a bottle of wine, poured himself a drink, and stood there, glowering.

'What's wrong, Jon?' asked Kate.

'I've just spent the last three hours at bloody Kings Cross police station, that's what's wrong,' he replied.

'What did you do, mate, stick up a bank?' asked Oliver. His mother quelled him with a glance.

'The cops pulled me over—for a faulty muffler, they said—and the bastards searched the car. And me.'

Oliver and Lucy exchanged a guarded look.

'But why?' asked Kate. The boy shrugged. 'You didn't cheek them, did you?'

Jonathan dropped his eyes. 'Not really.'

Oliver and Lucy sniggered, and Kate threw them a withering look. 'What did they find?' she asked.

'Just some dope.'

'Oh, no,' groaned Kate.

Rachel's heart sank. Christmas Day, a couple of patrol officers angry at having to work on a holiday, spoiling for a fight: it was a recipe for revenge.

'Why on earth didn't you call someone to get you out?' asked Alec, more exasperated than sympathetic.

'They wouldn't let me make a phone call. When I asked, they laughed. Said I'd been watching too much TV, that this wasn't America.' He stared down at the table and said softly: 'They body searched me.'

There was a horrified silence.

'What happens now?' asked Alec, finally.

'I have to go before a magistrate next month. In the meantime, I suppose I've got to contact the folks in London and tell them. The old boy will throw a fit.'

'It's not as bad as it looks,' said Rachel, trying to restore calm. 'You won't go to jail for a first offence. At your age and with your character references, they'll put you on a bond under Section 556A. That means it'll be recorded as proven, but with no conviction: you won't have a criminal record.'

She regretted it immediately. All eyes swivelled in her direction.

Reaching across the table for the wine bottle, Lucy said sweetly: 'You'd think with a madman running around loose the police would have better things to do with their time, wouldn't you?'

'Lucy! That's enough!' said Kate.

Rachel held up her hand, silencing her friend. 'Please, it's OK. I know some police take advantage of their uniforms. It's a big organisation, and sometimes the wrong people get in. But the police are undereducated and badly paid, and I'm afraid you get what you pay for.'

Jonathan tried to interrupt, but Rachel stared him down. 'I'm sorry your Christmas was spoiled, Jonathan, but you were caught holding a prohibited substance, and it sounds as if your car was unroadworthy.'

'But...' said Jonathan.

'I know you think the drug laws are hypocritical and unworkable, and I'd tend to agree with you, but until they're changed, you're taking a risk breaking them.'

'But they only busted me because I was driving an old car and had long hair,' protested Jonathan.

'I know, but look on the bright side. In a couple of years you'll probably be driving an imported car and wearing a suit, and the police won't notice you unless you run over their feet.

Your chances of ending up in jail are almost zero. So spare a Christmas thought for the no-hopers who don't have the luxury of dropping back into the boring old middle class. They'll keep getting busted, and they'll probably end up in jail.'

'Go, Rachel!' said Oliver, thumping the table.

Jonathan looked from one face to another, mystified.

'She's a cop, you idiot!' said Gabriel, taking pity.

Then Jonathan blushed painfully, and his cousins laughed with the healthy callousness of youth. The tension ebbed, and Jonathan was soon jollied out of his black mood. The evening had been ruined for Rachel, though. She'd hoped for sanctuary in the Westwood home, neutral ground, but it seemed as if she couldn't escape crime and punishment for even a few hours.

Later, when she took her leave, Kate accompanied her to the front porch to see her off. 'I'm sorry, Rachel,' Kate said, taking her friend's hands and looking into her eyes.

'Stop worrying, Kate. You can't make the whole world right. I'm sorry, too. I shouldn't have come down so hard on Jonathan: he's just young.'

'And foolish,' said Kate, and they laughed.

But Rachel hadn't fooled Kate, and as she drove off, she caught a snapshot of her friend's face, full of concern, in the rear-vision mirror.

She probably thinks I'm going home to slit my wrists, she thought. Maybe I should. 'Merry Christmas, Rachel,' she said to her reflection.

Next day being a public holiday, Rachel was thrown on to her own devices. Unable to face going into work again, she rang the yoga school on the off-chance there would be someone lonely or dedicated enough to take a class on Boxing Day. She was in luck.

Arriving at the nondescript building in Bondi Junction slightly late and agitated from the heavy traffic, Rachel inhaled the familiar smell— sweat and a slight mustiness overlaid with the lavender oil one of the instructors sprinkled on the carpet to freshen the room. She quickly undressed and pulled on tights and a faded maroon T-shirt—the sorts of people who practised yoga weren't interested in glamorous gym wear—and joined the class. By this time, they were on to virasana suptavirasana, a resting pose. She did some quick warm-ups on the ropes and settled on to the floor and felt her body beginning to unknot.

It wasn't till the class was almost over that she noticed a new face among the regulars. Or was it? Something about the woman seemed familiar.

The school's owner, Carol, was running the class, so it was concentrated and disciplined—no standing about chatting. Two hours later, invigorated but rather more relaxed, Rachel was passing the time of day with an old hand called Nikki, when she noticed the new student edging closer. When Nikki left, the woman approached and said: 'Do you remember me?'

'Yes, but remind me...'

The woman was well-fleshed and strong-looking.

'The hospital,' the woman prompted. 'You interviewed us about Lisa Broderick. I'm Judy Rowlands.' She seemed nervous, but police have that effect on some people, and murder has it on almost everybody.

'Of course. You look different in leotards.'

The woman laughed sardonically: 'Fatter, you mean? Do you have time for a coffee?'

'Sure.'

Lisa Broderick's colleague had something on her mind. It might be just an obsessive need to talk about the murder of her friend, but it could be a lead. They strolled along the mall, found an open coffee shop, and went in. Not wanting to lose the sense of well-being the yoga had given her, Rachel stuck to orange juice. Coffee made her speed at the best of times. They chatted about yoga for a while, comparing schools and teachers like experts.

'I just can't do headstands,' complained Judy.

'It's partly upper body strength, partly nerve,' said Rachel, waiting patiently for Judy Rowlands to come to a decision. 'It'll come; don't push it.'

'Don't push the river, you mean?' said the nurse, and they both laughed: of all the Buddhist teachings, it was probably the most useful. If you could manage to practise it.

After fifteen minutes of shilly-shallying, Rachel made her move. 'Judy, do you have something you want to tell me about Lisa Broderick?'

The woman kept her eyes on the hill she was constructing in the centre of the sugar bowl: 'It might be nothing. I don't want to make trouble if I'm just imagining something.'

'There won't be any trouble. If it seems promising, I'll look into it myself. Does that help?'

Judy Rowlands sighed. 'OK. It's just that Lisa and I were on the same shift two weeks before she died, and she said something odd to me. I only remembered it after you talked to us, then I thought I might have imagined it, or got it wrong. It's so hard to remember...'

'What did she say?'

'She was looking out into the corridor and someone went by, and she sort of hugged herself and said, "I think I might have done the wrong thing there." I looked up, but I couldn't see anyone. I said "What do you mean, the wrong thing?" And she said, "I just don't seem to be able to get rid of people." '

Rachel's pulse quickened: the incident seemed to bear out her intuition about Lisa Broderick's character. 'That's all?'

'I think so, but I wasn't paying all that much attention. An old woman was dying. I wasn't too worried about Lisa's social life.'

'Who was she talking about?'

'That's the problem. I don't know. I wasn't fast enough. Whoever it was had moved out of sight. And it didn't seem all that important at the time.'

'But now it does?'

The nurse shrugged: 'If it was a woman, it was just a throwaway remark, but if it was a man, maybe she thought that she'd led him on, raised his hopes.' Almost as an afterthought, she said, 'But she was always doing that.'

Rachel's pulse quickened. 'What do you mean?'

'Taking on lame ducks and being nice to them.'

'Why do you suppose she did it?'

'I think she was superstitious. She'd been so lucky in her life...I don't know how to explain. Maybe she thought if she put something back in, she'd be able to keep what she had. That's only a guess from someone with one year of psych in nurse training. I'm no expert on people's motives. I don't know why I do things half the time.'

Or maybe it was simple goodness, thought Rachel. It's becoming so rare people refuse to believe it when they see it. Or feel it.

'Do you remember exactly when it happened, Judy?'

'No, but it's easy to check. It was the night Mrs Saunders died.'

'So we can find out who else was on that shift, and who might have been in the area when you were in Mrs Saunders' room?'

'I can tell you who was on in our ward, pretty much, but there's always lots of through-traffic. It's a big hospital.'

Don't I know it, thought Rachel. And now I'll have to go back in there.

'Where can I reach you, Judy?'

The nurse gave her work and home phone numbers and wrote down the names of the people on the crucial shift. As they parted, she asked: 'Did I do the right thing? You don't think I'm being silly?'

'You did the right thing. I don't want to frighten you, but I'd advise you to act as if one of the men working in the hospital killed Lisa.'

The woman looked shocked: 'Should I tell the others?'

'I think you should let it drop in the staff room that the police haven't ruled out hospital staff as suspects. And I wouldn't walk around the grounds alone at night.'

Rachel was tempted to call Mike at home to tell him the news, but decided it would be out of line. He'd probably be with his family...And what if a woman answered the phone?

7

Throw Your Arms Around Me

Riding the phone all morning, Rachel hectored out of the hospital bureaucrats the roster of ward 3B for December 3 as well as any other staff who might have passed Mrs Saunders' room that evening. As far as they could remember, there were five: a male nurse, a gerontologist, a man visiting his dying mother, a physiotherapist and one of the maintenance staff fixing a broken doorhandle.

She showed the list to Mike. 'You call the specialist and I'll do the others,' she suggested. 'You know what male doctors are like. He'll call me girlie and patronise me. I've had a rough enough day without that.'

Mike smirked, but agreed.

After another marathon phone session, they were able to clear the doctor, who'd been at a send-off for a colleague leaving to teach at Harvard Medical School. It had been held on the other side of the city, north of the Harbour Bridge, and lasted till midnight.

'He couldn't have made it to Crossley in time,' said Mike, sounding a little disappointed. The medico had been as rude as Rachel had predicted.

The visiting son turned out to be gay, and said he'd been at home with his housemate all night. They'd stayed in and watched the 1937 version of *A Star is Born* on video. He and Rachel agreed it was miles better than the Streisand/Kristofferson travesty. By the time she put down the phone, Rachel had cheered up considerably, and crossed him off her list.

Damien Grant, the male nurse, was unreachable, on holiday, trekking in Nepal. They put a question mark beside his name. Peter Lucas, the physiotherapist had been to a movie with his girlfriend, getting out at 11 p.m. He'd then taken her home and they'd gone to bed. The girl's flatmate verified their story.

'What about this maintenance man?' asked Mike. 'Was that the creep with the keys we saw the other day?'

'I think so. According to the roster he was on duty till eleven.'

'If he doesn't have proof of where he was after eleven, he could be a player. Do we have an address for him?'

Rachel checked her notes.

'Newtown.'

'That means he could have got to Crossley by the time Lisa's train came in.'

'What do you think?' asked Rachel.

'I think we've got to talk to him, and the trekker.' Remembering the incident in the hospital, he offered to interview the janitor. She coloured slightly, but agreed.

That afternoon Brett Marcantonio, who'd been running a background check on the men Judy Rowlands had seen in the hospital corridor, reported that Damien Grant had a police record. Two years before, his estranged wife had brought charges against him for rape. She'd been badly beaten as well, spending a night and a day in hospital, but had later dropped the charges.

'Let's talk to her,' said Mike, picking up the phone.

At first Jeannie Carmichael adamantly refused to discuss her former husband, but yielded when they mentioned Lisa Broderick's murder. She agreed to talk to them at closing time at the flower shop she owned in the city. By the time Mike and Rachel had fought their way through the commuters and found a parking space, she was locking the door behind her last customer, a businessman sheepishly clutching a bunch of red roses.

'I thought you weren't coming,' she said, letting

them in. While the florist gathered up stalks and leaves, put scissors and vases away, wiped down the counter, all the time watching them nervously, Rachel stared about her. Jeannie Carmichael had talent: her arrangements were original and arresting, with unexpected choices of plants and unusual colour combinations. Rachel breathed in a heady emanation of flowers, eucalyptus leaves, lavender, ferns, wondering what it would be like to work in such idyllic surroundings. But obviously the deep, calm breath of the blooms had failed to soothe the soul of Jeannie Carmichael, who was too thin, too blonde, too highly strung.

'I don't know what I can tell you,' she said, when Mike asked her about Damien Grant. 'I haven't seen him since I took out a restraining order on him after the…assault.'

'Tell us about that,' said Mike.

The woman wrung her hands, then realising what she was doing, dropped them to a vase of glowing purple irises and began to rearrange them absent-mindedly. 'The first few years were good. I put Damien through university by selling flowers. We were happy…at least I was. But about three years ago he changed. He started spending all his money on drugs and all his time trying to score. He kept promising to stop, but he couldn't. I kept hoping…

'Then one day he brought a friend to the house.

Rory, his name was. He was a dealer; even I could see that. This Rory went on and on about how much money he made selling drugs. That wasn't the worst, though. He bragged about how he broke people's kneecaps if they didn't pay their bills. He thought it was funny. And Damien was going along with it because he wanted to stay on the right side of this...animal. Damien's supposed to be a healer. That was it for me.'

Lulled by the beauty of the blooms, half-intoxicated by the scent of flowers, Rachel was brought back to earth with a thud by this too-familiar story of human greed and stupidity.

'So you left,' prompted Mike.

The woman laughed. 'Eventually. I had some mad idea of making Damien move out of the house, but he just dug in. I didn't feel safe around him any more, so I eventually cracked and left. Then it started. He rang me, he followed me, he broke into my flat. I got so frightened I went to the police, but they said they couldn't do anything: he hadn't committed a crime.'

'This was before the stalking laws were tightened up, I take it,' interrupted Mike.

'Yes, about two years ago.'

Rachel understood now why the woman looked so strung-out. What would it be like to be hunted down by someone who professed to love you, to become a desperate man's obsession? You'd start to wonder which of you was mad.

'He found out I'd been to the police,' continued Jeannie Carmichael. 'They must have gone to see him. That's when he broke in and raped me and beat me up.' She paled and trailed to a halt.

They waited. She found her voice and said: 'I think he was daring me to take it further.'

'Which you did,' said Mike.

'I had no choice. It was out of my hands by then. My next-door neighbour heard me screaming and rang the police. They called the ambulance and the whole thing took on a life of its own. I let them talk me into laying charges.'

'But you dropped them,' said Rachel. 'Why didn't you go through with it?'

The woman hugged herself and rubbed her bare, brown arms. 'He put on his white coat and name tag and came into my hospital room in the middle of the night and told me if I went ahead with it, he'd kill me. He said the police had taken him in and humiliated him, and that I'd have to pay. He half-smothered me with a pillow, and when I got my breath back, he said: "What are you going to do now, Jeannie?" Of course I told him I was going to drop the charges. I'm not crazy.'

'Is he still stalking you?' asked Mike.

'No. I got a lawyer to write a letter telling him I'd charge him with attempted murder as well as rape if he ever came near me again.'

'And it worked?' asked Rachel.

'It did when I moved in with the lawyer,' the woman answered, deadpan.

Mike and Rachel exchanged glances: in less ghoulish circumstances, it would be funny. 'Is he capable of murder?' asked Mike.

Jeannie Carmichael's busy fingers turned a length of white satin ribbon into a perfect bow. 'I've been asking myself that all day. I'll admit it crossed my mind when I heard about the murder and realised Lisa Broderick worked at his hospital, but I decided it wasn't Damien's style. He's very good-looking and superficially charming...Have you met him? No? Well, he has no trouble attracting women. If he'd wanted Lisa Broderick, he could probably have had her. He wouldn't have had to kill her.'

'But what about his violence towards you?' said Mike.

'I think it was a combination of things. It was a sort of temporary insanity, I suspect. I'm probably the only woman in his life who could make him that angry. He'd bottomed out on drugs, he was broke, he was worried about his job. My withdrawal was the last straw. We were high-school sweethearts, you know. He was always too dependent on me, though he'd never admit that. Or even recognise it.'

Rachel was impressed. The woman had obviously thought long and hard about her marriage: perhaps counselling had helped. 'Has he done anything about his problems?' she asked.

'I heard he'd dried out and was paying off his debts,' said the woman. 'I don't want to know, really. I don't care any more. I've been in therapy ever since the rape. All I want to do is not feel anything for him.'

But she isn't quite there yet, Rachel thought, watching the nervous hands.

There was nothing more to learn here. Mike signalled that it was time to go. Rachel nodded agreement and said: 'You've got a wonderful eye, Jeannie. Could you do me some flowers?'

The woman seemed surprised, but pleased. 'Of course, what would you like?'

Rachel's eyes roved the shelves and locked on to a bucket of sweet peas. She could never smell the unassuming little flowers without a wash of bittersweet nostalgia: perhaps they'd grown in her parents' garden. Rachel pointed, and the florist made her a posy of mauve and white sweet peas and baby's breath.

Rachel's choice was a revelation to Mike. He would have expected her to favour strong, spiky flowers like tiger lilies or prehistoric-looking Australian native plants. But sweet peas were so...innocent.

Belatedly, he realised Rachel had bought the flowers for Jeannie Carmichael as well as for herself: the woman was smiling when they left.

'What do you think?' he asked as they drove off.

Lifting her reluctant face from the flowers Rachel said, 'I wouldn't cross him off the list just yet. Look at all the killers whose wives didn't suspect a thing.'

'Or say they didn't,' replied Mike.

On her way to Woollahra for her second appointment with the psychiatrist, Rachel turned on a rock radio station and got an old Hunters and Collectors' song. It was about a joyous lovers' reunion, and one of the lines ran: 'You will make me call your name and I will shout it to the blue summer skies'. She sighed. Nobody had ever written a song like that for her, and it was unlikely anyone ever would.

She took her flowers into the doctor's office: they wouldn't last five minutes in this heat in the locked car. The doctor took them from her and put them in the sink in the little kitchen behind her office. 'Remind me to get these before you leave,' she said. 'Though I think I could bear to take them home.'

She came back and sat down, noting how melancholy Rachel was today, how disinclined to get down to business.

'You're sad. What's wrong?'

'Just some silly song about some woman throwing her arms around her lover. I was thinking how long it's been since anyone's wanted to throw their arms around me.'

This wasn't the direction Persia Lawrence had intended to take, but it was fortuitous: Rachel was attractive and smart and apparently kind; if she didn't have men in her life, it must be by choice. But why? 'Is it possible people have wanted to do it, but you haven't let them?'

Rachel thought about this, skirted the question: 'I've had lovers.'

'Had?'

'Now I just seem to work.'

'Was that a conscious decision?'

'It must have been. There are plenty of men out there, but it doesn't seem worth the effort.'

'Why not?'

'The relationships I had didn't make me happy. A couple of those men thought they loved me…or maybe they just wanted me, but what they wanted was some notion they had of me. They didn't have any idea who I really was. They didn't even know they didn't know me…'

'Was that their fault?'

'How do you mean?' asked Rachel, knowing full well what she meant.

Persia played along. 'Do you think it was them

112

failing to connect with you, or you refusing to let them?'

Rachel pondered that. It was always easier to dole out blame than to accept it, but love is a two-handed game. 'Both, I suppose. How's that for honesty?'

The psychiatrist smiled: honesty was a movable feast. 'Did you give up on love because you didn't feel anything, or because you did?'

It was a clever shot. Rachel came to attention: this psychiatrist would make a good police officer. That didn't mean she wanted to answer the question, though. 'That's too hard, Persia,' she feinted. 'Can I take a rain check?'

Persia Lawrence had prised open tougher nuts than this with a pointed question. 'Do you dislike men, Rachel?'

No matter how women felt about men, few except feminist separatists would come out and admit they didn't actually like the other sex. Though Rachel was no braver than most, she resisted the temptation to deny it automatically. 'I don't know if it's dislike. I'm not used to them, I suppose. I grew up in a female household, went to a girls school. Men didn't really play much of a role in my life till I got to university, and by that time it was too late to be relaxed around them. They seemed like aliens.'

'How long did that last?'

'I'm not sure it's ever ended. I can socialise with men, and even go to bed with them, but I'm not comfortable having them in my space. They seem to take up so much room...And I've never been totally happy about going to sleep with a strange man in my bed. I'd much prefer they went home.'

'You'd consider a man you're sleeping with a "strange" man?'

'Why not?' asked Rachel. 'How can you tell? The first thing you learn in homicide is that the person most likely to harm you physically, even murder you, is the person you sleep with.'

It was a flip answer, and the doctor ignored it. 'Do you have any idea where this distrust of men came from?'

'I used to think it was because my father died when I was young.' Like all new psychology students, Rachel had analysed herself obsessively, applied every new theory to herself, come down with the symptoms of every neurosis, before she'd learned critical distance. The most obvious answer was a sense of abandonment, but she wasn't going to volunteer it.

She didn't have to. 'Did you feel he'd abandoned you by dying?' asked the doctor.

'Yes.'

'You said you used to think that? Have you changed your mind?'

'It doesn't hold up as a reason for mistrusting

men. My mother died in the same accident—abandoned me, too, if you like—but I don't have the same sort of problem with women.'

'Was your father responsible for the accident?'

'I'm not sure. My aunt implied that he drank too much, and they had a head-on collision, so it's a possibility.' She knew what Persia Lawrence was getting at. 'I don't think I blame him.'

A sense of abandonment was more likely to lead to poor self-esteem and depression than the anxiety this young woman was feeling. The doctor was certain there was something else. 'Would you say you're frightened of men?'

The question put Rachel on the defensive. Nobody likes to admit fear, especially not a female member of the Homicide Squad. 'Why should I be frightened?'

'I don't know. Are you?'

The silence lengthened as Rachel thought back over her relationships with men. They always ended the same way, with her withdrawal. Eventually men made her claustrophobic. It was partly emotional, but partly physical, too: their size, their superior strength, their maleness, threatened her somehow. It was too complicated to go into.

'Any woman who doesn't fear men is a fool,' she said. 'Men are dangerous. It's an objective reality. I see it every day in my job. If they're not bullying people emotionally, they're beating them up, killing them, exploiting them sexually.'

'Are all men like that?'

'I suppose not, but how do you know what any man's capable of?'

Persia Lawrence couldn't argue with any of this, but dealing in abstractions wouldn't solve Rachel's problem. 'Was your father violent?'

'Not that I've ever heard. I can't remember him. From what my aunt's let drop, I got the impression he was unreliable, didn't like responsibility. That sort of thing.'

The psychiatrist digested this new information. It might account for Rachel's unwillingness to rely on men, but didn't explain her sense of physical danger around them. She tried another tack.

'Tell me more about your job, Rachel. Why did you join the police force?'

'I wanted to stop them. I wanted to stop men hurting people.' As she said it, Rachel realised it was more honest than the answer she'd given Mike Ross. But then, he was a man.

'So it was an ideological decision?'

Rachel was startled: 'Why do you say that?'

'From what you've told me, there were no violent men in your life; there's no evidence of sexual assault, unless you've repressed it; and you were brought up by a supportive woman, so it couldn't have been based on personal experience. So where do you suppose it came from?'

Rachel shrugged. Put like that, her career choice seemed inexplicable. She couldn't even attribute it to example, as she'd had nothing to do with individual police officers—apart from one speeding ticket—before she joined up.

The therapist had some ideas about Rachel's motives for joining the police force, but it was essential that Rachel figure it out for herself. There was a lengthy silence. Persia Lawrence watched Rachel's face, saw that a struggle of some sort was going on. She saw it often, when a patient trotted out a cherished formula and watched it disintegrate under the harsh light of scrutiny. But Rachel surprised her by saying: 'Persia, I had a nightmare a couple of nights ago and wet the bed.'

The psychiatrist's interest quickened: this was more like it. 'Tell me about the nightmare, Rachel.'

Rachel recounted the sense of being hunted down. Even retelling it made her anxious and sweaty-palmed.

'Did you wet the bed as a child?'

'Yes, after I came to live with my aunt. It lasted about two years.'

'Did she talk to you about it? Try to explain it?'

'No. She pretended it wasn't happening. She didn't even take me to a doctor. It was our dirty little secret. Or that's how I felt at the time.'

'Did you ever get round to talking about it?'

'No, and now we never will.'

'Because she died.'

Rachel nodded.

'Tell me about your aunt's stroke.'

Rachel remembered the surge of panic she'd felt when Mrs Cripps, her aunt's neighbour, had called to tell her that Louise was in hospital. Mrs Cripps had noticed the newspaper still on Louise's porch at midday and had investigated, finding Louise on the floor beside her bed. Rachel had driven to the hospital and picked her way through the labyrinth to her aunt's ward in a sort of dream, suspended, not knowing what she'd find. Mrs Cripps had implied it was a bad stroke, but Rachel hadn't wanted to consider the possibility that her aunt might die. Or that she would be paralysed and unable to speak.

But the unthinkable was what she'd found. Louise had looked impossibly small and helpless in the hospital bed. Eyeing the life-saving tubes snaking out of the thin body, Rachel had suddenly realised how irrevocably illness reversed traditional roles. Now she was the adult; now it was her turn to do the caring.

Then her aunt had opened her eyes and seen Rachel, had tried to speak, but could only make terrible, strangled sounds that froze Rachel's heart. For weeks, every time Rachel closed her eyes she saw Louise's terrified eyes staring up at her

118

beseechingly. Help me, Rachel. Make it better. But nobody could make it better. In intensive care a week later, Louise had suffered another, catastrophic stroke and was dead before Rachel could reach the hospital.

Recounting this to Persia Lawrence, Rachel said: 'It's as if the last link with my past has gone. I've been cut adrift. The last of the line. Now I'll never find out what my parents were really like. While Louise was alive, there was always the possibility I'd get the courage to force her to talk to me, that she'd unbend and give me a history, but that's gone now. I'm completely alone.'

She looked up at the psychiatrist: 'I wonder if people who pretend they want to be free realise how frightening it can be.'

'What did you do about coming to terms with Louise's death and the loss of your history, Rachel?'

'Nothing, really. I talked about Louise to Kate Westwood, who'd met her, and I spent some time with Louise's neighbours and her priest, but mostly I just got on with organising the funeral and clearing out her house.'

At the time the funeral had been a godsend: a practical task to keep her mind off the sorrow, the waste. Louise had only been sixty-five. She should have had a good ten years ahead of her. The funeral had been surprisingly well attended. There were women from the charity where Louise did volunteer work, some workers from a homeless men's shelter where she occasionally helped out in the kitchen, members of the church, and neighbours. Rachel wondered if she'd have such a big turnout. At least if she was killed in action, there would be a huge police funeral with appropriate pomp and ceremony and official hypocrisy.

Some kind of chemical response, adrenalin perhaps, saw her through the funeral, but clearing out her aunt's house—the house where she'd grown up—was an ordeal of a higher order. The helpful friends had returned to their lives, and she found herself alone. The clothes were easy: she sent them all to her aunt's charity. After she'd picked out any furniture she wanted—a splendid circular Australian cedar table, a walnut sideboard, some glassware and silver and a Royal Doulton dinner set—a second-hand dealer took the rest away.

She sorted the books and records, kept some and gave the rest to the library her aunt had patronised for thirty years and where Rachel had read her way first around the children's section and later the adult collection. Some powerful echo of her aunt's proscription made her leave Louise's personal papers till last.

Then one night, sitting on her aunt's bedroom floor, she opened the cedar box of documents that

Louise had always kept locked in her little escritoire. There were Rachel's report cards, lovingly tied with a red ribbon, and birth certificates for Rachel, Louise, and Rachel's mother, Claire. Claire and Tom Addison's marriage certificate was there, along with their death certificates. The full circle, thought Rachel. A whole life in three official forms. And there was a passport belonging to Louise, who must have been a keen traveller before she'd suddenly become a foster-mother. It bore entry stamps to England, France, Italy, Germany, Turkey, Greece, Spain and Morocco.

Turkey! thought Rachel. Morocco! She suddenly saw the sedate, buttoned-up Louise in another light. Maybe she'd been different before the tragedy had changed her life, before she'd taken on the responsibility for a damaged child. She wanted to cry, but the tears would not come, as usual.

Louise, did I ever thank you properly? she wondered. I tried to show you how grateful I was by being a good girl, by coming top of the class, by never giving you a bad moment. It was too much responsibility for both of us.

As she packed up all the photographs of her life with Louise to take home, Rachel became convinced there had to be more. And there were. Louise had bundled them into a shoe box and pushed it to the back of the top shelf of the wardrobe in the spare room—pictures of Louise and Claire as children, photos of their parents, Rachel's grandparents, who'd died when their daughters were in their teens and twenties. They hadn't lived to see the next generation. But most precious of all were the photographs of Rachel's parents: a backyard wedding with Claire dressed in what looked like an old ivory lace wedding dress from the forties cut down—daring for 1965—with flowers in her hair beside Tom Addison, burly and bearded in an obviously borrowed suit; numerous photos of Claire and Tom Addison and baby Rachel in the backyard of their house in the country. Rachel stared long at the photographs, mesmerised by the long-denied reunion with her parents.

She told Persia Lawrence all this.

'How did you feel about Louise keeping the photographs from you?'

'I don't know if I've worked out exactly how I feel yet. Intellectually, I know she probably justified it on the grounds that she was protecting me from my unfortunate past, but emotionally, I'm confused and angry about it. Maybe it was herself she was protecting. Louise probably hadn't wanted her sister to marry some mad American and live out in the bush. She was hurt, I suppose, and angry at Tom for causing my mother's death.'

Time was up.

'Next time I want us to talk about the nightmare, Rachel. See if we can find out what it means. Will this time next week do?'

'I think it should be sooner, if you can fit me in,' said Rachel. Instinct told her time was short. Whatever was out there waiting to pounce fed on weakness and ignorance: knowledge would be her best defence.

Driving home, she played over the interview in her mind, like a contestant who'd failed a quiz by forgetting a familiar fact. Deep down she knew that she held the answers, locked in her memory. She had a sudden vision of a savage dog hurling itself at a door, howling. Did she dare set it free?

The thought of going home filled her with dread. Shut up all day, the house would be suffocating, and she was too restless to settle to anything. Detouring through the city to the Domain, she grabbed her swimming gear out of the back seat and entered the Boy Charlton Pool. The serious swimmers were here this time of the evening, ploughing up and down the pool doing laps. That was the beauty of swimming, you couldn't gnash and worry: the simple effort of breathing regularly and churning through the water was a form of meditation.

After twenty laps she was calmer, the worry washed away. Smelling of chlorine, she sat on the side of the pool in the twilight watching the activity at the nearby naval dockyard. This was an oasis. The great trees of the Botanic Gardens breathed gently behind the pool, and an evening breeze filled with the smell of the harbour rippled its surface: elsewhere, the city sweltered under a poisonous temperature inversion. There was something eerie in the atmosphere, a sense of things coming to a head.

8

Even the Stones Would Mourn

Rachel was at her desk pretending to work, brooding over her nightmare and its effects. In this job more than most you had to rely on your body, and hers had let her down. Feeling more than a little paranoid, she was rattled and slightly alarmed when a young policeman came to her desk and said the Chief wanted to talk to her.

The police force's idea of good management was to kick arse when something went wrong, so she'd assumed the silence after her TV appearance signified approval. What now? she thought.

She was finally ushered in after cooling her heels for fifteen minutes while the Chief Inspector dealt with some emergency.

'Good job on that documentary, Addison,' he said. Before she could do more than nod, he added: 'I hear you're a good interrogator.'

It was unanswerable. Rachel sat tight. If there

was anything this job had taught her, it was the value of strategic silences.

Checkmated, he said: 'They tell me you can get hardened old lags crying on your shoulder.'

'I think that's a bit of an exaggeration, Sir.'

'Be that as it may, how do you do it?'

The process was entirely intuitive with Rachel. She'd refrained from analysing it out of superstition, believing in letting well alone. What it came down to, she realised, now she was forced to think about it, was judging the moment when the need to share the experience—either through guilt, remorse or sheer boastfulness—became irresistible, and giving the suspect the opportunity to confess. It was the quality of attention, the ability to listen, a skill most women absorbed with their mother's milk, a survival skill in a hostile world. And it was something to do with trust: rightly or wrongly, men trusted women more than their own kind.

Aware of the need to choose her words carefully with this old-style copper, she said: 'It's about listening, I think, Sir.'

Suspecting she'd edited her reply to suit her audience, but totally unable to fault her demeanour or the answer, the Chief realised why his men trod lightly around this woman. 'Listening, eh?' he said. 'Well, I want you to go and listen to this little girl's husband, what's his name?'

Rachel was elated. 'Tony Broderick.'

'That's right. We need to know what really happened in that marriage. Who left whom. How he felt about his wife seeing other men. Go and have a talk to him. But clear it with Dick Kellett first, will you, or he'll get his knickers in a knot.'

'Thank you, Sir.'

'This isn't by way of being a favour, Addison. On your way.'

At the door, Rachel hesitated.

'What else?' asked her boss.

'Could I talk to Roger Blair as well, Sir? He's Tony Broderick's best friend, and Kellett thinks he may have been having an affair with Lisa.'

The Chief laughed. 'In for a penny, in for a pound. Go for it.'

He waved her out, his mind on more important things than her problems with Dick Kellett.

Rachel decided to get the inevitable showdown with Kellett over quickly. She found him in the courtyard out the back, leaning against the wall in the shade, having a smoke. Seeing her coming, he flicked his cigarette on to the cement, ground it out and prepared to leave.

'Can I talk to you, Dick?' she said, forestalling him.

He shrugged. 'Talk.'

'The boss has asked me to interview Tony Broderick. I thought I should clear it with you first.'

'Clear it with me? Tell me, you mean.'

'Let you know as a courtesy, then,' said Rachel.

'I like that. You think it's courteous creeping around my back convincing people you can do a better job than I can, do you? I've got another word for it.' Kellett's voice was as cold as a shard of ice.

'Like what?' asked Rachel, provoked.

'Disloyalty.'

'Since when have you been loyal to me, Inspector Kellett?'

Kellett laughed. 'You haven't got a clue, have you, girlie. I could break you'—he snapped his fingers—'just like that. So far you haven't been important enough for me to bother with, but I could change my mind.'

'Doesn't finding this murderer mean anything to you, Inspector?' asked Rachel.

'Lisa Broderick is just another dead girl, Addison. She's not going to help you out in a tight spot. Your mates will do that. If you have any left after your little starring role.'

'I was ordered to go on television,' protested Rachel.

'Maybe, but you loved it, didn't you? Your fifteen minutes of fame.'

Outraged, Rachel turned to go, but Kellett got the last word, of course. 'It doesn't pay to go behind my back, Addison.'

Sweaty-palmed and trembling, Rachel spent five minutes alone recovering her composure before she went in search of Mike. She found him in the tea room. Mike was elated initially, but then the implications sank in. 'How did Kellett take it?'

'Badly. Accused me of disloyalty.'

'Kellett's a bad man to cross, Rachel. I thought you handled him well in the pub the other night, but I'd lie very low after this little episode. He's watching you now, and if you put a foot wrong, he'll make sure everybody knows about it.'

Rachel considered her reply. The Chief had put her in a difficult position, but he'd also given her a chance to prove herself. And Rachel was ambitious. 'I'll handle it,' she said, and grinned at him. 'Just stand behind me, OK?'

On their way to interview Tony Broderick, Mike said: 'Do you believe in clairvoyants?'

Clairvoyants occasionally surfaced in major murder inquiries, and sex murders were a magnet for weirdos, professional confessors, amateur criminologists, informers and malicious snoops. In this business healthy scepticism could quickly harden into a closed mind, but Rachel was aware of the dangers of writing something off out of blind prejudice.

'My first reaction is that it's rubbish, but then I'm not into all that new age stuff, you know, crystals and pyramids,' she said. 'But I've heard stories about clairvoyants turning cases around. I just don't know, Mike. My aunt was dead against that sort of thing. I had my palm read once in high school, and she hit the roof.'

'What did it say?' asked Mike.

'An old woman did the reading. She was a bit scary, actually. You can see why old women frighten some people: they know too much and they've got too little to lose.'

Suddenly, she looked in the rear-vision mirror, accelerated and veered across two lanes of traffic to turn right. 'Nearly missed the turn-off,' she explained to Mike, who was clutching the dashboard.

'You haven't told me what she said,' he prodded, when he'd relaxed sufficiently to speak.

Rachel shrugged. 'She said I'd end up on the side of light, though there would be a long tunnel in the middle. I mustn't despair, but I must remain vigilant. She told me to remember that it's easy for the hunter to become the prey when the wind changes.'

Mike turned and stared at her. 'Christ!'

Rachel laughed. 'Relax. It's nonsense, like the I Ching and astrology.'

She wasn't going to admit the reading had scared the hell out of her, that she'd made up something innocuous when her aunt had pressed for details. Taking her eyes off the road for a moment, she gave Mike a hard look: 'What's this all about, anyway?'

'A clairvoyant's been ringing me every day, driving me nuts, that's all.'

'And you want me to say it's OK to talk to him?'

'Yeah, I suppose so,' he said, caught out. The bloody woman was laughing at him. 'It's a her, by the way.'

'What do you think?'

'I think it's hokum, but...'

'But what if this person really knows something and we ignore her and she turns out to have been right and then we're left with egg on our faces?'

'Something like that.'

'OK, Mike. I give you permission to talk to the clairvoyant.'

Rachel sneaked a look at his face: he was grinning. 'Good, I've already teed up an appointment for Monday morning. For both of us.'

Rachel grimaced. 'Don't they usually need something belonging to the dead person? Have you got something of Lisa's?'

'I think they'll let me have one of the sandals she was wearing when she was killed. It's got no evidentiary value.'

'Good God, how did you manage that?'

'The old man's a bit superstitious, I think. I sent the idea up the line, and he said we might as well

131

try anything. I think the Commissioner's giving him a hard time. And someone said he was on a case once where a clairvoyant helped.'

Rachel didn't answer, and Mike sensed her scepticism. 'You think this is a wild-goose chase?'

'Probably. But it isn't the first, and it won't be the last. Do what you have to do, Mike.'

Chagrined, not sure whether he'd won or lost the round, he slotted a tape in the car stereo, cutting off any further conversation.

Lisa Broderick's ex-husband was living in an expensive but characterless high-rise flat in Neutral Bay, a dormitory area on the lower north shore. The only decoration was a framed blow-up of a photograph of the couple taken on a yacht in happier times. Tony Broderick was in his early thirties, tall and nice-looking in a forgettable sort of way, with light-brown eyes, even features and fair to medium colouring. There were purple shadows under his eyes, and he'd cut himself shaving.

Rachel had realised, as Tony Broderick answered the door, that the man was half-mad with anger, grief and God knows what other complex emotion a murder victim's estranged husband was likely to feel. She knew it would take him months, perhaps years, to work out a way of living his new life. He'd need careful handling.

The police officers introduced themselves, and Mike faded into the background to observe, to watch Rachel Addison in action, to witness the famous interviewing technique.

'I don't see why I have to be questioned again,' said Tony Broderick, lighting a cigarette, the first of many.

Because you've got no bloody alibi, thought Mike.

'You were shocked and probably under a strain when Detective Inspector Kellett interviewed you just after the murder,' said Rachel. 'Now that you've had time to think, you may have remembered something that could help us find your wife's murderer.'

'She wasn't my wife,' said Broderick. 'She left me, remember?'

'Could I ask why?'

'I didn't beat her, if that's what you're thinking.' It was still a sore spot, it seemed. 'She wanted kids; I didn't.'

'Because you were worried about a genetic disability, is that right?' asked Rachel.

Tony Broderick looked stunned, then flushed deeply. 'Where did you get that idea? I just didn't want the noise and the mess.'

Why did Lisa lie about it? wondered Mike.

By this time Tony Broderick had recovered his bravado. 'Neither of us would give in. She went off to find the father of her children.'

'But you still loved her, didn't you?' asked Rachel.

Leading the witness, thought Mike, as shocked by this approach as Tony Broderick. He couldn't imagine asking another man such a question. Where was Rachel taking this? The two men's eyes met, then Broderick looked down. Rachel waited.

'Of course I still loved her,' he said finally.

Love was a meaningless word in this business: usually it meant possession. The police officers had heard numerous villains professing love for a wife or child they'd killed rather than let go. Rachel allowed none of this to show on her face.

'Then you want to help us find the killer.'

'It's nothing to do with me,' he said. 'She'd moved on. She was seeing other men. Maybe she chose the wrong one. Ask them.'

Rachel ignored that: 'Mr Broderick, did you see Lisa's body?'

Rachel had. She'd never forget the shock and pity she'd felt at the sight of the body—violated, torn, bloody, dirty—and her anger at the waste. Even the stones would mourn Lisa Broderick.

He turned shifty. 'No. I thought her father should do it.'

A coward, judged Mike.

'That's too bad,' said Rachel. 'I know you're angry now, but I think if you'd seen Lisa's body you'd find yourself pitying her...' (Not a chance, thought Mike. He'd rather hate her.) 'And you'd be a lot more anxious to help me find her killer.'

'I thought you'd decided it was me,' Broderick said.

'Why should I think that?'

'It's usually the husband, isn't it?'

'Most of the time it is,' said Rachel. 'But to be honest, this doesn't look like a domestic killing to me, Mr Broderick.'

Good move, thought Mike.

Broderick was hooked. He knew no more about the crime than the newspaper reading public. 'Why not?'

Rachel was on thin ice here, unable to disclose details of the killer's modus operandi the police were keeping secret, but needing a peace offering, a wedge. 'There was an element of ritual about the crime,' she said. 'You don't usually get that sort of thing in a crime of passion.'

Mike watched the emotions ripple over Tony Broderick's face, and wondered how he'd react in the man's place. Would he want to know, or would he prefer blissful ignorance? It was a gamble: would the truth be worse than the imaginary scenes he faced every time he closed his eyes?

Tony Broderick stubbed out another cigarette and made his decision. 'Like what?'

Mike's gaze flicked to Rachel. If she disclosed a

confidential detail and Broderick went to the papers, she'd be history on the case. And any other.

'He took some pubic hair as a souvenir,' said Rachel.

Mike let out a breath. It was the right answer. If Broderick was innocent, he'd keep his wife's sad little secret; if he'd killed her, he wouldn't want his sexual fetish broadcast.

Tony Broderick's jaw dropped. 'Good Christ,' he murmured. 'He's a real sicko.'

'Maybe,' said Rachel, 'but he's also evil.' She moved in for the kill. 'Is there anything you can tell us that could help?'

Broderick lit another cigarette. 'We kept in touch, had dinner once a month. I don't think she cared whether she saw me or not, but she wouldn't tell me to piss off and get on with my own life. She was too nice, that was her problem. Any other woman would have just got pregnant and made me deal with it, but Lisa thought it would be dishonest.'

'That must have frustrated you,' said Rachel. 'If she'd got pregnant, you really would have had the upper hand.'

It was said so quietly Mike wondered if he'd imagined it. It was a king hit. Broderick paled, then flushed. 'You bitch!'

Mike made a move, but Rachel raised her hand

136

slightly and stopped him. They were finally getting somewhere.

Rachel let the silence run. When Broderick realised that glaring at her wasn't going to make her leave, he got up and went into the bedroom, returning with a small black diary. He thrust it at her and sat down, sullen-faced. Rachel flicked through it, noting the asterisks beside some of the initials. She looked up.

'The asterisks meant she went to bed with them,' said Broderick.

'How do you know?'

'We had a fight about it. I took the diary out of her purse. She got angry. I'd never seen her like that. Then I got mad...That's why I've still got it.'

So maybe he did do it, thought Mike. The worm turned.

'Did she say anything about any of them?'

'She said one of them was worse than me. Something about thinking you know people and then finding out they're complete strangers. She wouldn't tell me any more. I think she was afraid I'd go in there and beat the shit out of him.'

Mike almost snorted with derision, but stopped himself in time. This was Rachel's show.

'I've been thinking about him,' Broderick continued. 'Wondering if he was the one.'

And if she gave him the flick and he didn't like it and bided his time, thought Mike. They'd have

137

to check all the initials in the book against Lisa's known associates.

'But you didn't feel the need to tell us,' said Rachel coldly.

'I've already told you I don't know his name,' shouted Tony Broderick, grateful for an excuse to vent his anger.

Taking pity, Rachel brought the conversation back to more mundane details about Lisa's habits and kept Tony Broderick talking till he'd calmed down. Mike found himself feeling a little sorry for the man: he wouldn't fancy being carved up psychologically by Rachel Addison.

'What was that business about kids?' he asked as soon as they were out of earshot.

'I think Lisa was hurt that her husband didn't want her to have his children, so she made up an excuse, but not for herself, for him. She was ashamed of him, and probably embarrassed that she'd married him.'

'But why on earth did she marry a shit like him?'

'He's good-looking; to an unsophisticated girl he'd seem charming...' Rachel paused: 'And he probably told her he needed her.'

Lisa Broderick's little black book was burning a hole in Rachel's handbag. In the privacy of the police car, they examined it more thoroughly, checking the initials against the names of men they'd interviewed in connection with the investigation.

'There it is!' said Rachel. 'DG: Damien Grant. Back in October. It's got an asterisk, too.'

'Do you really think she would have been having it off with a scumbag like Grant?' asked Mike.

'That probably depends on what he's like now. Jeannie Carmichael says she'd heard he was off the drugs. Maybe he's cleaned up his act. We won't know until we talk to him.'

'What about Roger Blair? Kellett reckons they were lovers.'

'Wait a minute.' She flicked through the pages. 'His initials are here, but no asterisk. And there are several other sets of initials I don't recognise. We'll have to get them checked out with her family and friends.'

'We must be losing our marbles,' said Mike. 'Initials and asterisks will never stand up in court, even if we can match them with real people.'

'Has anybody talked to the woman Lisa shared her flat with, the one who went overseas?' asked Rachel. 'She might know who Lisa was seeing. What was her name again?'

'Susan something or other. Nobody's been able to locate her. She's backpacking, apparently, doesn't call home, just writes and picks up letters poste restante. She probably doesn't even know Lisa's dead. It's going to put a damper on her holiday when she finds out.'

Rachel stowed the precious diary away, started the car and drove off. Mike drifted off into a private world.

'You're very quiet,' remarked Rachel, curious.

'I'm thinking.'

'What about?'

'What happened back there. What did happen back there, by the way?'

Rachel looked into his eyes. The pupils were huge, making his eyes look black. Excitement? Sexual arousal? Either would do. It was a welcome change from cool professionalism...She felt herself responding.

'Radical surgery,' she answered. 'He'll hurt for a while, but at least there's a chance he'll get over it now. He might even grow up.'

'How did you know all that about him?'

'I've seen his type before. He's incapable of empathy. Lisa's dead, but he's the one who's demanding attention. He's hurt, he's angry; tough about her, she's only dead. Lisa might have been nice, but she was tough enough to realise he wasn't good enough for her. He knows that, and he can't forgive her.' She ran out of breath.

Mike digested her analysis of Tony Broderick. 'Remind me never to ask what you think of me,' he said.

9

Morning Was a Long Time Coming

Roger Blair agreed to see them at his home the next day. A partner in a major accounting firm, he was not keen to be seen talking to the police at his office: people might suspect embezzlement. The house was the sort of unpretentious bungalow on the north shore that cost the same as an apartment building in the western suburbs. Like the man, it was understated, comfortable and designed to last.

Not short of a dollar, thought Mike, catching sight of a top of the line BMW through the garage door. But then, chartered accountants were seldom poor.

Blair would have been about tall enough for Lisa Broderick, as long as she hadn't worn heels. He was casually but tidily dressed, with fair hair thinning on top, and answered the door with reading glasses in one hand. Although he had it well under control, a trained eye could detect some nervousness about Roger Blair.

Because he's a murderer, or just a guilty conscience about not having told the whole truth? wondered Mike.

Inside, in Blair's tastefully decorated living room, Rachel explained that she was reinterviewing some witnesses in the light of new information.

'What new information?' asked Blair.

'Information that you and Lisa Broderick were rather more than friends.'

Roger Blair jumped in too quickly. 'Who says?'

Rachel waited. Blair looked to Mike for help, but Mike simply stared back, unresponsive as a rock.

Rachel persisted. 'Were you and Lisa Broderick sexually intimate, Mr Blair?'

'I don't see that that's any of your business.'

'Mr Blair, I know it's a sad reflection on love, but women are more likely to be murdered by someone close to them than a perfect stranger. If you were close to Lisa, we should know about it.'

That smoked him out. He leapt to his feet. 'You don't seriously think I had anything to do with this, do you? I loved her.'

Progress, thought Mike, signalling him back into his chair.

When Roger Blair had seated himself again and regained his composure, Rachel said: 'No, I don't think you had anything to do with the murder, but you haven't told us everything you know, have you?'

He flushed. 'All right, we were lovers, but it was very recent. We only...made love once. Just before she died.' He dried up.

'But you'd been friends for some time, hadn't you, through her husband?'

Obviously embarrassed by the inference that he'd stolen a friend's wife, Blair protested: 'I knew the history; she came to me for help...'

'Which you gave?'

'I've known Tony since high school, and Lisa since they started going steady.' He paused, perhaps remembering them all, younger, happier. Alive. 'I'm finding it very difficult to believe all this has happened to us. We're so...ordinary.'

'Most murder victims are,' said Mike.

Rachel frowned at him, but Mike had his own agenda. He hadn't liked Lisa Broderick's ex-husband at all. 'Why did she marry Tony Broderick?' he asked.

'He's not just a pretty face,' said Roger Blair. 'When he's not drowning in self-pity, he can be very funny. I've seen him do spontaneous stand-up routines that made people fall on the floor laughing.'

'He wanted people to like him,' observed Rachel.

Blair stared at her. 'I never thought of it that way, but I suppose you're right. I don't think Tony's all that confident, deep down. He's never sure that people will like the real Tony Broderick, so he becomes what they want him to be. Plays the role.'

'Did Lisa know that?'

'I think so, but I don't think that was the problem. It was more fundamental than that. Tony didn't have the self-discipline to give up booze and drugs and running around with his mates. He wanted Lisa to lay down the law and make him behave—this is speculation, you understand—but Lisa didn't want to be his policeman...Sorry, you know what I mean. She was smart enough to know that's the wrong basis for a marriage. For an adult one, anyway.'

Rachel found herself warming to the man, understanding his appeal for Lisa Broderick after her showy, unreliable husband. Lisa had eventually figured out she'd married the wrong member of the triangle, but the realisation had come too late. The man must be going through hell...

'Did Lisa confide in you, Mr Blair?'

'How do you mean?'

'Did she ever accuse Tony Broderick of violence?'

'No. Tony's not like that. He was more likely to cause a fight then go off and get drunk and get into trouble and make Lisa feel guilty. That's his style.'

'What about other men?'

He flushed again. 'I don't think she's been seeing anybody except me for a couple of months.'

'Think, Mr Blair,' said Mike. 'This is important. Did she ever talk about any of the men she worked with at the hospital?'

Roger Blair looked helpless, then said: 'Can I get you a cup of tea, or something?'

Mike looked at Rachel. 'That would be nice,' she said.

Roger Blair went into the kitchen. As soon as he was out of earshot, Rachel murmured: 'I think he knows something, but he's sensitive about the fact that she was on with someone before him. Let's give him a little time.'

Roger Blair returned, rattling cups to alert them to his presence. They wasted a few minutes over the tea ceremony and small talk, and when there was no longer any way of staving off the inevitable, Roger Blair said: 'She did once mention someone she called the social climber.'

'The social climber,' said Mike. 'What did she say?'

He shrugged. 'We were talking about judging people, you know, how you can make mistakes, and she said something like, "Yes, I work with someone like that. I thought he was genuine, but he's turned out to be just a social climber." '

'How did she say it?' asked Rachel.

He pondered. 'Bitter, I think. That's why I didn't want to remember it. I got the impression she'd been quite keen on whoever it was and had been let down.'

As Lisa Broderick's last lover didn't seem to have anything else to tell them, they took their leave.

'Damien Grant, Nepal, social climber,' said Mike, when Roger Blair's front door closed behind them.

'That's what I thought,' said Rachel. 'Let's greet him at the airport when he gets in…' She checked her notes. 'Friday week.'

'I reckon we should drag him home.'

Rachel snorted. 'Who's going to climb Mount Everest to get him? You or Dick Kellett?'

Rachel and Mike spent the next few hours trying to put names and faces to the initials in Lisa Broderick's diary. They got no further. Lisa, it seemed, guarded her privacy jealously. Knowing what rumour mills institutions were, and detesting being the butt of gossip herself, Rachel applauded the woman's caution. But it made their job difficult: the killer could be hiding behind one of these sets of initials.

She was wearily making a cup of coffee late in

the afternoon, when Brett Marcantonio came in and mumbled something about a girl who had evidence about Lisa Broderick's murder. 'She wants to talk to a woman,' the constable said.

'A witness with taste,' replied Rachel, perking up. If the girl was embarrassed, her evidence probably had something to do with sex. Maybe this was a victim who'd lived to tell the tale. Waiting for her in an interview room was a small, scrawny teenager dressed in one of those short shapeless shifts that passed for uniforms in some schools, and black lace-up shoes and white socks.

'This is Elena Dimitriadis,' said Brett, who seemed inclined to hang about. From the details he'd taken, Rachel read that the girl was sixteen: she looked younger.

'Thank you, Constable,' said Rachel, giving him a meaningful look. He withdrew in some confusion.

She turned to the girl. 'I'm Rachel Addison, and I'm working on the Lisa Broderick investigation. Do you have something to tell me, Elena?'

Twisting one leg around the other, the girl peered out from behind a curtain of thick dark hair. Perhaps someone had once told her it was cute.

'I don't know,' she said.

Rachel picked up a pen and fiddled with it, then looked out the window. This was a ritualistic dance: the girl wouldn't be here if she hadn't made up her mind.

Finally Elena tired of waiting for Rachel to reply: 'I don't want to get in trouble.'

'Why would you get into trouble, Elena?'

'I shouldn't have been there.'

'Where?'

The girl squirmed: 'You got to promise not to tell my parents. My father, he'll kill me. He still thinks we're back in the old country.'

Rachel said: 'Look at me, Elena.'

The girl obeyed, giving Rachel a look at a pair of lustrous, knowing brown eyes. Suddenly she seemed a lot older.

'Why did you come to see me, Elena?'

'Because I felt so bad...' The girl's voice broke. 'I think I saw her. I didn't realise till I saw that thing on TV, you know, where that lady was pretending to be Lisa Broderick...'

'The re-enactment?'

'Yes.'

'So you've been following the case.'

The girl nodded, back behind the wall of hair.

Time to get tough, thought Rachel. 'So you know what an animal this man is. And he's still out there. Nobody's safe until we catch him.'

'I know,' wailed the girl. 'Ever since I figured out what I saw, I've been too scared to go out. It's like he knows. I'm frightened he'll come after me.'

She burst into tears: 'I didn't know what to do.'

Rachel patted the girl's arm: 'Wait here.' She went to the door, beckoned to Brett and sent him out to get an espresso for her, a Coke for the girl and some doughnuts. Comfort food. Then she went back into the room. The girl had recovered slightly.

'Tell me about yourself, Elena.'

The girl was surprised: 'What do you want to know?'

'Anything.'

'I'm sixteen. I go to Abercrombie High. I hate it, but my father, he won't let me leave. Says there's no jobs.'

'What do you do for fun?'

The girl shrugged. 'Hang out. Go to the movies, go drinking. It's boring out there where I live. It's a hole. I can't wait to get out.'

'What would you do?'

'Get a job selling clothes. My cousin's got a shop in Strathfield.'

And marry a nice Greek boy and settle down near your parents, thought Rachel. At least that's what they hope.

There was a knock at the door, and Brett entered with the food. The girl caught his eye, and he blushed and retreated.

'This boy, is he Greek?' asked Rachel, when the door closed.

Elena sprang to attention. 'Which boy?'

'The one you were out with when you saw Lisa Broderick, the one your parents don't know about.' She pushed the food across the table to the girl.

'How did you know?'

'As I'm too old to remember what love is like, I must have seen something like it on TV,' said Rachel, deadpan.

The girl paused, doughnut in midair and stared at Rachel. Then she laughed. 'You're all right,' she said.

'So you're ready to tell me?'

Elena took a long slurp of Coke and launched into her story. 'I was at Crossley shops the night Lisa Broderick disappeared, in my boyfriend's car. We were fighting. Donny wanted to go somewhere to park, you know…but it was getting late. I was staying over at my girlfriend's house…Becky's mother lets us go to the club, you know, go dancing, but we have to be home by twelve thirty. Not like my parents. They don't let me go to places like that. I wanted to get back to the club, but Donny was being stupid.

'We were still sitting there arguing, when the train came in. A few people got off and went home. Then I saw this girl walking down the street by herself.'

'And you think it was Lisa Broderick?'

The girl nodded. 'I watched her because I thought she was nuts, walking around there at night.'

Rachel was elated: finally some testimony placing Lisa Broderick at Crossley railway station.

Elena said: 'I said to Donny maybe we should give her a ride, but he said if I wasn't careful, I'd be out there with her, walking home.'

The girl gave a little sob. Rachel was looking forward to talking to Donny. He wouldn't quickly forget the experience.

'What happened then, Elena?'

'A car drove up beside her. She stopped and talked to the driver, then she got in.'

'You saw her get in of her own free will? He didn't drag her in?'

The girl looked puzzled. 'No. They talked. She got in. It looked like she knew him.'

A surge of adrenalin threatened to lift Rachel to her feet. Controlling her voice, she said: 'Can you describe the car?'

'It was blue. A small Japanese car, I think. But I don't know much about cars. Beat up a bit. Old, dirty.'

Let's hope Donny knows more about cars, thought Rachel.

'Will this help you find him?' the girl asked.

'Elena, your evidence is very, very important. Up till now we weren't even sure whether Lisa got to

Crossley, and we didn't know whether she'd accepted a ride or been abducted off the street.'

The girl shuddered. 'It could have been me.'

Rachel went around to Elena's side of the table and sat beside her, looking directly into the brown eyes. 'It wasn't you. You're safe. But please be careful. Don't talk about this to anyone, not to Donny or your girlfriend or anyone. We don't want the media getting hold of this.'

The girl started in alarm. 'You think he might come after me?'

There was no way to sugar-coat this: 'He's a vicious animal, Elena. He killed Lisa Broderick, and he might have killed other women. We just don't know. But he's still out there. You've been very brave, and I want you to go on being brave.'

The girl stared at Rachel, big-eyed, pale, a half-eaten chocolate doughnut still clutched in her hand: 'Are we finished?'

'Not quite. I'm going to type up your statement and get you to sign it. Then I'll get the constable to drive you home.'

'No! My parents would chuck a fit if I turned up in a police car!'

'Fine, he'll drop you off somewhere and you can get a cab.'

The teenager was still anxious. 'Will I have to tell them?'

'Yes, because when we catch him, you'll have to be a witness.'

'My father will kill me,' said the girl, hopeless, resigned.

'Would it help if we sent out a police officer to talk to your parents?' asked Rachel.

Hope flared: 'Would you?'

Rachel nodded.

'Will you come?'

'You said your father's Greek?'

'Yes.'

'In that case I think we'd better send a man.'

She took out a card and wrote her home number on the back and handed it to the girl. 'Any time you want to talk, day or night, ring me. I mean it.'

Later, as a happy Brett Marcantonio ushered the girl out of the building, Rachel shook Elena's hand and thanked her. The girl walked away.

'Elena!' called Rachel.

The girl turned.

'Give Donny the flick.'

Shock rippled across the girl's face, then she laughed. She'd survive.

At eight o'clock, Rachel left the office and headed for the gym, where she did an hour-long workout with one of the martial arts teachers and swam off the twinges in the pool. It was late when she got in. On the way home the traffic had been heavy, the roads laden with holiday traffic.

Riffling through her mail, Rachel listened to the messages on her answering machine. One was from a builder, telling her he'd worked up a quote for paving part of the backyard and asking her to call back. She'd forgotten all about it: it belonged to life before Lisa Broderick. Then there were a couple of hang-ups—people who refused to talk to machines, she assumed—and finally, a long silence. Or was it? She turned up the volume and paid attention: now she could hear someone breathing. Time stopped, and the hair on the back of her neck bristled.

Just then the phone rang, and she jumped, reached for it, changed her mind, stepped backwards, then pulled herself together and picked up the phone.

'Hello?' she said. She usually gave her name, but the breather had thrown her. Instead of answering, the caller breathed hoarsely into her ear, then put a hand over the phone and laughed. It was a man's voice, someone trying to be sinister. And succeeding, she had to admit. There was something vaguely familiar about the timbre of the voice. She wouldn't swear it in a court of law, but she was almost certain she'd heard it before. Maybe it was the killer. She wished she'd had the foresight to record the call.

Watching the late news, she realised the tone of the Lisa Broderick story was changing. Short of new leads, the media were beginning to turn on the police. Police incompetence was always popular with the public. For the team it could only mean more pressure from the Minister's office, and that promised longer hours and shorter tempers. If that were possible.

Before she retired, Rachel double-checked the doors and windows, and despite the heat, locked her bedroom door and pulled a chair under the doorknob. She'd have to change her phone number.

That night she dreamed she was in the main street at Crossley watching Lisa Broderick walking from the station. A blue car stopped, words were exchanged, the door opened, and Lisa Broderick hesitated. Rachel tried to shout a warning, but couldn't make a sound, as if her throat was full of mud. Sensing something, Lisa turned around and scanned the street, but noticing nothing out of the ordinary, stooped and got into the car. Rachel tried to run after it, but her feet were rooted to the ground. Morning was a long time coming.

Friday was the day of Lisa Broderick's funeral. It was being held at the little local Church of England where she'd married. The media would be there in full roar, and a senior Minister was attending on behalf of the Premier, who was in China, trying to drum up business for the state. Rachel hadn't the slightest desire to attend, but the Chief had made it clear he wanted all the Nightingale Task Force members on hand to keep an eye on the crowd.

'Does anyone really believe Lisa Broderick's murderer is going to go to her funeral with every reporter in Sydney on hand plus half the cops in New South Wales,' asked Brett Marcantonio, who didn't like funerals.

'Why not, he might fancy himself as a TV star,' said Kellett, and Rachel flushed.

'Who knows?' said Mike. 'He might decide to come along to gloat.'

To relive the thrill, the sense of power, thought Rachel.

'Yeah, but how will we know him if we see him?' asked Brett.

The police officers looked at each other and grinned sheepishly. 'Well there is that, young Brett,' said Kellett. 'But you know the old saying, Ours not to reason why...'

Brett looked mystified, until Rachel muttered: 'Ours but to do or die.'

They went early, in a convoy, and spread out through the church and grounds.

'What are we looking for exactly?' asked Steve Midgely, seeking some shade under a tree beside

Rachel, who'd been daydreaming, imagining what this ceremony would be like for Lisa Broderick's relatives and friends.

'Something incongruous, I suppose,' she said.

People arrived in a trickle, then a torrent. Every seat in the church was full, and the crowd spilled out into the grounds and on to the street. Reporters pushed and shoved, trying to get footage of the Brodericks, senior police, politicians and grieving friends. It was turning into a circus. Through it all, the Gallaghers remained dignified, though Lisa's father looked as if he hadn't slept for a week, and her mother was red-eyed and wobbly, supported on one side by her husband and on the other by her former son-in-law.

'The husband's here,' remarked Midgely.

'And there's Roger Blair, her new boyfriend,' said Rachel, pointing. Blair was ashen, hiding behind sunglasses. The media, who didn't know about his relationship with the victim, ignored him. 'And the one on crutches is Denise Young, one of Lisa's friends, with her mother, Marian. Mike and I interviewed them.'

When the sounds of organ music reached her, Rachel took leave of her colleague, went round to the back of the church and let herself in through the vestry door. Standing in the wings behind the altar, she could see everyone in the church. It was hot and claustrophobic, with the scent of the wreaths and the flowers piled on Lisa's casket warring with women's perfume and sweat. Some mourners fanned themselves with the program, and a few mopped their brows with handkerchiefs. Many wept. The distress was palpable.

Lulled by the heat and the atmosphere into a sort of waking doze, Rachel was startled by the sound of children's voices singing the Twenty-third Psalm—'The Lord is my shepherd, I shall not want…' It came from the choir loft, from a group of schoolgirls, many of them in tears, in the uniform of Lisa Broderick's old school.

Something oddly familiar about the scene unnerved Rachel. She even knew that the strains of 'Praise my Soul the King of Heaven' would accompany Lisa's casket out of the church. It's just déjà-vu, she told herself. Her aunt had been cremated, her ashes scattered in her beloved rose garden, so if she'd seen this service before, it must have been at her parents' funeral. But she couldn't call up a picture: she could imagine it, but not remember it. Would her aunt have let her attend the funeral? She simply didn't know. Some people saw the funeral ceremony as closure, others believed in shielding children from the harsh realities of death.

Suddenly the church became too oppressive, and Rachel slipped back outside and joined Mike outside the gate.

'Any of our suspects in there?' he asked.

Rachel realised with a small, scalding shock that she hadn't bothered to look. 'Uh, I don't think so,' she said, and Mike looked at her oddly. 'What about you?'

'I think I saw the hospital janitor on the other side of the road for a few minutes, but I wouldn't swear to it. Probably just curious.'

Just then the pallbearers appeared at the church door with the coffin and the media went into a frenzy. 'Let's get out of here,' said Mike, and vastly relieved, Rachel nodded. They fought their way through the throng and went back to work. Lisa Broderick's last rite of passage may have been celebrated, but her death remained unavenged.

That night Rachel dreamed of funerals. This time her parents' caskets held pride of place in the aisle, and she and her aunt were the chief mourners, frozen in shock and grief in the front pew. A choir of tearful children from her mother's school sang like angels and the church was full of mourning townsfolk—her mother's pupils and their parents, shopkeepers, farmers her father had crop-dusted for, his pilot friends—but no reporters were there to record their passing nor dignitaries to pay their respects. It was just another anonymous tragedy. Rachel awoke headachy and depressed.

10

The Irrational Shame
of the Victim

The meteorologist on the radio was threatening a blast-furnace day. It had been hot since 6 a.m. Drought had the outback firmly in its jaws, and rain was becoming an unreliable memory even on the coast. If the wind kept up, bushfires were forecast for the national park to the north of the city.

Woken early by the heat, Rachel drove to Bondi Beach. The surf was up, pollution was low and the water green and cold. Plunging about among the waves and riding them to the shore, mind blissfully empty and joyful as a dolphin, Rachel forgot all about Lisa Broderick's murder, her own troubles and Kellett's malice. Cleansed and new, she bought the Saturday papers and sat in a noisy beachside cafe catching up on other people's problems, occasionally eavesdropping as locals and blow-ins discussed surfing conditions and property prices. She also considered, for perhaps the hundredth time, moving to the beach.

Back at home, the phone was ringing as she let herself in. Breathless, she picked up the receiver and gave her name.

'Rachel, is that really you?' said a voice. The years dropped away, and she was a teenager again, huddled in a blanket in the living room of their dingy flat, clutching a cup of cocoa and a cigarette, lit by the dim glow of an electric heater, discussing life and love and the future with Holly Frazier.

'Holly,' she said faintly. 'Where are you?'

'In the Blue Mountains. Just up the road.'

Rachel smiled to herself. Perhaps it was, if you'd just flown in from India. Famous for their blue eucalyptus haze and majestic rock formations, the Blue Mountains were part of a spiny range running almost the length of the country and dividing the temperate coast from the continental outback. The area was about an hour and a half west of the city along congested highways.

'Are you home to stay?' asked Rachel, hoping against hope. At the beginning, when Holly had been wrenched out of her life, she'd missed her friend as badly as an amputated limb, and gradually the pain of the loss had turned to a dull throb, then an emptiness. With no-one to call a best friend, and nobody to confide in, Rachel had kept her feelings to herself, and now reticence had become a habit.

Holly hesitated, guessing how this would hurt. 'No, I'm married to an Indian and settled in now. Apart from you, there's nothing here.'

Rachel swallowed her disappointment. 'Who's the man?'

'A Buddhist teacher, Ananda. That means bliss in Sanskrit.' She giggled. 'He's giving a course at a meditation centre in the Blue Mountains. I'm sort of along for the ride.'

'What's he like, Holly?' asked Rachel, remembering some of her friend's romantic disasters.

'Just lovely. As mild as milk; you know, one of those amiable men who just let things go over their heads. Nothing like me. Spiritually, he's as tough as an old boot. You'd like him, I think, though he does giggle a bit. I know how Westerners hate that.'

Rachel said: 'And being a Westerner, you don't giggle, of course,' and they both laughed the way they used to.

She's happy, thought Rachel.

'I've got two boys, too, Rachel,' Holly said. 'Four and six. They're with their grandparents. I would love you to have met them, but it was too far and too expensive. One's like me and the other is like his father. At least one of them has a fighting chance.'

'How long has it been?' asked Rachel.

'About ten years. Oh, that makes me feel old. But I want to see you. Can you come up here today? I did the family yesterday—wait till I tell you about that!—and the course starts tonight. After that I'll be tied up helping Ananda till we leave.'

Rachel gave it all of ten seconds thought. She could go into work, but the long hours, the funeral and the subsequent dream had enervated her. 'Of course I'll come. Where is it?'

On the drive out west, along a highway clogged with weekend traffic, Rachel relived her long friendship with Holly, remembering the confident girl who could never resist a dare, the mercurial, popular teenager, then the morose, troubled young woman.

There but for the grace of God, she thought.

As a girl, there had been times when Rachel had feared she'd fly into a million pieces, but somehow the centre had held. But at what price? She'd tried to solve her problems by studying psychology, but Holly, it seemed, had found peace in the embrace of the Buddha. Or was it the arms of the lovely Ananda? Certainly the cool, intellectual Anglicanism they'd been taught at their expensive school had offered neither of them any spiritual solace.

Stewing in the heavy west-bound traffic, Rachel replayed her conversation with her old friend,

163

imagining, as far as she could, Holly's life in India, and wondering what she'd be like now. She'd sounded reassuringly normal on the phone: the neurotically self-absorbed teenager had disappeared, but India didn't seem to have turned her into a blissed-out hippie.

Rachel had been profoundly disturbed by her friend's disappearance all those years ago. Although she'd known Holly's parents were behind it, that Holly was alive, if not well, somewhere, the sense of unfinished business had nagged. She realised now the loss had rekindled the buried grief about her parents. Holly's resurrection was an unexpected gift.

Heat-dazed and sluggish, the line of traffic wound its way up the mountain to the village of Blackheath. From Holly's directions, the meditation centre was about fifteen minutes drive away, three or four kilometres down a dirt track off the main road. Summers here in the mountains were notorious: bushfires swept through the eucalyptus forests and menaced the small settlements with terrifying regularity. Despite the heat, Rachel turned off the air-conditioning and opened the windows. A searing wind rushed in, redolent of the mountain—dry grass, gum trees, a faint hint of smoke. Nostalgia for picnics in the bush, farmers burning off paddocks—for childhood innocence, perhaps—swept over her.

A discreet green sign announced the centre and Rachel slowed. Before turning, she checked her rear-vision mirror, and realised, with a small shock, that a car had slowed behind her, a small, battered white Japanese sedan. Where was it going? The driver seemed as confused as Rachel. When she turned off the main road, he slowed down then stopped. Though mirror sunglasses, a baseball cap and a downturned sun visor obscured his face, she could feel the man watching her. He might simply be a curious motorist wondering what lay hidden down the dirt road, Rachel told herself, or a resident returning home. On the other hand, it could be somebody following her. Lisa Broderick's murderer, for example.

The back of her neck prickled a warning, and a rush of adrenalin made her heart thump: a deserted bush track was a perfect place for an ambush. She eased her gun out of her bag and drove on, monitoring the white car anxiously in the rear vision mirror. The man made no attempt to follow her down the track, however. The relief was immense.

The meditation centre, which commanded a stunning view over mountains and valleys, was ominously quiet when Rachel arrived. She checked her watch: three o'clock. Please let someone be here, she thought.

Her prayers were answered. At the sound of her

car, a thin, nut-brown woman with honey-coloured hair in a long heavy braid appeared in a doorway, squinted into the sunlight, hitched up her sari and approached tentatively. Rachel climbed out of the car and the two women stared at each other.

'Holly?' asked Rachel, and the woman's face broke into a grin.

'Rachel!' she shouted, and they ran into each other's arms.

'God, look at you,' said Rachel, through tears. 'You look like an Indian.'

'An associate Indian,' amended Holly. 'I'm married to one and my kids think they're Indian.' She laughed. 'Tough about their blue eyes.'

Rachel held her friend at arms' length: 'You're happy.'

'And you're not,' said Holly. 'Come inside out of the sun. You're as pale as a toadstool.'

She drew Rachel into a sitting room shuttered against the glare. A quiet young European woman in a sari and a nose ring padded in barefooted with lemonade, unloaded the tray without speaking, and left.

'Ruth's an old student,' said Holly. 'She's started observing the silence already. The rest of the students aren't here yet. The course starts this evening.' She picked up a glass of lemonade and passed it to Rachel. 'I hear you're a cop. It fits, somehow.'

'How do you mean?'

'You were always obsessed with being a good girl.'

Rachel grimaced and Holly laughed. 'Tell me about this case you're on. I hear you've become a media sensation.'

Rachel recounted her part in the Lisa Broderick investigation, omitting the frightening telephone calls and her fears about being followed.

'So you like your job?' asked Holly.

Rachel nodded. 'It makes me feel useful.'

'So what's making you so unhappy?'

Rachel was disconcerted: 'What are you, a mind-reader?'

'No, but I've had vast experience of unhappiness, remember. I can smell it from fifty paces.'

'What do you smell here?'

Holly leaned over and took Rachel's hands. 'You were an anxious little girl, a repressed adolescent and a grind at university. You were never happy all the time I knew you. Maybe it's become a habit.'

'Happiness never seemed an option,' said Rachel, startling herself. 'I just wanted to get past the worst stuff and lead a quiet life.'

'Chasing crooks is hardly quiet.'

'I mean emotionally,' said Rachel.

'Are you telling me you've given up men?'

Rachel laughed. 'What's this sudden interest in my sex life?'

'It's hardly sudden. I got an earful of your sex life when you were having that torrid affair with David whatever his name was.'

'Gardiner,' interrupted Rachel.

'Yeah, David Gardiner. The golden boy.' Holly laughed wickedly.

Rachel blushed, realising what it must have been like for Holly, trying to sleep on the other side of the bedroom wall.

'What happened to him? I thought you two were headed for the altar.'

'Everyone did. I got a lot of flak when I left him. People kept asking me what had gone wrong.'

'What did you tell them?'

'Nothing.'

Holly waited, but Rachel remained silent. 'For God's sake, Rachel,' said her friend. 'It's me, Holly. What happened?'

It was an effort for Rachel to break her long silence about David Gardiner. 'Everything was fine at the beginning, but then he got moody, charming one minute, aggressive the next. He was doing drugs of course, I know that now. God, I was so naive in those days.'

'He didn't hit you, did he?'

'No, he didn't have to. He used to control me with anger and sarcasm. I woke up eventually. We had a terrible fight one night over the car keys. He was out of it and I wouldn't let him drive...I thought he was going to attack me.'

'Why didn't you tell me?' asked Holly. Then she shook her head. 'Don't answer that. Let's face it, I was too far gone to listen to anyone else's problems, and you knew that better than anyone, but you could have talked to someone.'

'I was ashamed.'

'Of what?'

'My bad judgment, I suppose...No, that's not even true; I blamed myself. I was like some beaten woman out of a case history, suffering the irrational shame of the victim. It was Kate Westwood who got me through it eventually.'

This was a revelation to Holly, who'd never known Rachel to ask for help as long as she'd known her. 'Good old Kate,' she said. 'She saved me from myself more than once. Do you still see her?'

'Yes, she's the closest thing I've got to family now. I even got her to refer me to a shrink.'

Holly's eyes widened. 'Do you want to talk about it?'

As it seemed impossible not to confide in this calm, wise reincarnation of her oldest friend, Rachel recounted the emotional turmoil of the past few weeks.

Shocked, Holly said: 'It all sounds too dangerous to me; maybe you should get yourself taken off this case.'

'I can't. It would mean the end of my career.'

'A career isn't much use to you if you're dead, Rachel. My advice to you would be save yourself. There's something very unattractive about martyrdom.'

'Is that what the Buddha would advise?' asked Rachel.

'Definitely. He said if every individual saved herself, there would be no more trouble in the world.'

Trumped, Rachel changed the subject. 'What about you, Holly? What happened to you? One minute you were there, the next you were gone.'

'The parents got sick of the suicide attempts and the drunken displays, and whisked me off to a high-priced sanatorium and had me zapped with chemicals. I was a zombie. Two years of my life...' She shook her head to dislodge the memory. 'I ran away with a psych nurse, finally.'

'They wouldn't tell me where you were,' said Rachel.

'I know that now, but at the time I thought the whole world had abandoned me, so I was easy game for Luke—that was the nurse's name. Thank God for him, sleazy con man that he was. If he hadn't got the hots for me and sprung me, I might still be there. It was his idea to go to India, and it sounded good to me. I was so angry in those days.'

She paused and looked back at her younger self. 'I broke into the house and got my passport and stole some money from the old man, and that's all she wrote.'

'Hardly.'

Holly laughed. 'Except for the fact that Luke dumped me for another hippie chick, in Calcutta of all places. With no money. The Buddhists took me in and haven't been able to get rid of me since.'

'It makes my life look pretty boring,' said Rachel.

Holly shook her head. 'Different battle tactics, that's all.'

'Holly...' Rachel wasn't sure how to ask the question.

'What made me do it?'

'Forget it. It's none of my business.'

Holly shrugged. 'It's OK. You have a right to know; you cleaned up after me often enough. It was my father. He was a violent drunk.'

'I never realised...'

'It was a deep, dark secret. His partners covered up for him at work, and we covered up for him at home. Especially my mother...But that's another story. I suppose I was just acting out all the anxiety and stress. My brother wasn't so lucky. He started drinking in high school, a chip off the old block. I've talked him into coming to this retreat, but I don't know how long he'll last.'

They gazed at one another. 'But what about you, Rachel?' asked Holly. 'What made you so scared? I never could work that out.'

'I don't know yet. I'm working on it. This murder seems to have triggered something...'

'Stay till tomorrow night,' her friend urged. 'Meditation has a way of bringing bad stuff to the surface. It could be useful.'

'I don't know...'

'Come on, Rachel. Dare a little. The food's good, and you might learn something. And it's free.'

'Free?'

'You only pay if you want to. We've got some very generous benefactors.'

Rachel resisted, not sure she could relax enough to let go, afraid part of her mind would be mulling over the murders and worrying about her own emotional state, or standing off, observing and criticising the method. Besides, she hated to be preached at.

Before she could refuse, Holly clinched the argument. 'And I'd like you here for my sake.'

By 5 p.m. about fifty people had turned up, some of them obviously old friends. The atmosphere was festive, and the vegetarian dinner, the last meal before the commencement of ten days of silence, was a social occasion. The students were a mixed bunch, some of them obviously conspicuous spiritual consumers who'd tried every sect and self-improvement method on the market; others were there to try to kick smoking, alcohol or drugs. There was also a core of serious Buddhists present, exuding calm.

Rachel renewed her acquaintance with Holly's brother, Jack, whom she remembered as a glamorous, debonair figure, but who was now a wreck looking a decade older than his forty years. When he asked her what she was doing these days, she told him she was a psychologist. It made life easier.

A gong summoned them to the meditation hall, and the chatter dried up. Sitting cross-legged on small cushions, they listened as Holly explained what would happen during the course, and gave a brief description of the meditation method, while Ananda beamed beside her. This was another Holly entirely: a contented woman who'd worked her way through the pain and confusion to self-knowledge and peace. Rachel despaired of ever catching up.

When Holly had finished, her husband, who was small, plump and beatific, gave a simple spiritual lesson.

Buddhism for beginners, thought Rachel.

But after dropping her defences and really listening, she had to admit the wisdom of the teaching. He told them most unhappiness came from living in the past and the future; contentment came from observing the moment, that each of us can begin again this very minute. As a means of personal salvation it made sense to Rachel, but its political quietism disturbed her. As a woman who'd infiltrated a male domain, she saw activism, not prayer, as the driving force behind social change.

Ananda also told them that suffering was infectious, that often anger was simply a conditioned response to someone else's. With meditation and self-knowledge, they would stop reacting blindly and learn to reject these poisonous gifts and hand them politely back to the donor.

This struck Rachel as eminently sensible. I'll try this out next time Kellett patronises me, she thought, then grinned. She'd already perfected concealing her anger and hurt; learning not to feel these emotions required discipline of a higher order.

At 10 p.m. they were dismissed and filed quietly into their rooms. Day two would start at dawn. The digs were simple, the meditation rules forbidding comfortable beds as well as smoking, strenuous physical exercise, stimulants and sexual activity, though Holly had confided that it was not unknown for students to sneak out for a coffee or chocolate hit. Others cut and ran when the going got tough.

Despite the altitude, the night was hot and breathless. Rachel tossed and turned, unable to get the details of the case out of her mind, replaying interviews, wondering if the man in the white car had been a threat or if she was simply seeing danger everywhere. Finally she rose and walked in the grounds till the gong sounded for the first session of the day. In a lesson on controlled breathing they were warned that their minds would wander and that they would initially find it impossible to concentrate on their breath for more than a couple of seconds at a time. Nonetheless, Rachel was surprised and humbled by the shortness of her attention span. Some of the students simply gave up and snoozed gently.

It was hot, dim, close and perfectly silent in the hall. After a time, the atmosphere and exhaustion lulled Rachel into a state somewhere between sleep and wakefulness and she drifted into a lengthy erotic daydream about Mike Ross. She imagined touching his skin, which she decided would be warm, burying her face in his neck and inhaling his scent. After riding with Mike in the police car for the last couple of weeks, Rachel felt she could identify him blindfolded: his spoor was subtle, the simple scent of clean, healthy male unadorned by cologne or aftershave.

The gong shattered her reverie, and feeling like a guilty child, she rose and joined her fellow students for a breakfast of muesli, yoghurt, fruit and herbal tea. Fighting down a longing for a cup of strong coffee, she found a seat in dappled shade under a tree full of rowdy birds. What was going on in her head? Holly had warned her that unexpected emotions would bubble to the surface in this course, but Mike Ross! She wasn't even sure he liked her.

The second morning session was uneventful, though Rachel decided that meditation was by far the most difficult learning experience she'd encountered. It was a pity she wouldn't be able to complete the course: anything this hard had to deliver a major pay-off. But the afternoon session seemed different almost immediately, as if she were finally getting the hang of the method. She found she could concentrate longer before her mind flew off into distractions.

In one of these rare periods of perfect quiet, a face leapt into her consciousness. It was a young woman, perhaps twenty years old, with a long, sensitive face, tortoiseshell glasses shielding pale eyes, and a waterfall of straight hair.

'Alison,' said Rachel. Propelled to her feet by shock, she stumbled over knees and cushions in her haste to escape. Outside, she leaned against the wall and breathed deeply. Who was Alison? All Rachel knew, at some deep visceral level, was that a terrible memory attached to Alison, some inconsolable grief. Whatever it was, a protective callus had grown over the details long ago, sealing it off from her conscious mind.

Holly, who'd seen her leave, came over. 'Bad?'

Rachel nodded. 'I've been having odd flashes of memory, and I think they're connected to something bad. There's a battle going on inside me between wanting to know and not wanting to know.'

'You're halfway there if you know you've been hiding something, surely. How good did you say this shrink was?'

'Very good, I think.'

'Then stay with it, Rachel,' said Holly.

Rachel was close to tears. Holly took her hands and kissed her on each cheek and they exchanged a long look: neither knew if they would meet again.

'I must go back in,' she said. 'Let me know how you're getting on. Jack's got my address in India.' She grinned: 'Would you mind terribly taking him down the mountain with you? He's in pretty bad shape.'

Worse than me? wondered Rachel, and watched her friend disappear back into her new life. Holly's ruse was transparent, but she was grateful for Jack's company, nonetheless: the stranger in the baseball cap could be waiting somewhere on the road back to the city.

Secure in the knowledge that the nearest pub was only fifteen minutes away, Jack Frazier was excellent company, entertaining Rachel with his journalistic exploits on a tabloid newspaper. Their mood darkened, though, when she tuned into the radio news. Bundjalung National Park in the north of the state was burning, with more than a hundred fires blazing over a wide front. Scores of campers had been evacuated, their Christmas break ending in chaos.

11

Everything Was Red

As Rachel entered the incident room, she almost bumped into Mike Ross coming out. Embarrassed by the memory of her imaginary encounter with him at the meditation centre, she had trouble looking him in the eye. Feeling her confusion, he gave her a searching look and noticed the faint flush on her cheeks. What's all this about, he wondered, registering, too, that she was looking good.

The public holiday skeleton staff were grateful for the air-conditioning today, especially those still suffering from a hangover from New Year's Eve parties. Outside, it was 37 degrees Centigrade and the strong winds of the weekend persisted. Fires were burning in the Hunter Valley, threatening the vineyards and the profitable wine industry, and a major blaze had been extinguished in Sydney's south-west.

The talk turned obsessively to the fires.

'They're saying the whole state's going to burn if we don't get rain,' said Brett Marcantonio. He was worried about his mother's sister and her family, who lived in Gosford on the Central Coast, a closely settled strip that served as a dormitory area a ninety-minute drive north of Sydney on the freeway. So far the fires were contained in the national park adjoining Gosford, but if the flames escaped and raced down the hills surrounding the town, the townsfolk could be pushed into the sea.

'Grafton's gone up, too,' said a constable who'd grown up in the northern town. 'About three thousand hectares gone in the Nymboida, last I heard. I probably won't recognise the place when I go back.'

He turned on a small transistor radio, and silence fell for a special news bulletin. 'A fire has swept through bushland in Newcastle's west, threatening the commercial centre of Charlestown,' said the announcer. 'Thousands have fled their homes. Dharug and Brisbane Water National Parks on the Central Coast, and closer to Sydney, Ku-ring-gai Chase, Lane Cove National Park, the Royal National Park are closed to the public.'

The Fire Chief told a reporter that two thousand volunteers were fighting the fires. 'It's only the efforts of the firefighters that have prevented massive property loss,' he intoned. Then his bureaucratic poise crumbled: 'It's horrendous out there.'

On the Lisa Broderick front, there was jubilation at pinning Lisa's disappearance down to Crossley station, but the boyfriend of Elena, their teenage witness, hadn't been able to throw much more light on the blue car. Denying Rachel the pleasure of teaching the teenager some manners, Ray Larsen had interviewed him on the weekend. 'A horrible little shit,' he reported. 'Dressed to kill in all the latest basketball gear, he was. I asked him if his school had a special team for midgets and he got real upset. Thought he might cry.'

The men sniggered, buoyed by one small victory against the young punks who borrowed their bogus street sophistication and defiance of authority from black American rap singers and homeboys they saw on television while leading safe lives in the suburbs.

Listening to the discussion with one ear, Rachel toyed with the idea of mentioning the white car that had frightened her in the Blue Mountains, but caution won out. She couldn't prove anything, and nothing had happened, after all: it would be career suicide to get a reputation for jumping at shadows.

On the way to the clairvoyant's house, while Mike was retailing his conversation with Elena's parents, she almost succumbed to the temptation to confide. She refrained, however, realising she didn't know how she'd want him to react. The memory of the daydream at the ashram was so strong she had a momentary, overpowering desire to lay her head on his shoulder and ask him to make it all go away. Horrified, she dragged herself back to the present, to the real world, where she'd never even touched his skin.

'It's the same old story,' he was saying, oblivious. 'The parents still think it's 1970 in Thessalonika. They're determined to keep their girls locked up until they're safely married off, but the kids go to Aussie schools and see all their friends having fun and going out at night and they go nuts.'

'Elena's parents are like that?'

'The father is. He's the Greek. The mother's Australian. She's frightened of the old man and worried about the kid. Stranded in the middle of the culture gap.'

'What's going to happen?'

'I made it pretty clear that physical violence wouldn't be tolerated, but I don't think little Elena's relationship with her dad is ever going to recover. My guess is she'll be kept under lock and key for the duration.'

'That mightn't be such a bad thing,' said Rachel. 'She's the only one that came close to getting a look at our man.'

'Maybe, but there'll be fun and games when we catch him and the kid has to testify. All the juicy details will be in the papers for all the rest of the

Greek community to see. She'll never live it down.'

'For God's sake, she's a bloody heroine! She should get a medal. If I hear of anybody giving her a hard time, they'll have to answer to me. And that includes her father.'

This was the closest to an emotional outburst Mike had heard from the Ice Queen. He was impressed: there was passion there after all. But he'd noticed she unleashed it only in the defence of others; when attacked herself, she responded with icy cool.

'Go for it, Tiger,' he said, po-faced, and Rachel blushed.

Bridie Casey, the clairvoyant, lived in a small weatherboard house in an anonymous street in a dead flat, featureless western suburb. Surveying the stunted trees, the small front yards with their regulation patch of lawn, the lookalike houses, Rachel said: 'How could anyone live out here?'

'Money, they were born here, they work nearby. All sorts of perfectly good reasons,' said Mike Ross, who had grown up in a suburb not unlike this. Now a Vietnamese ghetto, it had been like a country village in his childhood, with chicken farms, creeks, open paddocks and a polyglot population dumped in temporary housing thrown up by the government for the waves of European

183

immigrants imported to service the postwar economic boom.

Curtains in several front windows twitched when they pulled in and parked in front of the clairvoyant's house. The woman herself turned out to be short, plump, about fifty, with soft white, powdered skin, dyed blonde hair and vivid make-up. She greeted them at the front door clutching under one arm a beribboned Maltese terrier, which barked enthusiastically but subsided when Mike patted its shaggy head.

Before the real business could begin, the two police officers were required to make a fuss of the dog, drink a cup of tea and try Bridie Casey's cream cake. It reminded Mike of the time his mother had taken him along to a tea-leaf reader in a dowdy arcade in a failing part of the city when he was about ten. He'd enjoyed himself thoroughly, and the reader, who was done up like a stage gypsy, told him he'd end up in uniform. Every time he'd misbehaved, his mother had reminded him, predicting it would be a jail uniform.

Realising he was grinning, Mike tried to look official, but the effort was wasted as the women, murmuring away quietly, hadn't even noticed. Ignored, he amused himself by examining the clairvoyant's photographs and knick-knacks. You could learn a lot from people's memorabilia. Bridie

Casey obviously had a talent for getting next to celebrities: she'd had herself photographed with television talkshow hosts, a beauty queen or two, and several soap stars. Were these all clients?

His rude inspection was interrupted by the clairvoyant's peremptory demand: 'What have you got for me?'

Mike obediently handed over the sandal, preserved in a plastic bag, and Bridie Casey unwrapped it reverently and held it, closing her eyes. Mike chanced a quick look at Rachel, but she refused to meet his eye. This was your idea, her face said. If you're going to do it, do it properly.

With the curtains drawn, the room was hot, claustrophobic. It was quiet in this back street, and the real world seemed a long way off. They waited. Bridie Casey went into a trance, muttering and moaning. For Rachel, the eerie atmosphere and the sight of the lone sandal triggered a full-colour vision of Lisa Broderick's defiled body. Could a clairvoyant really intuit Lisa's last, terrible hours from a relic? Do terror and pain leach out into their surroundings like blood, or simply rise, unanswered, to the heavens?

What would it be like, Rachel wondered, the dawning realisation that you were at the mercy of a monster, that he needed to hurt, humiliate and degrade you, that it gave him pleasure. Suddenly understanding that begging and pleading and promising not to tell would only heighten the thrill, but not able to stop, desperate to reach any vestige of humanity in the man, praying he still had a shred of conscience. And then realising you were going to die, when you hadn't done anything yet, hadn't lived. All your plans stillborn. Your mind flashing to your parents, maybe even calling out to your mother.

Then the pain of the beating and the tearing, and finally, the sharp shock and the agony of the knife. And all the time this thing on top of you, invading your body, his foul breath in your face, his hands on you, the stink of his sweat. Pumping up and down on you, grunting like a pig, while the blood and the life leaked out of you.

I know you, Rachel thought. I can almost see you.

She must have started, or gasped, for she suddenly felt Mike's hand on her arm, its reassuring pressure. When she forced a smile, he relaxed slightly and withdrew his hand. Her arm burned where it had rested. She resisted an impulse to touch the place.

Apparently impervious to their little drama, Bridie Casey returned to the present and looked around, as if wondering where she was. Then her face turned grim. 'He's evil,' she said. 'He's done this before.'

Mike shot Rachel a covert glance. They could have figured this out for themselves.

Rachel had questions for Bridie Casey, but was suddenly dizzy and tongue-tied. It was too hot in this room, and there were too many intense emotions clogging the air.

'Anything else?' asked Mike.

'Everything was red.'

'Blood?'

'No, something else.' The woman closed her eyes. 'I can see it now. The hair. She was a redhead, wasn't she?'

'Yes.'

'I can see red hair black with blood.' The clairvoyant's voice strengthened. 'The hair is the key; that's why he chose her. He likes redheads.'

A tremor passed through Rachel's body, as if her nerves were going to implode. She went hot, then cold. She couldn't breathe. Mike didn't notice. While he thanked Bridie Casey and rewrapped the evidence, he was thinking about that television documentary.

What the fuck have we done? he thought. If this loony is hot for redheads, we've offered him one on a plate.

One of the suspects Rachel had interviewed could have been fantasising about her all the time, might even be enjoying murderous sexual fantasies about her right this minute. Wondering if she'd already figured that out, he felt slightly ill. And guilty: why hadn't he stopped it? Reckless endangerment...

Picking up on the emotional turmoil she'd let loose, Bridie Casey said to Rachel: 'I'd be extra careful if I were you, my dear.'

Outside in the sunlight at last, in the open air, back in real time, Rachel felt the ground sway beneath her feet. Before she could fall, Mike took her arm. 'He'd have to get past the entire New South Wales police force, Mrs Casey,' he said. 'Let's go, Rachel, we're late.'

On the ride back to town, Mike was silent, giving Rachel time to recover and himself time to think. For a moment in Bridie Casey's front garden he'd been afraid she was going to lose it the way she'd done in the hospital the day they'd interviewed Lisa Broderick's nursing colleagues. He didn't blame her; nobody wanted to hear they might be on a psychopath's wish list.

He cast his mind back over the events in the hospital. Something had spooked her there, too, and it wasn't an old woman pointing the finger like a witch out of a melodrama. What was the common denominator, and did it have anything to do with the case? He couldn't shake the suspicion that Lisa Broderick's death had unleashed some of Rachel Addison's private demons. And if she were in danger, that preoccupation would make her vulnerable. He decided to keep a very close eye on his partner.

He broke the silence when they neared the city centre. 'It's just speculation. We don't know that Lisa Broderick's red hair had anything to do with her murder. The old girl was probably just being dramatic.'

'Let's pretend she's right,' said Rachel, determined to appear cool and controlled, knowing they could take her off the case for her own protection, and that Mike Ross's opinion would count. 'The question is: can we justify taking another look at all sex crimes against young red-headed women on the word of a clairvoyant?'

'Why not?' he said, relieved that she'd recovered so quickly. 'It's not as if we've got much else to go on.'

They returned to their own thoughts, then Mike said: 'How do they do it?'

Rachel jumped slightly. 'What do you mean?'

'Clairvoyants, fortune-tellers.'

Rachel, who had become interested in the paranormal during her psychology degree, had given the phenomenon some thought. Most of the time it was pure charlatanry, but occasionally someone came along who had a real gift.

'Some of them are just canny old birds making a buck dispensing tea and sympathy,' she said.

'They provide rituals for people who don't believe in religion, confession for people who don't believe in priests. They probably don't do much good, but they don't do any real harm either. They deal in hope. In their own way they're psychologists, I suppose. Better than some, actually, because they're not pushing any ideological barrows.

'Then there's the con artists in the stage shows; that's just sleight of hand. But what the good ones have, the ones people pay to go back to time and time again, is empathy, a heightened intuition about people.'

She paused for a moment, formulating her theory. 'It's based on an ability to receive stimuli, I think. We all give out millions of clues that most people can't interpret: the gifted ones can. If ordinary folk are crystal radio sets, then these people are sophisticated electronic listening devices. Plus they're experts at reading body language and placing people socially and culturally by the way they talk, the way they dress.'

'Like you,' said Mike.

'Me?'

'I've watched you questioning people. You hear things they don't say.'

Rachel stared at him, taken aback.

'And you don't ask the things everybody else asks,' Mike went on.

'Like what?'

'Well, you've never asked me a single question about myself, where I grew up, what sort of school I went to. That sort of thing.' He looked at her slyly. 'My marital status.'

Rachel, who knew he was single from tea-room gossip, filed the remark away. 'That's not information: it's static,' she said. Then she took a calculated risk: 'Anyway, I know everything about you I need to know.'

He didn't answer, but something in the quality of his silence reached her, and she turned to look at him. He took his eyes off the road and met her gaze. His pupils were huge, making his eyes even blacker. She'd seduced him with words.

'Everything,' she said.

12

Their Blind, Mindless Determination

Now that the office had gone quiet, Rachel began reluctantly to work her way through a pile of neglected paperwork. Among the jetsam that had washed up on her desk was an urgent message from Senior Constable Jenny Cole from the Rape Squad.

Rachel and Jenny Cole had met on a course the previous year and become friends. Though the subject of sexual orientation had never arisen, Rachel had immediately recognised her colleague as a lesbian in deep cover. Jenny Cole's reticence was eminently sensible—though two very senior women were widely believed to be gay, the force was far from ready for sexual show and tell. When a highly qualified female was passed over for a top position in another state, there had been broad, if tacit, agreement that lesbianism had cost her the job.

Rachel glanced at the clock: six-thirty. Jenny was a workaholic, so there was an even chance she'd still be in her office. 'It's Rachel Addison here, Jenny. You called me?'

The voice was tired. 'Yeah, Rachel. How's it going?'

'Not so good. This case is grinding me down, to be honest. And we're getting nowhere fast.'

'You might be interested in this, then. I think someone tried to abduct a woman at the university on Friday night.'

Rachel's pulse quickened. It might be a random sexual attack, but it might be Lisa Broderick's killer trying again. 'Did you investigate it?'

'No, more's the pity, but when I saw the details I thought it might be worth another look.'

'What happened?'

'Somebody grabbed a student off a path and dragged her towards the car park nearby. There's thick shrubbery along that path, so if he'd just wanted to rape her, he could have done it right there, but he didn't. She got away when a bunch of joggers ran into them. Literally.'

'Could they ID him?'

'Hardly. They all fell in a heap, and by the time they'd sorted themselves out, the man was gone.'

'No other witnesses?' asked Rachel.

'No, although the path is well lit, apparently. The university did a security audit recently and upgraded the lighting to discourage just this sort of thing.'

'Looks like they wasted their money.'

'On this guy, anyway. If it's our man, he's getting more careless. Or more desperate.'

'What sort of shape is the girl in, Jenny? Can I talk to her?'

'I imagine she's freaked out of her brain, but the attacker didn't have time to do anything but bruise her arms where he grabbed her. The hospital didn't even keep her in overnight. She's at home, being treated by the family doctor.'

'How did the parents react?'

'The father's Roland Parker, the QC. He's making noises about suing the university.' She snorted. 'Typical Phillip Street prima donna. The mother's just grateful the girl wasn't badly hurt. Lisa Broderick's murder has made people very tense, you know.'

'If you'd seen the photographs you'd know why,' said Rachel.

'Are they bad?'

Rachel would never forget those stab wounds: the killer had concentrated on Lisa's breasts and genital area, and had almost severed her head in his fury. That's what the experts meant by a murderous frenzy. 'They're bad. If this guy really was Lisa Broderick's killer, your student is a very lucky girl.'

The two women exchanged some gossip and promised to meet for lunch some time. Before she rang off, Jenny Cole said: 'You won't forget who gave you this tip, will you Rachel?'

Aware of Jenny's ambitions, Rachel grinned to herself. 'I'll buy you a drink when it's over. If it ever is.'

Rachel took down the victim's details, sorted through the rest of her messages, made a few phone calls, and called it a day. Walking out of the building into the heat was like hitting a brick wall. She took off her jacket, slung it over her shoulder, and looked around. It was an odd, deserted pocket of the city, with few cars and no pedestrians at this time of the evening.

Spooked, she hurried to the underground car park and waited for the elevator to her floor. When it didn't arrive, she gave up and took the stairs. Halfway down, she paused in the graffiti-daubed stairwell, almost suffocated from the stench of old urine, convinced she could hear footsteps. But as soon as she stopped, so did they.

It's just an echo, she told herself.

Sweat running between her breasts, shirt clinging damply to her skin, she pushed open the heavy door and found herself in pitch darkness. Fighting panic, she ran blindly along the rows, trying to remember where her car was parked. Behind her, the door to the stairwell slammed shut. Finally she located her car, fumbled with the keys and fell inside, immediately locking the doors and switching on the ignition and the lights. The sudden flash of the headlights picked up a man standing beside a car two rows away. He immediately turned away and melted into the darkness. Tyres screaming, Rachel accelerated away. Then she was in the street, breathing fast.

Every fibre of her being wanted to flee, but her training overcame her instinct at the end of the street and forced her to stop at a red light. Anxiously, she checked her rear-vision mirror and felt a hot rush of fright as a dark car erupted from the parking station and pulled in behind her, too close, its headlights on high beam.

'Damn you,' she said, trying to block out the glare with her hand. When the lights changed, she took off and made for the freeway, the dark car in close pursuit. The driver, invisible behind his shield of blinding light, stuck like a burr, and Rachel, who prided herself on her driving skills, was unable to shake him. She sped up, longing for the relative safety of the well-lit, busy freeway.

Once on the freeway, she calmed down a little. The driver had made no attempt to overtake and force her off the road: maybe he was waiting for her to panic and peel off into a side street and make a run for home. If so, he'd misjudged Rachel:

she was too smart to abandon the safety of the freeway.

Suddenly, as several vehicles exited, Rachel found herself alone with the stalker. Alarmed, she put her foot down, caught him by surprise, and put some distance between them. At that moment several cars emerged from a side road, one of them sliding deftly into the space between them. This gave Rachel her chance. Forcing herself to concentrate, she tried to visualise the map of metropolitan Sydney. The answer came to her just as the freeway began to peter out.

Ignoring the horn blast and rude gestures of the driver behind, she cut into the outside lane and increased speed, leaving her pursuer stranded in the inside lane. There was a cacophony of outraged horns as he tried to catch up. Then Rachel threw a sudden, dangerously late left-hand turn, and sped through the suburban streets, wheels screaming, well above the speed limit, to pull on to the footpath in front of a police station. The dark-coloured car rounded the corner too fast, realised at the last minute what she'd done, swung out with a blast of his horn, and disappeared down the street. Jumping out and craning after the speeding vehicle, Rachel recognised it as a dark red Ford Falcon, but the numberplate, smeared with dust, was indecipherable.

Before a police officer could emerge to find out

what the racket was about, Rachel took off again, and made her way home through the back streets, keeping a wary eye out for dark-coloured Fords. By the time she reached the eastern suburbs she was coming down from the rush of the chase, and was starting to wonder what it all meant.

Safe in her own driveway, she got out of her car, legs shaky, fumbled in her bag for her keys with trembling fingers, and froze. Someone had drawn a heart with an arrow through it in the dust on the rear window of her car. It hadn't been there that morning.

She considered reporting the incident, but what would she say? That someone had drawn a heart on her car? That a nasty man chased her on the freeway? The man in the parking station hadn't done anything but stare, and the maniac in the V8 might simply have been having fun at a woman driver's expense; after all, the roads were full of men who used their vehicles as weapons, who regarded women drivers as prey to terrorise. Her colleagues would regard the graffiti as a joke or a message from an admirer and wonder what all the fuss was about. They'd whisper that she was seeing shadows, cracking up. Being female.

Inside, the house was suffocatingly hot. Desperate for some air, she threw open doors and windows and unlocked the French doors to her tiny backyard. A ripe, rotten smell assailed her.

The rubbish tin had fallen over—dogs probably; the area was full of dog lovers and ranging pets— and garbage had spilled out on to the paving stones. Sighing, she went over to clear up the mess, and stopped, transfixed. The remains of last night's steak had escaped its newspaper wrapping and was a seething mass of maggots.

Rachel gagged and leapt backwards, eyes riveted on the busy grubs. Some had escaped and were making their way towards her back door. Their blind, mindless determination horrified her. She told herself they were only grubs, but her feet wouldn't move.

Just then an ambulance rushed past, and the wail of its siren broke the spell. Released, Rachel backed into the house, found a dustpan and broom, scooped up the wriggling mess, wrapped it in newspaper and put it back in the bin, grimacing in distaste. Her appetite no match for the heat and the maggots, she poured herself a glass of chilled white wine, kicked off her shoes and settled down, nerves twitching, skin prickling, to watch the news.

It wasn't good. Arsonists had been busy, and a deliberately lit fire on Mangrove Mountain behind the Central Coast was now threatening the small settlement of Kariong. A blaze had even broken out within the Canberra city limits in a pocket of bushland. So far there had been no property damage, but an Emergency Services spokesman warned that worse was to come unless the weather broke. That didn't seem likely: the Bureau of Meteorology was predicting more hot dry weather.

At 3.30 a.m. Rachel woke in front of a black and white war movie, parched and stiff. Jack Hawkins, brave and stiff-upper-lipped, was castigating the perfidy of the Nazis, as usual. She switched off the TV set and climbed the stairs. A cold shower helped, but she slept fitfully, smoke, flames and running people filling her dreams, until the light drove her out around dawn. Turning on the radio news while she cut up fruit for breakfast, she learned that the fire threat had worsened overnight.

The newspaper, when it arrived, was full of the fires. Though Australia's isolation protected it from many man-made catastrophes, nature compensated with fire, floods, cyclones, and recently an earthquake. This was a dry, inhospitable country, settled by humans at their own risk. Intimidated by the empty, echoing deserts, dry lakes and haunted mountain ranges inland, most Australians clung to the coast, to the narrow strips of green, to the illusion of a benign nature.

The fear of bushfires was deeply burned into the national psyche. Old people spoke in hushed tones of Black Friday 1939 and of the fires that killed hundreds of people in New South Wales and Victoria and devastated huge swathes of bush and farmland, and every teenager remembered Ash Wednesday 1983. The fires of 1994 seemed destined to go down in infamy, too.

In the incident room, the buzz of rumour and speculation masked a palpable sense of dread. The danger was becoming real now, close, not something that only happened out in the bush. Glued to a transistor radio, Sheree called for quiet and announced that fires were crossing the Hawkesbury River on the northern outskirts of the city.

A news bulletin announced that parts of the Blue Mountains, where Rachel had spent the weekend, were ablaze. Worried about Holly, she called Jack Frazier at his newspaper to be told that the meditation centre had been evacuated and Holly and Ananda were safe with the Fraziers. For the time being, anyway: fires were threatening parts of the north shore where they lived.

The fire at Kariong was eventually contained, but new blazes were popping up faster than the firefighters' ability to respond. Of the two team members who lived on the Central Coast, only Larsen had made it into work.

'It's all eucalyptus in that national park, and the ground's covered in dry fuel,' he explained. 'If the wind changes, we've had it. The fire will roar down those hills like a bloody express train. We'll probably end up standing in the surf at Terrigal watching the mountains burn.'

Rachel reflected that inner-city living had its advantages at times like this. You longed for more trees sometimes, desperately missed the greenery, the shade and the birds, but were also spared the fires and the worst fury of the storms.

Tearing herself from the fire reports, she told Mike what Jenny Cole had passed on about the attack on the university student. 'It might be the same man. It's a long shot, I know, but maybe we can get a physical description.'

They agreed that Rachel would follow it up.

Emma Parker lived with her family in a mock Tudor mansion in Wahroonga, one of the old northern suburbs favoured by professionals and conservative business people. The streets were clean, quiet and tree-lined, with houses hidden behind carefully tended gardens and manicured lawns, the only hint of imperfection the lingering smell of smoke from the bushfires. It was un-naturally quiet. Though the purr of a well-main-tained European car occasionally broke the stillness, no unaccompanied dogs or children were visible. Girls brought up here were used to safety, privilege and serenity, and dreamed of taking out good degrees and marrying young men from

202

similar backgrounds. They certainly didn't expect to become the victim of a sex criminal.

Harriet Parker, the girl's mother, greeted Rachel at the door, and served up perked coffee and Dutch cookies before withdrawing discreetly. Rachel quickly took in the ambience: the interior of the house was modelled on the English cottage look, with deep stuffed couches covered in flowered chintz, Axminster carpet, silver-framed family pictures on little polished tables and the faint smell of pot-pourri in the air. And a piano, of course.

In some ways Emma Parker lived up to Rachel's preconceptions. Taking after her artist mother, she was self-confident, tall and attractive, with clear skin and expensively straightened teeth. What Rachel hadn't foreseen was the nose ring and the hair dyed a deep black and highlighted with henna. Nor had she expected the girl to be more outraged and angry than distressed.

The girl told Rachel she'd failed a subject and was at the library cramming for a supplementary exam. 'I left about eight and took the path beside the chemistry building to the car park. It's well lit; I wasn't afraid. But then I never am.' She shrugged. 'Maybe I should be.

'Then this guy leapt out of the bushes and grabbed me. I couldn't do anything, because I had my arms full of books. They fell on the path. At first I thought he was after my shoulder bag, but he wasn't interested in money. He yanked my arms behind my back, grabbed both of my wrists with one hand and put the other over my mouth.'

She rubbed the blue fingermarks on her bare arms. 'You always wonder if you'll be able to scream if somebody attacks you…Now I know. It was so fast I didn't have time. But I did kick him in the shins: it must have been a reflex.' She laughed. 'He'll have a few bruises to remember me by: I was wearing my Docs.' She stopped, seeing it again.

'What happened then?' prompted Rachel, caught up. The girl had a good voice and used her hands—an excellent story-teller.

'He started dragging me through the bushes towards the edge of the car park. But then a bunch of joggers ran smack bang into us. I took off like a rocket back to the library and got them to call the police. I wasn't game to go into the car park.'

'What happened to your assailant?' asked Rachel.

'Assailant,' the girl mocked. 'You police must be the only people in the world who use that word.'

'You're taking this well, Emma,' said Rachel.

The girl's mood changed. 'Not as well as I'm pretending. I'll be all right for a while, then I realise how close I came and go cold all over.' Playing with an earring and avoiding Rachel's eye, she asked, 'What was he going to do to me?'

'Rape you, at the very least.' said Rachel. The girl was too intelligent and perceptive for kind half-truths.

Just then a breeze ruffled the curtain and a ray of sunlight fell on the girl, lighting up her hair, and Rachel shivered.

'What's wrong?' asked Emma, alarmed.

Risking puncturing the girl's brittle composure, Rachel said: 'Would you be prepared to come back to the university with me tonight and re-enact the crime?'

Emma looked uncertain. 'Why?'

'I'd rather not explain until I see where it happened.'

The girl paled. 'Do you think it was...?'

Rachel cut in. 'Let's just wait and see, shall we, Emma. Can you do that for me?'

The girl was silent, thinking it through. 'OK, but don't tell my mother what we're doing. She's just holding it together. My life's going to be difficult enough as it is, knowing she's worried every time I go out the door.'

Rachel returned to Wahroonga that night and collected Emma, who'd told her mother they'd be looking at mug shots at headquarters. Emma's father, Roland Parker, was home. A bulky olive-skinned man with the high colour of someone who had eaten too many expense account meals and taken too little exercise, the barrister was a famous wit reputed not to suffer fools gladly. Testing out the rumours he'd picked up around the courts, Parker quizzed Rachel about the Lisa Broderick murder. When she parried his questions politely but firmly, he eventually gave up, telling her he hoped he'd never have to deal with her in the witness box. She decided to take it as a compliment.

'He's a terror, isn't he?' Emma said on the way to the university.

The man was a bully and Rachel had disliked him, but his daughter didn't need to know that. 'He's just doing his job.'

'That's the problem. He never stops. He wanted me to go into the law, but I refused. He's never forgiven me.'

'What are you studying?'

'Drama.'

It fitted. 'Acting isn't that different from what he does for a living,' Rachel said. 'Tell him that.'

Emma laughed. 'You're all right. You're not like any cop I ever met before.'

There was no answer to that sort of backhanded compliment.

'What's your background?' the girl asked, unabashed.

'An MA in psychology, Police Academy, the beat, Homicide,' Rachel replied.

The girl nodded. 'I guessed some of that from

the way you handled Dad. He intimidates most functionaries.'

The relationship between those who made the laws and those who enforced them would always be complicated. The Australian middle classes looked down on the predominantly working-class police, but tolerated them out of need. Unchecked, the police in many states had turned into a necessary evil. Until the last ten years or so, police corruption, racism and incompetence had been overlooked in the interests of a quiet life, but police attitudes and practices were now under constant attack from the parliament, commissions of inquiry and the media.

Rachel, as an honest cop and a product of the middle class, often found herself caught up in contradictions. She survived by lying low, by keeping her opinions to herself.

Emma wasn't the type to take silence for an answer, however. 'What on earth made someone like you join the police, Constable Addison? You could be making a fortune in private practice. And everyone knows the cops treat women like dirt.'

'I'm interested in crime,' said Rachel.

Emma was unimpressed. 'So am I. So's Dad. But it's a different matter being on the front line like you are. What if you come face to face with this nutcase who cut up Lisa Broderick? What will you do?'

'Pretty much what you did, I suppose,' said Rachel. 'Plus I'd hope I could get to my gun in time.'

Rachel had hoped that the mention of guns would end the interrogation, but Emma Parker had an axe to grind. 'You just seem wrong for the police force, somehow,' she insisted.

'How?'

'You're the wrong class, to put it bluntly. I mean really, Adam Dalgliesh and Shakespeare-quoting coppers like…What's his name, again?'

'Inspector Wexford,' said Rachel.

'Yeah, Wexford. Well, they're OK in novels, but the fact is, most of the cops in this country wouldn't have read a book since high school.'

Rachel could have pointed out that this was changing, but the charge was true enough to demand a serious answer. 'In case you hadn't noticed, the privileged classes aren't all that inter-ested in doing dirty work like picking drunks up out of gutters or breaking up domestics or talking down armed robbers,' she said. 'They'd rather somebody else did it.'

The girl flushed. 'I'm not putting it down. I just wondered why you're doing it.'

There were all sorts of reasons Rachel could give—contributing to a better society, keeping the streets safe, blazing a trail for women—but they were only part of the truth. Though she was coming to realise that she'd joined the force out of fear and a compulsion for order, this was nobody's business but her own. Choosing her words carefully, she said: 'I wanted to make the world a safer place.' For myself.

'Doesn't it scare you?' asked the girl.

Until recently the police force was the only place Rachel had felt safe, but her demons had somehow breached the blue line. 'Of course I get scared sometimes,' she said. 'But your imagination can be your worst enemy in this job. You can't afford to demonise the enemy: you have to understand them.'

'How do you mean?'

'Most criminals aren't monsters; they're poorly socialised and impetuous—people who don't understand consequences—or they're just plain stupid. If they want something they can't buy because they don't have a job or don't think they should have to work or don't earn enough, they take it from someone else.

'If something or someone makes them feel angry or sad or stupid, they head-butt it. If the other person is weaker, they might get away with it; if not, they end up injured or dead or in jail. Let's face it, there aren't many smart people in jail. The smart ones get away with it.'

'God that's depressing.'

'Is it? Maybe it's just the natural order. The

good cops know we're never going to get back into the Garden of Eden, return to some mythical state of grace when there was no sin in the world. The most you can do is try to keep some kind of balance between good and evil.'

Emma looked sceptical. 'Is this the police department's philosophy?'

Rachel laughed. 'I doubt it.'

Then, to her relief, they arrived at the university gates. After Rachel parked the car, they found the path, which was brightly lit and, since Friday night's attack, empty.

'Women aren't game to walk anywhere on campus at night without an escort now,' said Emma. 'It's a bloody outrage. The sooner you catch him, the better.'

Rachel examined the area where the man must have waited, but if there had been any clues left behind, the investigating officers had already found them. She signalled Emma to walk towards her. Just as she'd expected, the tungsten lights made the girl's hair look dark red.

'What was that really about?' asked Emma, as they reversed out of the parking space.

'The first thing that struck me was that the assailant'—they both smiled—'didn't try to rape you on the spot. He could have dragged you into the bushes, but he was trying to get you to the car park.' She reached out and touched Emma's arm. 'I don't want to frighten you, Emma, but I think your attacker might be Lisa Broderick's killer.'

The girl's hands flew to her mouth. 'Why?'

'For one thing, Lisa was abducted, and I see this as an attempted abduction, not a simple rape. If there's such a thing. Most rapes are opportunistic; done on impulse, on the spot, when the conditions are right. Abducting a woman is just too risky for most rapists: they have to keep the victim quiet until they get to the hideout, and they might get stopped by the police or have an accident on the way. And then there's the hair.'

'But Lisa Broderick had red hair!' protested Emma. 'Mine's black.'

'In this light it looks red. When I saw the sun shining on your hair today, I suspected you'd look like a redhead under some lights. That's why I wanted to bring you here.'

'Stop the car,' said Emma. When Rachel pulled into the side of the road, she jumped out and ran furiously along the grass verge. Rachel moved to follow, then stopped. Eventually the girl ran out of steam, bent over with her hands on her knees and gasped, then straightened up and walked back to the police car.

'Sorry about that. I thought I was going to explode,' she said sheepishly as Rachel opened the door.

As they neared the Parker home, Rachel asked Emma if she could identify her attacker. The girl shook her head. 'I doubt it. It was all too fast, and he grabbed me from behind. While he was getting away, I was too busy picking myself up from the ground and fighting my way out from under those idiots to get a look at him.'

'They might have saved your life,' said Rachel.

The girl flushed. 'I know.' She faltered. 'I've just remembered something about him, something I didn't tell Jenny. He stank.'

Rachel went very still. 'How?'

'Like an animal that's been hibernating in a lair. Skin grease, BO, cigarettes, sweat. Ugh, I think I'm going to be sick.' Rachel slowed down, but the girl regained her composure.

'What should I tell the parents?' asked Emma, when they pulled up in front of the house.

Rachel considered Emma's father, his power, the aggression behind the veneer of charm, the ethics of the situation. 'I can't make that sort of decision for you, Emma, but I wouldn't advise you to go about alone at night until we get this thing cleared up.'

The girl's voice rose: 'Is that going to happen? I can't creep around for the rest of my life because some bastard wanted to kill me!'

The rage is good, thought Rachel, always the psychologist. She'll be OK.

'I can't promise that we're going to catch him,' she said. 'We catch some; some stop for their own reasons, or go to jail, or die. But there's a very committed team working on this.' Even to Rachel it sounded like a press release.

'What about you? How do you feel about being used as bait?'

'What on earth are you talking about?'

The girl floundered. 'I...I just assumed...I mean, you're redheaded and good-looking. And they've been parading you on television...'

It's just a coincidence, thought Rachel, but doubt had taken root.

'You've probably interviewed him,' continued the girl. 'He might have been close enough to touch you.'

By this time, Emma was out of the car. She hesitated, then leaned in the window and said: 'Be careful, Rachel.'

With that, she ran up the path to the house and pounded on the front door. The door opened, and Rachel saw the light spill out, watched as the girl's mother embraced her. Then the two women turned and looked back. Rachel drove off alone.

13

The Janitor's Wife

According to the television news, well over a hundred fires were blazing throughout the state, many of them deliberately lit, prompting a passionate denunciation of arsonists by a spokesman from the firefighters' union. Graphic footage of walls of fire and retreating firefighters in yellow slickers with sooty, exhausted faces, cut to shots of the burned-out truck in which a volunteer firefighter had died. Another volunteer, a middle-aged father of eight, had been killed by a falling tree at a godforsaken place called Mount Horrible.

Turning on the radio, Rachel was hit by a blast of invective against pyromaniacs on a talk show. She shuddered and switched to a station which was giving minute-by-minute updates, but there was nothing new. Thoughtful, she turned off the radio; from what she knew about sex murderers, there was a good chance Lisa Broderick's killer had lit the odd fire in his teenage years. The bushfires were probably keeping him in a constant state of arousal.

All night Rachel tossed and turned, her dreams filled with fire and confusion. In one dream, an image of Alison's appeared, her face contorted in fear, calling on God for help. Rachel woke with a start, sweating and shaky, burdened with a sense of helplessness and loss. Who was Alison?

Wednesday dawned hot and windy, with no prospect of rain.

At police headquarters, Rachel had to interrupt a discussion about the fires to tell the team about Emma Parker. 'It wasn't just your run-of-the-mill rape attempt,' she said. 'She's convinced the man was trying to drag her to the car park. I think it might be the same man who killed Lisa Broderick.'

There was an uproar, and Mike said: 'Why?'

'The fact that he tried to abduct her: most rapists see an opportunity, commit the crime and beat it. Our man likes his privacy and he likes to take his time. And there's the hair. I walked Emma Parker through the crime, and under the lights on that path, her hair looks red. She's tall and good looking, too, like Lisa.'

'But you said she didn't see him,' said Kellett. 'So what good does it do us?'

Heading off a confrontation, Larsen changed the subject. 'Have the media picked it up?'

Rachel shook her head. 'The father's a QC. He'll nip any publicity in the bud.'

'So it's that Parker,' said Larsen. 'What a know-all bastard he is.'

There was a murmur of agreement from others who'd been victims of Roland Parker's forensic skills in the courts.

'If it was our man, he went after the wrong member of the family, if you ask me,' said Kellett, to general merriment.

As the meeting broke up, Larsen drew Rachel aside. 'How do you know he's targeting redheads?'

'I don't know for sure,' she said. 'We don't even have any proof he's a repeat offender. But if he is, he'll have patterns. I don't think we should dismiss it out of hand.'

'You'd better watch your step, Rachel,' he warned. 'You've been on TV. He knows about you.'

Rachel watched Larsen walk away, and thanked God there were still a few like him in Homicide. He was a Catholic, a good family man, and she'd heard he was active in the St Vincent de Paul Society. She'd never once heard him putting a woman down or spreading vicious rumours.

'Yeah,' said Kellett, striding past. 'With that red hair, you might be next.'

'What did Dick Kellett say to you?' asked Mike when the conference broke up.

'He warned me I might be next.'

Mike grimaced, remembering Kellett's cold smile and the clairvoyant's words. He searched Rachel's face, but it was locked.

'Didn't you mention someone you interviewed smelling bad,' she asked. 'Who was it, can you remember?'

Mike racked his brain. 'It was the janitor from St Bart's, I think. Why?'

'Emma Parker said her attacker stank.'

Mike whistled.

'What was he doing the night Lisa Broderick was killed, Mike, can you remember?'

He pulled out a notebook. 'At home, he said. His wife backed him up.'

'That's not much of an alibi. What was he like?'

'The sort only a mother could love, a mother hyena preferably. He wasn't uncooperative exactly, more a passive resister. Never volunteered anything. Answered in monosyllables. Very guarded, come to think of it. Like a big black dog on a leash waiting for an opportunity to bite your leg off.'

'Think he could have done it?'

Mike shrugged. 'Maybe. There's definitely a lot of banked-up aggression there.'

'Tell me about his wife.'

'A frightened doormat. She stayed in the background and jumped whenever he barked at her.'

'Abused?'

'There were no bruises, not where I could see them anyway, but she's obviously scared of him.'

'Think we should have another talk to her, without him this time?'

'Why not?'

Newtown was an inner-city area full of mean, working-class terrace houses. After the war, waves of Greek, Italian, Lebanese, Turkish and now Polynesian immigrants had rolled through the precinct, isolating the Anglo-Celt first settlers on small islands. And although gays were moving in, gentrifying some streets and transforming bloodbath pubs, cheap cafes and discount shops into boutique pubs, trendy eateries and yuppie interior design establishments, pockets of the suburb remained defiantly down at heel. It was in one of these narrow, seedy streets that the St Bartholomew's Hospital janitor and his wife lived.

After repeated knocking, the curtains twitched and a pale face appeared at the window, then withdrew. They waited for the woman to come to the door, but nothing happened.

'What on earth is she doing?' asked Mike as the minutes passed. 'It's bloody hot out here.'

'What makes me think she's not going to come out?' asked Rachel.

'We'll see about that,' said Mike, pounding on the door. Hysterical barking started up in the back of the house, and the next-door neighbour came to her door, glared at them, and demanded to know what they wanted.

'We're the police, Madam,' said Mike, holding up his badge. The woman retreated indoors, unwilling to get involved. The constabulary wasn't popular in this neighbourhood.

Mike gave the door another thump and the commotion smoked the woman out. Despite the heat of the day, Eileen Brady's thin body was shrouded in long-sleeved shapeless shift in the sort of shiny fabric that made Rachel's blood run cold. Reluctantly, the janitor's wife let them in, and they found themselves in a tiny, gloomy front parlour. The furniture was old and faded, and in pride of place over the bricked-in fireplace was a gaudy picture of Jesus with a crown of thorns dripping blood down his agonised face. The house smelt of mould and trapped cooking smells.

Chop grease, thought Rachel, wincing. She refrained from imagining what the kitchen looked like.

Despite the appalling heat, the windows were tightly shut, and the woman made no move to open them. A blue cattle dog slunk into the room and lay down beside its mistress, panting. It badly needed a bath.

'We'd like to ask you a few questions, Mrs Brady,' said Mike. At the sound of a man's voice, the dog flattened its ears and pressed its body against the floor.

'I've already told you all I know,' the woman said querulously, eyes downcast.

Seriously depressed, thought Rachel, noting the slow speech, the lack of affect, the inability to look people in the eye.

'We're just checking a few details,' said Mike. 'I wondered if you could tell Constable Addison here what you told me about the night Lisa Broderick died.'

'There's nothing to tell. Neville was here all night. He came home from work about a quarter past eleven, had a late supper, watched the telly and went to bed.'

'And he didn't go out at all that night?' asked Rachel, suppressing the urge to fan herself with her notebook.

The woman shook her head, didn't look up.

'Did your husband ever mention Lisa Broderick to you, Mrs Brady?' asked Rachel.

Eileen Brady jumped slightly at the name of the murdered girl, and her bony fingers began picking tufts of faded velvet off the arms of her chair. 'No, never. He never talks about work to me.'

'What do you talk about?' asked Rachel.

Surprised, the woman looked up and stared at Rachel, then shook her head helplessly.

'What shift is your husband working this week, Mrs Brady?' asked Mike.

The change of subject confused her, and she stared around, searching for someone to help her. 'What do you mean?'

Mike was inexorable. 'Just answer the question, please, Mrs Brady.'

It was an effort, but the woman finally got it out. 'Four till midnight.'

She's scared, thought Mike. Frightened she might be giving the wrong answer.

'You're sure about that?' asked Rachel.

The witness's voice rose: 'That's what he told me!'

Rachel adopted a soothing tone. 'Where is your husband now, Mrs Brady?'

'Out.'

'Where?'

'I don't know.'

There didn't seem to be anything more to say, and the miasma in the house was making them both nauseous. When they'd escaped into the open air, Mike spat in the gutter. 'I've got to get the stink of that dump out of my nostrils. Let's find somewhere with air-conditioning and have a cold drink.'

'She's terrified of that husband of hers,' said Rachel.

'Yeah. And what about that weird dress. She probably wears it to cover the bruises.'

Rachel nodded. 'So is he on nights or not?'

'Only one way to find out. If he isn't, he's lying to her, and if he's lying, why?'

They drove back to the shopping centre and strolled along Newtown's main street looking for a place to eat. Dozens of Thai restaurants had sprung up in the last few years, but it was too hot for spicy food. Eventually they found a pub in the main street that had been a notorious criminal hang-out until a couple of gays had gutted it, redecorated and put in a new restaurant. Over a seafood salad, Rachel recounted her talk with Emma Parker.

'You liked her,' said Mike.

'Yes, I did. She's a bit cheeky, but she's nice, too. At the moment she's acting tough, and there's sure to be some sort of emotional backlash later on when it all sinks in, but I don't think she's going to let the attack ruin her life.'

As they lingered over cold drinks, Rachel said: 'Mike, do you think the department is using me as bait?'

Mike was suddenly alert: 'Has something happened?'

Rachel shook her head, but it seemed less a

denial than a desire to shake off a disturbing thought. Mike was tempted to push, but realised bullying wouldn't work with this woman. He had to content himself with asking why she thought she'd been set up.

'It was something Emma Parker said. I'm superficially similar to Lisa Broderick—same height, redheaded...'

'Good-looking,' Mike added.

'Be serious,' said Rachel.

'I am,' said Mike. 'But the answer is no. I think they had another agenda altogether.'

'Like what?'

'You haven't heard the rumours about a sexual harassment charge against the Minister by one of his female staffers?'

Rachel's eyes widened.

'It's not public yet,' he cautioned. 'Very hush-hush. I'd be willing to bet they wheeled you out because you're a woman in an elite squad. You know, to prove there's no discrimination. That's the conspiracy theory, but it's just as likely that they're hiding behind your skirts.'

'What on earth do you mean?'

Sometimes she's just a babe in the woods, thought Mike. It must have been that private school. 'I think they're parading you as the human face of the police force because you're a woman, not in spite of it. They're hoping the media will think twice about criticising us for not finding Lisa Broderick's killer because it would look like an attack on you. They haven't noticed that chivalry is dead.'

The cynicism was breathtaking. 'Where did you get all this?'

Mike smiled enigmatically. Chewing it over on the way back to the office, Rachel realised it would have come from the old boys' network, his former colleagues in the Special Branch. She couldn't decide whether to be outraged or relieved, but the fact was they'd put her at risk, whatever their motives. Maybe the threat she was feeling was real, not imaginary.

Back at headquarters, Mike got on to the hospital and discovered that Neville Brady was on day shift, 8.30 a.m. till 5.30, which meant he could have been the university attacker. He was jubilant.

'What do we know about his car?' asked Rachel.

Mike looked it up. 'It's a 1985 Toyota Corolla, white.' He reeled off the registration.

Rachel's stomach lurched. A white Japanese car. Was Neville Brady the man who'd followed her to Blackheath?

Mike had seen the shudder. 'Are you all right?'

She nodded. 'A goose walked on my grave, that's all.'

'Trouble is, that little Greek girl…'

'Elena! Her name's Elena. Helen in English.'

'Thank you for that invaluable fact, Constable,' said Mike. '*Elena* swears the car that picked up Lisa Broderick was blue.'

'So what? Maybe he has one car registered in his name and one in his wife's.' She logged into the Roads and Traffic Authority's registration files under Eileen Brady's name and came up with a 1983 blue Mitsubishi Sigma.

'So where is it?' asked Mike.

'Let's find out.' Rachel dialled the Brady house, and after a lengthy delay, Eileen Brady picked up the phone, answering hesitantly, as if she seldom received calls. She dithered and dodged Rachel's questions, but finally admitted she had owned the car, but that her husband had sold it several weeks ago because she never used it.

As soon as Rachel put down the phone, Mike, who'd picked up the gist of the conversation from Rachel's end, said: 'Brady doesn't know we're on to the car yet, so he wouldn't have dumped it. What's the bet it's stashed in someone else's garage near his house?'

When Rachel nodded agreement, Mike beckoned over Brett Marcantonio and told him to organise a house to house in Newtown and Camperdown to try to track down the blue car.

The constable was agog. 'Is this the murder vehicle?'

'It might be,' said Mike. 'But this is strictly need to know, Brett. If this gets out, he'll ditch the car, and we'll be back where we started.' He paused. 'And if it leaks, I'll personally cut out your tongue.'

The young policeman, who was used to this sort of abuse, saluted mockingly and bounded off to organise the search.

At six the next day, Rachel set off for Woollahra for her appointment with Persia Lawrence. On the way, she stopped on a ridge to look at the smoke billowing in from the north and south, imagining the fires racing towards the city.

The doctor apologised for turning on the air-conditioning, but Rachel was grateful for the respite from the heat and smoke. They discussed the fires for a time, speculating about the sexual connotations of fire-starting.

When they'd exhausted the topic, the doctor said: 'We were going to talk about a nightmare, the one that frightened you so much...'

'The one that made me wet myself, you mean,' said Rachel, grimacing. 'The man chasing me. How pathetically Freudian can you get?'

'It's not Freudian if it's real,' said the doctor.

Rachel couldn't help but grin, and thought, not

for the first time, that she'd been lucky in her choice of counsellor. 'It all started with the Lisa Broderick murder investigation. It's probably just my imagination working overtime, identifying with the victim.'

'But you don't believe that, do you?'

'No.'

'Tell me about the man.'

'There's not much to tell. I can't see his face, just his silhouette against the light. He's huge.'

'Do you think he looks like a giant because you're crouching down, hiding from him, or because you're small?' asked the doctor.

Rachel looked up sharply. 'Both. It's got to be both, Persia. I must have been a child when it happened. If it did. The new dream is connected with my childhood, too; I'm sure of it, but it's not frightening. It's sad.'

'Can you tell me about it?'

'The whole thing started as a sort of vision, a face that popped into my mind while I was meditating, or trying to meditate. It's a young woman—a girl, really: she's about nineteen—and somehow I knew her name was Alison. I was certain that something terrible had happened to the girl...She was like an unhappy ghost. I know there's been no-one like Alison in my life since my aunt brought me to Sydney, so if she exists, she's part of the old life, the one I've blocked.'

'How did you feel when you saw Alison, Rachel?'

'Galvanised. Shocked, desolate, grief-stricken. As if I'm standing on the edge of a black bottomless pit.'

'Knowledge,' said the doctor.

Rachel nodded. 'I'm frightened to find out what's down there, but I can't drag myself away either. My unconscious keeps pulling me back.'

'Tell me about the meditation, Rachel.'

'It was Holly's idea. You remember we talked about her?' Rachel smiled: 'It's as if you conjured her up by reminding me how much I'd missed her, Persia. She turned up out of the blue and rang me, and I drove up to Blackheath to see her. She's married to an Indian, a Buddhist teacher out here to give courses. She talked me into staying.'

'And you've dreamed about Alison since that first sighting?'

'Yes. She was calling out to God to help her, but of course he, or she—whatever—didn't.'

'You don't believe in God?'

Rachel's tone was bitter. 'No. Something in me always resisted when people talked about God. I think I lost faith in God when I lost my parents. I didn't understand how God could do that to a child. But maybe...maybe I just remembered Alison begging God for help and getting no answer...Which must mean I know—or I knew at some stage—what happened to Alison.'

'But you can't remember?'

'No, it's a dream, like the other one, the one about being hunted.' The doctor waited while Rachel added the next piece of the jigsaw. 'The dreams are connected, aren't they, Persia? They're part of the same story.'

'Only you know that, Rachel.'

Rachel sighed. 'But I can't remember, and there's nobody to ask. My aunt's dead, and there isn't anybody in Sydney who'd know if Alison ever existed.'

The doctor didn't offer any advice. If Rachel were remembering something that really happened, the answers lay in her birthplace. Physically, it was only a few hours drive south-west; emotionally, it might still be unreachable. The decision to go back there would have to be Rachel's.

Suddenly Rachel said: 'There's guilt there, too, Persia.'

There's always guilt, thought the doctor. Where would human nature be without it? 'What about?'

'I didn't help. When she called for help, I didn't answer.' Neither of us answered, she thought. God or me.

Rachel was becoming agitated. The psychiatrist said: 'Tell me what it was like seeing your friend again.'

The relief showed on Rachel's face. 'It was as if we'd never parted. She's totally different but the same, somehow. She's learned wisdom. I think it was always there, but she had to struggle so hard to get through to it.' She stopped.

'What are you thinking about now, Rachel?'

Rachel jumped slightly. 'I was thinking that everything is too hard and takes too long. All that time wasted in struggle.'

She was talking about herself, of course. 'Did seeing Holly help you in any way?'

'Yes, I finally confessed that I'd been an abused woman. That my university lover, the one everybody expected me to marry, had bullied and threatened me, and that I was too ashamed to tell anyone.'

'And you haven't trusted a man since.'

'No.'

'Does that seem extreme to you?'

Rachel leapt to her own defence. 'You wouldn't say that if you knew how hard it had been for me to trust him in the first place, Persia. All my instincts told me to stay away from men, but I didn't listen. And I paid.'

Her tone told the doctor not to persist. Changing the subject, Rachel said: 'The question is, are we dealing with dreams or memories here? We both know dreams aren't necessarily reliable memories; they distort reality. Like looking at your life in one of those fun-hall mirrors. Did something bad happen to me when I was a child, or am I manufacturing these nightmares because of what's happened to me since I was assigned to the Lisa Broderick investigation?'

'Exactly what has happened, Rachel?'

'I wish I knew. There might be a man in a white car following me; someone who's got hold of my unlisted number is calling me and breathing; somebody drew a heart with an arrow through it on my car. But it could be my imagination, or paranoia. Maybe it's all perfectly innocent, or just a series of coincidences. I know how stress magnifies everything. After all, the man in the white car didn't do anything, the phone caller didn't threaten me, and a kid could have drawn the heart. Or someone who fancies me. You see my dilemma...'

Paranoia was one thing, thought the doctor, but Rachel was a police officer working on a dangerous case—the threat could be real. 'Have you told anyone about all this?' she asked.

Rachel heard the concern in Persia's voice and looked up. 'No.'

'Why not?'

'I'm a woman.'

The doctor knew what she meant, knew all about double standards in the workplace, but too much pride was dangerous. 'What about your partner?'

'He thinks I'm acting strangely. He'd have to be blind not to. I practically fainted into his arms in the hospital, and I freaked out the other day when we went to see the clairvoyant. I tried to cover it up, but he noticed.'

'What happened at the clairvoyant's, Rachel?'

'She told me I was in danger because I was a redhead. In retrospect, you wouldn't need a crystal ball to work that out. I'm probably the only person in Australia it hadn't dawned on. Since then I've been wondering if the department is using me as a decoy to draw the murderer out of cover.'

This revelation disturbed the doctor. 'Do you suspect the killer might be behind these incidents?'

Rachel shrugged. 'Put it this way. I don't go anywhere without my gun and my portable phone any more.'

Time was up. The doctor was worried. She was beginning to believe Rachel was in some sort of danger, but was unsure whether the threat emanated from a real, live murderer, from her past, or from delusion. The young woman's fear could simply be the reaction of an overactive imagination under stress. The psychiatrist's intuition was that Rachel had suffered a massive trauma in childhood, but it was not clear yet whether the damage had been caused by the loss of her parents or something else. Where did Alison come in? Why was the little girl hiding in the nightmare, and who was the bogeyman stalking her?

As Rachel was the last client of the day, Persia Lawrence saw her out. From the doorway, she said: 'Rachel, if you need me, call me anytime, day or night.'

Rachel looked back, disturbed by the concern in the doctor's voice. Her throat constricted by emotion, she was only able to nod. 'And be very careful.'

14

He Felt As If He'd Come Home

Tired, edgy and restless, Rachel let herself into her house, hung up her jacket in the hall closet, kicked off her shoes and wandered into the living room. There was a message on the answering machine from Kate Westwood—'Just wondered if you were all right...'

All right? thought Rachel. No, I'm probably not all right. Was I ever?

To release the stuffy, hot air from the house, she opened windows and doors, then let herself out into the small back courtyard. The heady scent of some sweet, night-blooming flower reached her from a nearby garden. Sourly she noted that the privet which had invaded from next door was taking hold; one good rainfall would send it wild. She looked up at the sky—little chance of that.

Fortunately there was some wine left in a bottle in the fridge in her white, antiseptically clean kitchen. The cold slate soothing against her bare hot feet, Rachel poured herself a glass of Clare Valley Riesling and sipped luxuriously. Surveying the empty refrigerator shelves, she sighed, found a tin of soup in the cupboard and put on some toast. A colourful collection of neglected cookbooks watched her reproachfully from a shelf near the stove: one day she'd cook something out of them, become one of those earthy women who could conjure up feasts from leftovers and sheer ingenuity. One day.

It was time for the news. Carrying her meagre single's meal, she moved into the living room and turned on the television. Over a hundred and thirty fires were burning, and everywhere firemen were frantically backburning to create buffers to protect settlements and heavily wooded areas. Distraught holiday-makers were filmed fleeing a caravan park just ahead of the flames, army and navy personnel had been pressed into service, and firefighters were pouring in from other states.

From a helicopter high above a blazing reserve, a tearful reporter described the inferno below. A National Parks spokeswoman warned it would take the parks years to recover. The Bureau of Meteorology predicted worse to come: high winds and temperatures expected to reach 36 degrees Centigrade. The fires had all but erased Lisa Broderick's murder from the public consciousness.

Although she watched little television—who wanted to watch fictional cops chasing celluloid criminals?—tonight Rachel left it on for updates on the fires. In the menacing silence of the house, the tinny racket was oddly comforting.

Maybe a bath would help. Upstairs she ran a deep tub, added lilac bath oil, breathed in the steam, then changed in her bedroom, hanging her suit neatly in the wardrobe and throwing her soiled underwear and shirt into the clothes basket. Lulled at last by the healing power of water, some innocuous classical music on her transistor radio and the scent of lilacs, she almost dozed off.

Later, prune-fingered but cool in an Indian cotton robe, she pulled a textbook on serial murderers from the bookshelf in her study and put it on her bedside table. Not most people's idea of bedtime reading, she thought.

Creaming her face at her dressing table, she suddenly froze. There was something odd about the reflection in the mirror. Fighting a surge of fear, she went to investigate. It hadn't been her imagination: the bed was slightly rumpled. Most people wouldn't have noticed, but Rachel was obsessively neat. She made the bed every morning and remembered smoothing down the cover.

She ran her hand over the bedspread, then leaned down and sniffed the pillow. Somebody had been in her bed. Pulling back the covers, she found the proof: there, coiled like a question mark, lay a lone black pubic hair.

Feeling faint, she slumped to her knees. Her heart thumped: she was having trouble catching her breath: she couldn't move. A car backfiring in the street below roused her, and she fled to the bathroom and brought up the wine, soup and toast.

As soon as she recovered, she grabbed her gun and ran downstairs, afraid to remain on the top floor, trapped and vulnerable. Had she locked all the windows? In a panic, she ran from window to window, door to door, checking, closing the curtains.

Locking the door after the horse has bolted, she thought, calmer now, searching the ground floor for signs of entry.

He'd entered boldly through the laundry window, simply smashing the glass and climbing in. Because her backyard was secluded, and the neighbours all out at work, he hadn't had to worry about being seen. Glad to have something to take her mind off her fear, she found some pieces of wood left over from the renovations, and hammered them into place over the window.

Upstairs, she contemplated the bed. Then she went into the bathroom, found some tweezers and an empty pill bottle, picked up the hair and deposited it in the bottle. Evidence. Shuddering, she stripped the bed and remade it with fresh linen, replacing the pillows with two from the bed in the spare room. Tomorrow she'd dispose of them.

She considered calling in the local police, but what good would it do? Although the back window was broken, nothing had been taken. To an objective observer, nothing had even been disturbed. The police would think it was local kids. If she said she thought some strange man had been in her bed, they'd think she was neurotic. After her years in the force, she could script the jokes they'd make about her sex life, or lack of it, as soon as they were out of earshot.

The house was deadly quiet: she could have been in a space capsule. No sound came from the neighbours; apart from the occasional car accelerating up the hill, the street was deserted. This was the main reason she'd chosen to live here, but now it seemed like folly. Bolt upright in a chair in the living room, Rachel tried to think rationally. There were plenty of people out there with good reason to hate her, to frighten her: men she'd questioned in investigations, villains she'd helped put away, their friends and families. Any one of them could be toying with her, trying to frighten her.

Or it could be someone far more dangerous.

If this break-in were the culmination of a campaign of intimidation, though, a number of incidents made sense now—the overturned rubbish tin and the maggots that had made her flesh crawl, the sense of being followed, the nagging feeling she was being watched. She was sure somebody was hunting her, but who? If it was Lisa Broderick's killer, what did this latest invasion mean? Was it a tease, a promise of worse to come, or had the killer been indulging in some secret ceremony, not realising he was leaving evidence behind?

The dread deepened. She was afraid to stay in the house, a stationary target, but was loath to leave the safety of four walls, no matter how illusory. He could be out there, waiting. She sat on, paralysed. From time to time her eyes went to the phone. Finally, she pulled it on to her lap and dialled. When he answered, she simply said: 'I need you.'

He didn't need to ask who it was, and he didn't waste time asking questions. 'Give me twenty minutes.'

Twenty minutes, she thought. A lifetime.

The urge to lock herself in the smallest, safest place she could find became almost irresistible. Maybe I could hide in the broom cupboard, she thought.

It seemed horribly funny, suddenly, and she gave a snort of laughter. It would be like a goldfish trying to hide in a bowl; and she was a police officer, for God's sake. Instead, she lay down on the floor and did yoga breathing exercises, trying to empty her mind and slow her heart. It worked to a degree: ordinary fear replaced the panic.

At least when Mike Ross arrived, Rachel was no longer shaking and stuttering, though he noticed that her pupils were huge and her eyes almost black against her pallor. She drew him into the living room without speaking. He looked around, noting the clean lines, the pale walls, some original watercolours, no clutter. It seemed too tidy to him—no piles of newspapers or magazines, no coffee cups—but the order wasn't a surprise. He wondered briefly how she'd handle his dusty, disorganised flat: if she ever had reason to enter it, of course.

He sat down: 'What's wrong?'

'I think someone's after me.'

'Who?'

'Whoever killed Lisa Broderick.'

'Jesus Christ! Are you serious?'

'Yes.'

He stared at her: 'I know I'm being slow, but you'll have to explain.' He'd been right, then, suspecting she was holding something back.

'Somebody's been in my house. He got in through the laundry window, and he was in my bedroom.'

'That's a break-in, not a murder attempt,' he said. 'What's missing?'

'That's just it. Nothing.'

240

'So they were disturbed.'

'He, not they. He lay on my bed.'

He thought of his own bed. It didn't get made from one wash day till the next. A biker gang could have an orgy on it and he probably wouldn't notice.

She saw the doubt in his face. 'I can tell. Look at this room. If I came in here and one magazine was out of place, I'd know. That's the way I am. Someone's been sleeping in my bed.'

'Maybe it was Father Bear,' he said, and instantly regretted it. She didn't smile.

'That's what it smelled like.'

Mike ran his hands over his face, not knowing what to say. Rachel was aware of how tenuous it all seemed. 'I know it sounds mad, but I promise you: I could smell someone in my bedroom.'

She got up abruptly and left the room, returning with a small plastic pill bottle: 'He left me a souvenir.'

Mike stared at the pubic hair with distaste. The vague thought that it could come from a lover crossed his mind. She read his thoughts: 'There's no tall, dark man, Mike. I've been celibate for a year.'

He suppressed an inappropriate desire to ask why, the close call making him blush. Rachel didn't notice: she was contemplating the hair as if it were a poisonous spider.

'Did you call the police?' he asked.

'Yes, Mike. I called you.'

His mind was racing. 'We've got to find somewhere safe for you to stay.'

He rose and paced out the ground floor, then ran upstairs and looked around.

'You can't possibly stay here,' he announced, when he'd finished his security check. 'There are too many ways in. There's glass everywhere, and someone could come up that tree and through the French doors upstairs. What about your family? I can take you there.'

'There isn't anyone.'

'No brothers and sisters?'

'No.'

'Friends?'

She shook her head. 'They've all got kids. I can't do it to them. I'll go to a hotel.'

He scoffed: 'A hotel would be the worst possible place to hide, thousands of people going in and out, nobody knowing who should be there and who shouldn't. You'd be safer here.'

'In that case, I'll stay here,' she said, resigned. 'If he'd wanted to kill me today, he would have just waited. He's unlikely to come back tonight.'

He hesitated, then said: 'I could stay here, if you like.'

She looked up, looked into his eyes.

'In the spare room,' he added.

'But what about, I mean, don't you...'

'I don't live with anyone, if that's what's worrying you,' he said. 'I don't have a dog, and my pot-plants gave up the ghost years ago. Nobody's going to miss me.'

The relief made Rachel light-headed. 'Well, if it's all right...'

'Really,' he said, and suddenly they were shy with each other.

After a cup of tea and some uneasy chat, Rachel made up the bed in the spare room, got him a fluffy towel (not threadbare like his), found him a new toothbrush in the back of the bathroom cupboard. Then she thanked him again and retired to her bedroom.

While he showered in the spotless bathroom—no grunge, no mould on the shower curtain, pearly looking shells on a shelf above the basin, some kind of lingering flowery smell—he mulled over what she'd told him. If the hair belonged to Lisa Broderick's killer, he'd probably had Rachel staked out since she appeared on television. Or if he was one of their suspects, since she'd interviewed him. He wondered if she'd noticed anyone watching her, or if she would have told him if she had. He cast his mind back over the people they'd interviewed about the murder. There were so many...Then he remembered that Emma Parker had remarked about the foul smell of the man who'd tried to abduct her at the university.

Realising the room was full of steam, he turned off the hot tap. The water from the cold tap was tepid because of the heat however, and he was sweating again as soon as he'd dried himself.

He eyed himself critically in the bathroom mirror—a tan suited him, he decided, helped offset the dark shadows under his eyes—then succumbed to the temptation to snoop. The medicine cabinet held tampons, drops for sensitive eyes, eye make-up in shades ranging from olive-green to brown, bath oil. He picked up the tiny bottle and sniffed, recognising the scent in the bathroom—a mud mask (women are so gullible), a condom (probably perished by now, if she's telling the truth), various skin lotions and a strip of a well-known brand of sleeping pills much favoured by junkies maintaining till the next hit.

So she has trouble sleeping, he thought. It fitted, somehow. She was a bit like one of those imprac-tical Italian sports cars that spend most of their lives in an expensive garage being fine-tuned.

I'm going nuts, he thought. Women as sports cars! What next?

As he padded by her room, he noticed that she'd left the door ajar and turned on a dim night-light. Odd. Most people gave up night-lights when they left childhood, but perhaps insomniacs found them comforting.

The street was quiet and the bed comfortable, so after giving in to a minor sexual fantasy about the naked woman almost within touching distance (inaccurately, as it turned out: Rachel always wore a T-shirt to bed), he drifted into sleep.

It was the noise of someone moaning that woke him. Not the noise, exactly, because it wasn't very loud: it must have been the change in the emotional atmosphere of the house. He wondered for a moment where he was, remembered everything in a fast flashback, then jumped out of bed to investigate.

Taking his gun out of its holster, he crept along the corridor. He pushed Rachel's door open with his foot and, holding the gun in both hands, pointed it into the room. In the glow of the night light, he could see Rachel throwing herself about in the bed as if trying to escape from some nightmare. She was alone.

Mike hesitated for a moment, lowering the gun, embarrassed, cold at the thought of her waking to find him naked, pointing a gun at her. But she seemed so distressed...Adjusting the safety catch, he put the gun on the floor and crept closer. He'd heard the old wives' tales about waking people from nightmares—or was it sleepwalkers?

As he reached her bed, she suddenly cried out and sat up. Seeing a figure, she began a scream, which he stifled with his hand: 'It's only me!' he said. 'It's OK.'

The wildness died in her eyes, and he took his hand away. 'I'm sorry. I heard a noise...I thought someone might be hurting you...You were moaning...'

He trailed off, aware of his nakedness and her vulnerability. Irrationally, he felt like a rapist caught in the act, then realised she was too embarrassed about waking him with her thrashing about to notice his bare arse.

'I have these nightmares,' she said, her eyes locked on his. For a moment he thought she was going to say more, but the habit of a lifetime was too strong.

Then she dropped her eyes, and they widened a little: 'I must have frightened you,' she said. And— a miracle—she smiled.

Looking him straight in the eye, she said: 'Aren't you lonely out there?'

He slid under the sheet before she had time for second thoughts. She came into his arms and buried her face in his neck. It seemed perfectly natural, as if they'd done it a thousand times.

They're right, she thought. It is like riding a bike. You don't forget.

Her skin was hot, probably from the night terrors, and seemed to burn him; his, as she had known it would, smelled like sun-warmed grass, like toast, like new hay. He ran his hands down her back and across her buttocks, she sighed. Clasped her hands behind his neck, she drew his face to hers.

God, I've missed this, she thought. The feel of a man's body wanting me. Wanting him back. You couldn't be safer than this; having a policeman in your bed.

It gave a whole new dimension to the term bodyguard.

Then their mouths dissolved in long kisses, and her consciousness flew up and away, leaving her body free, ready, fearless. Mike had never been kissed like this before: he felt as if his will was being sucked out of his mouth along with his breath. He capitulated happily, became hard and urgent against her, and she reached down and held him in a strong hand. Then, no longer able to bear the tension, she eased her leg over his, gasping softly as he entered her and began to move slowly and rhythmically. It was then she realised she'd been planning this from the moment she'd first sighted him, caught his spoor across the room, all those months ago.

As for Mike, he felt as if he'd come home.

15

There Was No
Stopping It Now

Rachel woke with a sense of strangeness, and quickly realised why. Mike Ross was in her bed, sleeping still. He'd kicked off the sheet in the night. He was lightly built but well muscled, golden-olive of skin and smooth-chested. She could see the pulse beating in his neck, and touched it with her finger. He woke, grabbed her hand and pulled her down beside him, where she rested, her face against his chest, feeling his heart beating through his warm skin.

God help me, she thought. I'm in love. With a cop. Then he turned to her and she stopped thinking and followed her instincts.

They were a little shy with each other, kept bumping into each other and saying sorry, then grinning. Outside it was hot already, a dry wind blowing. Parched leaves frisked around Rachel's ankles as she unlocked the car. Somehow they got to the airport in time to meet Damien Grant's flight from Bangkok. Fortified with espresso and Danish from the coffee shop, they scrutinised the streams of grubby, exhausted travellers who trundled their trolleys down the exit ramp, looked around fearfully, and fell gratefully into the arms of friends and relatives. Others, travelling alone, headed confidently for money-changers and the taxi rank.

As always, at any airport, at any time, Rachel longed to board a plane and go somewhere. Anywhere. When they had Lisa Broderick's murderer locked up, she'd take a holiday, she vowed.

Damien Grant was far better looking than his hospital ID photograph; tall, lean, muscular and obviously fit from the trek, with grey eyes startling in his tanned face. Only the thinning of his fair hair at the temples betrayed his age. He stared at them blankly when they showed their badge and asked him to come with them.

'What the hell is this all about?' he said. 'Surely you don't think I'm smuggling drugs.'

'We're not the drug squad, Mr Grant,' said Rachel. 'We're investigating the murder of Lisa Broderick.'

He paled under the tan. 'Lisa's dead?'

'Raped and murdered on the night of Saturday, the 17th of December,' said Mike, who had taken an instant dislike to the man.

'I didn't know,' he said. 'I left the country on the Sunday morning...Christ Almighty! You don't seriously think I had anything to do with it, do you?'

'Mr Grant, we have reason to believe you may have been intimate with Lisa Broderick,' said Rachel. 'We'd like to talk to you about what you were doing on the night she was killed.'

'But I've been in the air for ten hours! Can't I go home and clean up first?'

'We'd prefer to get it over with now, if you don't mind,' said Rachel coldly, and Grant withdrew into silence.

Her own nerves still frayed from last night's fright, Rachel lapsed into an open-eyed sleep behind her sunglasses. Mike drove in silence, letting her rest, watching her covertly, still slightly amazed at what had happened between them. Suddenly her blush as she passed him in the doorway that day made sense, and he grinned to himself. Grant slouched sullenly in the back, staring out at the waking city.

At police headquarters, Rachel led Grant into an interview room, while Mike made coffee. 'Real coffee!' she called after him as he headed for the kitchen.

'I had nothing to do with it,' said Damien Grant, when Mike rejoined them carrying Rachel's Italian coffee-maker and three cups. 'I don't see why I should have to answer questions.'

Mike called his bluff: 'Would you like to call a lawyer?'

They watched Grant calculate the odds. Finally, he shook his head; calling a lawyer would make him look as if he had something to hide.

The men faced off: Grant angry, Mike implacable. Then Grant dropped his eyes. Mike and Rachel exchanged a look, part of the silent dialogue they'd been carrying on since last night. 'Where were you on the night of December the seventeenth at about half past twelve, Mr Grant?' asked Mike.

'In a pub in Kings Cross; pissed, I think.'

'You think?'

'Some of it's a bit hazy.'

'Which pub?' asked Rachel.

He named a notorious dive in the city's red-light district frequented by prostitutes, drug pushers, petty criminals and a variety of victims, most of them only too willing.

'That's a rough place for a member of the caring professions to be hanging out in,' said Mike.

'No worse than Somalia,' said Grant. 'And you'd be surprised who you run into at that pub.'

'No I wouldn't,' said Mike. 'Did anyone see you there?'

'Hundreds of people.'

'Anyone we could talk to?'

He shook his head. 'It was a big night. The place was packed.'

'You went alone?' asked Rachel.

Staring insolently into Rachel's eyes, Grant said: 'Why take a ham sandwich to a banquet?'

What an insufferable pig, thought Rachel, wondering how long it had taken Lisa Broderick to see through this lout.

'Did you go home alone?' asked Mike.

'No,' said Grant, but he'd hesitated a beat too long.

'Wake up, Grant,' said Mike, tiring of the game. 'You have a record of beating up women, you were intimate with Lisa Broderick, you've got the right blood group, and you've got no alibi. Put yourself in our position.'

The litany shook Grant. 'What makes you think I was having it off with Lisa Broderick?'

'She kept a diary,' said Rachel. Grant didn't need to know that the diary entries proved absolutely nothing.

Grant rolled his eyes heavenward. 'So I screwed her. So what?'

'So she's dead,' said Rachel.

'What was my motive? Why would I kill Lisa Broderick?'

'Why did you rape Jeannie Carmichael and bash her?' asked Rachel.

'You've got nothing on me. The charge was dropped.'

'We've spoken to your ex-wife,' said Mike.

That took the wind out of Grant's sails, but he rallied quickly. Palms-up in a belated effort at conciliation, he grinned and said: 'Look, I was crazy then. I'm clean now.'

It probably worked with the women he conned, but Grant's interrogators were impervious to his particular brand of charm. 'Tell us about Lisa Broderick,' said Rachel.

He shrugged: 'What's to tell? I knew she'd split up with her old man. She was a good-looking woman. I took a run at her and got lucky. We went to a movie, had dinner a couple of times and eventually I got her into the sack. But she wasn't my type. No edge; too goody-goody. And too desperate.'

'Desperate?' echoed Rachel.

'She was one of those women whose biological clock is ticking away like a time bomb, if you ask me, baby mad. I wasn't interested. When she figured that out, she cooled down pretty fast.'

'And you got angry and killed her,' said Mike.

'Give me a break,' said Grant. 'Do you know how many women there are at that hospital? In Sydney? In the world? Why bother with one suburban prude. You're looking for a madman, not me.'

'So you won't mind if we take a look around your house,' said Mike.

'Of course I mind, but what choice have I got? Can you at least tell me what you're looking for?'

'She was stabbed,' said Rachel.

Damien Grant's bravado slipped a little: 'Someone who likes his work,' he commented. 'Go ahead. You won't find anything.'

Leaving Damien Grant alone to cool his heels while the search team got organised, Mike said: 'What do you reckon?'

Rachel shook her head. 'He's an ego monster, and he dislikes women, but I don't think he's our man. He has no history of playing with knives, for a start; and secondly, he lied about his alibi.'

'Yeah, I thought so, too. That was weird. Why would anyone lie about having an alibi for a murder?'

'Because he went home with the wrong person.'

'A man?'

'Maybe. More likely an under-age female. If it is, I'd say he's going to keep it under his hat unless we force his hand. He's probably afraid of losing his job. It is against the law after all, and the medical profession is getting kind of twitchy about sexual misbehaviour. He's lucky he got away with beating up his wife.'

'And stealing drugs: I'll bet anything he's been

ripping off patients' drugs for years,' said Mike. 'I wonder if he's really clean?'

By this time the building was starting to hum with early starters. Mike had other business, so Rachel accompanied Ray Larsen and a couple of uniforms to search Damien Grant's apartment in Elizabeth Bay, a densely settled harbourside enclave within walking distance of St Bart's. A nurse's salary wouldn't go far in this area, where glimpses of the harbour cost as much as suburban houses in less fashionable suburbs. Grant's building was a box-like high-rise in an area full of gracious Art Deco apartment blocks, causing Rachel to wonder if taste or budget had dictated the choice.

The search didn't take long. Damien Grant was obviously camped out waiting for his new life to begin. The only furniture was a king-size bed, a two-seater couch, a television and sound system and a small table and two chairs; not that anything else would have fitted in. The only discovery of any interest was a stash of porn magazines under the bed and a very small amount of marijuana secreted in a shoe in the back of the wardrobe. No suspicious looking knives, no bloodstained clothes, no sign of blood in the plumbing. Neither did Grant's car, a cherry-red Mazda MX5 sports car reveal anything incriminating.

Disappointed, they gave Grant back his flat. He

watched them from his balcony, grinning, as they drove off.

'I'd like to nail that self-satisfied bastard for something,' said Larsen, speaking for all of them.

At headquarters, many desks were vacant. The freeway to the Central Coast had been closed the night before, stranding thousands on the road overnight: those who'd got through were unable to return to the city. Powerlines had exploded, taking out the phone system in some areas and cutting people off from relatives and friends.

A massive blaze had ignited at the northern end of Lane Cove National Park, and had quickly spread into some of the heavily wooded, exclusive inner northern suburbs. Farther north, on the outskirts of the city, suburbs backing on to Ku-ring-gai Chase were being evacuated. Fires now threatened the very heart of the metropolis, approaching in a pincer movement from north and south.

On a television in the incident room, they watched the Fire Chief telling the media that the fires were out of control. 'We are facing potentially the most critical situation New South Wales has ever seen,' he warned. A chubby, middle-aged bureaucrat who exuded confidence, he'd become an overnight celebrity after years of anonymity.

From Sheree's desk a radio blared warnings to

residents and experts offered tips on safeguarding houses from flames.

'Listen to this,' shouted Larsen. 'The northern end of the bloody Royal National Park's on fire!'

Silence fell. Lying between the city and Wollongong, an industrial city to the south, this magnificent reserve had somehow escaped the depredations of developers, and occupied a special place in the hearts of both cities. As the day wore on, the fire in the park raged out of control, and there were heart-wrenching scenes as the residents of Bundeena, a tiny waterfront settlement, were evacuated by boat. Eventually firefighters managed to burn off a wide enough firebreak to halt the fire and save the village, though the park continued to burn on several fronts.

The Minister for Police appeared on television calling the situation 'a catastrophe' and making Rachel wince: if the politicians couldn't keep cool heads, how could they expect the population to remain calm. The Chief Inspector alleviated some of the mounting anxiety by ordering home those with family or property in danger. Several people left at a run. He also called for volunteers to help local police evacuate reluctant home-owners from threatened areas, control the crowds and deter looters. Several officers, including Rachel and Mike, raised their hands. The Chief gave the nod to Brett Marcantonio and Kellett. Mike was obviously disappointed, but Rachel's immediate reaction was relief, as flashes of light at the corner of her vision had warned her that a migraine was imminent.

Amidst the ensuing confusion, Mike was called to the phone and returned, looking troubled. 'That was my brother, in Heathcote,' he said. It was one of those settlements clinging precariously to the ridges abutting the Royal National Park. 'He needs me down there...'

The Chief told him to leave immediately. Rachel's stomach plummeted. The authorities were putting a brave face on it, but already one firefighter had been killed, and in a southern suburb, a woman had been trapped between her house and swimming pool and burned to death in a flashfire. It was a miracle there hadn't been more casualties.

Tense and preoccupied, Mike came over to where Rachel was watching television. 'I'll be on my way,' he said.

'Be careful,' said Rachel. It was hopelessly inadequate, but they were inhibited by the audience. She fought back a fierce desire to embrace him, but couldn't resist touching him on the arm.

'You'll be all right here?' he asked.

She looked into his eyes, which were very black, and saw that he loved her. She nodded. Then he was gone.

By afternoon the Nightingale command centre was all but abandoned. Fearful expectancy hung over the city like the pall of black smoke from the surrounding fires. Tempers became febrile as the temperature soared. Hot dry winds whipped parched leaves into frenzied tarantellas in the streets, which were ominously quiet and empty as people cowered indoors hooked up to telephones, radio and television as to life supports, expecting the worst, hoping for the best.

Assailed by images of walls of flame, exploding houses, fireballs, weeping and fleeing householders, dazed and exhausted firefighters, overwrought police ordering out procrastinators, brave individuals on rooftops warding off catastrophe with only a garden hose and desperate determination, the populace watched, waited. Toughened viewers were undone by footage of scorched bats hanging dead from branches or dragging themselves painfully up tree trunks.

A red-eyed, tearful volunteer described a fireball that lasted five minutes as sounding like the roar of a jet overhead. Fed by dry undergrowth, walls of flame marched down mountains, sounding to witnesses like the approach of a thousand express trains. Flames flicked across the canopy, feeding on the eucalyptus gas erupting ahead. Embers jumped roads and rivers like malicious elves, gobbled up everything in their path and turned into voracious flames. Fires reignited. Roads became rivers of tar and firestorms melted the couplings on hoses.

In the hardest hit areas, volunteers set up kitchens in churches and halls to feed firefighters and refugees, and offers of help and supplies flooded in. Old hands wept. The country went on to war footing, the government flying in thousands of firefighters from other states. For the first time ever, Sydney, the nation's richest and most powerful city, was cut off by land to the north and south. Along a fifty-kilometre front, only a thin, yellow line of firefighters stood between the city and catastrophe. The Bureau of Meteorology predicted more hot days, denying the respite of rain.

Rachel's headache had evolved into a full-blown migraine, squeezing her skull like a vice. Throwing some pills down her throat in the washroom, she caught sight of herself in the mirror. All the signs were there: the greenish skin, the bloodshot eye.

'Welcome to my nightmare,' she said to her reflection, wondering how long she'd be able to function. With so few of them to hold the fort, she didn't consider deserting.

When she emerged, Sheree called out that the Newtown police wanted to talk to her. Her heart began to hammer: had they found Neville Brady's car?

'Gavin Duffy, here,' said the Superintendent of the Newtown police station. 'About the blue Sigma—your suspect was in here a few minutes ago reporting it stolen.'

'Someone's tipped him off,' said Rachel, wanting to scream. Or cry. Except that she never cried.

'Looks like it. He'll have burned it out in the bush or dumped it in a creek by now, don't you reckon?'

Rachel put down the phone, her head thumping. Brady was always one step ahead. He'd realised they were closing in when they interviewed his wife about his movements on the night Emma Parker was attacked. It was nobody's fault: there was no way they could have kept the search for the car quiet. Newtown had a core of old working-class residents who'd lived there all their lives—whose parents had probably been born there—and the bush telegraph would have been humming with the news the minute the police knocked on the first front door.

He's beaten us, thought Rachel. He's got an alibi; the car is gone; and if he's got any brains at all, he'll have ditched the knife.

The thought of the knife reminded Rachel that Emma Parker hadn't mentioned a weapon, but then, the attacker had been interrupted...

If Lisa Broderick wasn't his last victim, she

probably wasn't the first either, thought Rachel, fighting the pain in her head. Sex murderers usually began their criminal careers in their teens, when the hormones started to pop. That meant the killer could have a history of violence, maybe a record. Neville Brady was in his late forties now: his criminal history could go back thirty years or more. Even if he hadn't been connected with the crimes, he might have left his signature.

With growing excitement, Rachel ran through Brady's file, looking for ways to narrow the search. His background details, taken from his hospital personnel records, were sketchy: born on the outskirts of Melbourne; left school early; had a variety of unskilled jobs; moved to Swan Hill at the age of twenty; married a local girl and ended up in Sydney. Rachel logged on to the computer and did a search of unsolved rape-murders in Victoria in the relevant period. There was only one. The victim had been picked up hitch-hiking outside Swan Hill in 1966, raped and stabbed, her body left in a field. Lorraine Stanton, eighteen: eyes blue; hair auburn.

Elation lifted Rachel to her feet, and that's how the Chief Inspector found her when he came by to see who was still on duty, standing staring at the computer as if it were about to explode. Taking in her pallor, the unnatural brightness of her eyes and her distracted air, he said: 'You look like hell,

Addison.' His wife suffered from migraines and he knew the signs.

'I'm fine, Sir.'

'I think you should go home.'

Rachel made the mistake of arguing. 'But there's nobody else here...'

'It was an order, Constable,' said the Old Man and stalked off.

Rachel waited till he was out of sight, then went to a bookshelf, found an atlas, and looked up Swan Hill. As she had thought, it was on the Murray River in the Riverina, the lush, green farming area which straddled the border of Victoria and New South Wales. Almost against her will, her eyes were drawn north-east, to a town a couple of hundred kilometres into New South Wales.

She sat very still for a minute, then keyed one word—Alison—into the computer. There was no stopping it now.

16

Not Knowing Is Worse

Safely home, Rachel lay down in a darkened room and slept. When nausea and the heat woke her, she went into the bathroom and bathed her face with cold water. Slumped on the edge of the bath, she gave up for a few minutes, overcome by fear, grief and self-pity. Finally she rose, looked at herself in the mirror, grimaced, and set about making herself look human again.

Downstairs, with the living-room drapes closed against the light and the smoke, she thought about the murders. Then she picked up the phone and called the Chief with her suspicions. He wasn't entirely convinced, but when she told him she wanted to go to the Riverina to look into an old murder case, he didn't laugh the idea out of court.

'All right. You and Ross can fly down as soon as this fire emergency is over,' he said.

'I'd like to go right now, Sir.'

'Alone?'

'I don't think we can afford to waste time. The fires might go on for days.' She was reminding him of the pressure on them all to get results.

The Chief thought it over and made his decision. 'It's irregular, but these are irregular times.' Then, giving her the benefit of his thirty years on the force, he told her what to look for. She was still writing furiously when he said, 'Don't you come from that part of the world, Addison?'

'Yes, Sir, Corella. It's in New South Wales, across the border from Swan Hill, where Lorraine Stanton was murdered.'

Rachel hung up slowly and sat perfectly still, thinking, then picked up the phone and dialled Persia Lawrence's office. When the receptionist answered, she requested an emergency appointment, and after being put on hold for a few minutes, was told to come in immediately.

The phone rang just as she was about to leave the house. Remembering the heavy breather, Rachel's first instinct was to ignore it, then professionalism took over. It was Mike, shouting over a dense background racket of blaring walkie-talkies, crashing plates and howling children. 'I'm in a church hall, having a rest. Christ it's hot.'

'Are you all right?' asked Rachel, remembering the shocked, distressed faces of the volunteers she'd seen on television.

'Apart from being half-dead, I am. We managed to save my brother's house.' He laughed. 'Mind you, it's a bit scorched around the edges, and his famous garden's gone up in smoke. The plant nurseries are going to make a fortune out of this.'

'When are you coming back into town?'

'Not for a while. I've been dragooned into crowd control. Some of these idiots won't leave their houses. Up on the roof in shorts and bare feet with a bloody garden hose. It's a miracle nobody's been killed out here.'

Rachel refrained from pointing out that Mike and his family had been guilty of the same foolishness. They talked about the fire for a few minutes, then Mike said: 'Are you OK? You sound odd…'

'It's nothing, a headache, that's all. The Chief sent me home.'

Mike already knew this: when he'd tried to raise Rachel at the office, Sheree had told him she'd gone home sick. Maybe this wasn't the best time to deliver this blow, but she had to know. 'Rachel, the real reason I rang…I don't quite know how to put this…Have you had any strange phone calls? Has anyone been harassing you? Apart from the break-in, I mean.'

Guilt tied Rachel's tongue for a moment. He was her partner, and now her lover, but she hadn't confided in him, afraid he'd think she was becoming unreliable. Unprofessional.

Mike read her mind. 'Look, I'm too tired to care about the fact that you didn't tell me before. Tell me now.'

Relieved to be able to share the burden finally, Rachel said: 'Somebody scared me in the parking station and terrorised me on the freeway on the way home, and I've had some weird phone calls. It's got to be somebody I know, or someone with good contacts, because my number isn't listed. He laughed once, and I thought I remembered the voice, but I haven't been able to place it.'

'It was Dick Kellett and his mate from the Commissioner's office,' said Mike.

The shock of the betrayal made Rachel's head swim for a moment. She could see why Kellett would want to make her life miserable, but what would the Commissioner's dirty tricks specialist have to gain? 'I don't understand. What's in it for Len Cooper?'

'He's Kellett's bosom buddy, and Kellett hasn't forgiven you for taking over his witnesses.'

'Lisa's husband and her boyfriend?'

'Yes.'

What's wrong with these men? wondered Rachel. Playing vicious tricks on me while Lisa Broderick's killer is running around loose. We're supposed to be on the same side. She gave up trying to comprehend the irrational: 'How did you find out, Mike?'

Mike was embarrassed; perhaps he should have spoken earlier, but then, Rachel hadn't exactly been forthcoming either. 'I've been hearing whispers, and there's been some sniggering going on, but I wasn't sure till today. One of the cops I've been working alongside told me Kellett was boasting about it at a retirement dinner for some old Vice Squad heavy last week. Kellett used to be in Vice: that's where he learned all his moves. This guy's brother is the wine waiter in the restaurant where they had the dinner.'

'Why did he tell you?'

'We were at the academy together. He knows you're my partner, and he thought I should know we were being sabotaged.'

We, not you, thought Rachel. The old male freemasonry in operation. Mike's mate didn't give a damn about me; he just wanted to protect his buddy.

'Are you still there?' asked Mike.

'Yes. But I have to go; I've got an appointment.'

Mike picked up the cold anger in her voice. Was it directed at all men, at Kellett and Cooper, or at him for keeping his suspicions to himself? If they wanted any sort of future, they'd have to work this out, but now wasn't the time. 'Will you be around later in the weekend?' he asked.

'No,' she said. 'I'm going out of town.'

'Where?'

'Back to the place where I was born.' Rachel hadn't known this until the words were out of her mouth. Now it seemed inevitable.

'I didn't know you liked the country.'

'I'm not going sight-seeing, Mike. It's business.'

'Police business? Does this have something to do with the Broderick case?'

Rachel considered telling him what she'd learned, but there didn't seem to be much point. He was needed here, and besides, there were some things in life you had to face alone.

'Personal business,' she said and put down the phone.

To hell with them all, she thought. The Chief would brief Mike later, and he could find his own way there.

Outside, the air stank of smoke, and smoky cloud veiled a blood-red sun. It was eerily dark.

'I thought you'd be out fighting the fires,' said Persia Lawrence, by way of greeting.

'I feel too ill. My head's falling off.'

'A migraine?'

She nodded, then winced.

'What do you think brought it on?'

'Everything. The fires, whatever has been happening in my head. Lisa Broderick.' She paused: 'And I slept with my partner last night.'

'What made you decide to do that?'

'I got home and found that someone had been in my house. I convinced myself it was the murderer…I called Mike.'

All the doctor's worst fears seemed to be coming true. 'And was it the murderer?'

'I just don't know. But I think he's concentrating on redheads…And then there was the clairvoyant…'

'You mentioned that yesterday. Tell me about it.'

'She told me I was in danger.'

'And you believed her?'

'It wasn't really a matter of belief. What she said crystallised a lot of suspicions in my own mind. She made me look at what I wasn't facing.'

That's what this whole story is about, thought Persia Lawrence. Knowing and not knowing. She waited.

'That's why I'm here,' said Rachel, finally. 'I want to know.'

'How can I help you, Rachel?'

'Hypnotise me.'

'You know the problems here, don't you Rachel; that it's dangerous to place credence in memories retrieved under hypnotism?'

Rachel knew. The psychology profession had been rent asunder by the controversy about hypnotism and false memories. In the United States a flood of accusations and legal actions had followed controversial charges of Satanism and child abuse retrieved under hypnotism, sometimes years after the alleged event. Lives had been ruined and reputations lost, and a backlash against the method had begun to build.

'I'm aware of the dangers,' said Rachel. 'But I think I've already started remembering on my own. This case obviously triggered something in my subconscious. I'm sure the nightmares are all part of the process, but it's moving too slowly. I'm losing control because I don't have enough information. I can't fight whatever is going on in my life wearing a blindfold.'

'What if it's bad news, Rachel?'

'Not knowing is worse, doctor.'

Their eyes locked, and Persia Lawrence made her decision. 'I'll do it if you'll open up and tell me what's been happening in your life since you first came to see me. Everything.'

Rachel's first reaction was fear, fear of breaking the long habit of reticence, but she understood now that silence hadn't protected her, it had served only to conceal the truth and make her vulnerable. After an initial burst of panic, she calmed down and agreed. The minute she gave herself permission to speak, it all poured out, everything that had happened, all she'd felt and thought since Lisa Broderick's murder.. The relief was oceanic.

Persia Lawrence's post-hypnotic suggestion had ensured that Rachel would be calm when she emerged from the trance, but would remember everything that had happened. Re-entering the present, Rachel blinked and stretched, looked around and seemed surprised to see her doctor.

'How do you feel, Rachel?'

'As if my whole world had changed. Everything is different now I know.'

'In what way?'

'I finally understand why I'm like I am. I don't blame myself any more for not being like everyone else.' She paused and considered. 'This might sound crazy, considering what we found out, but I feel relieved.'

'What are you going to do now?'

'I'm going back to Corella.' She smiled. 'Returning to the scene of the crime.'

'You're on a bit of a high now, Rachel,' the psychiatrist warned, 'But you're bound to get a reaction. It's not going to be easy to go back there and face your past.'

Rachel stood up. 'I know, but I have to.'

Rachel Addison and Persia Lawrence shook hands, and Rachel thanked the older woman. 'Take care, Rachel,' said the doctor.

Rachel nodded politely, not really listening. In her mind, she'd left Persia Lawrence and her wise counsel, had left the old Rachel Addison behind, and was about to abandon the present for the past. Outside it was as dark as midnight.

Once through the clogged city traffic, Rachel drove fast and competently, on automatic pilot, scarcely noticing where she was. Her mind raced and swooped, her thoughts lighting on what she'd learned in Persia Lawrence's office and veering away wildly. Then she began to stew about her colleagues' treachery. Though no cop in his right mind would have broken into her house, even to curry favour with Dick Kellett, she was certain Len Cooper had made at least one of the phone calls, and it had probably been a policeman who'd terrorised her on the freeway.

Maybe it's just not worth it, she thought, but then realised that this was exactly what they wanted. She decided to stay angry.

Taking refuge in her memories of Holly, she relived their reunion and tried to come to terms with losing her friend a second time. Perhaps Mike could help ease the grief. Mike. She'd been unfair to Mike, but she loved him and believed he knew it. He would still be there for her when this was over, she was sure of that.

Turning on the radio, she searched the network till she found an update on the fires. The news was all bad. Don't let anything happen to him now, she prayed. It would be too much.

On the outskirts of Yass, her headlights picked up a girl standing on the side of the road with her thumb out. Rachel had heard all the warnings against picking up hitchhikers—that they might rob you at knife point, steal your car—but the girl was so young and the road was so godforsaken...Besides, it would distract her from the cacophony in her head. She stopped.

The girl ran up, stared in the window, approved of what she saw, opened the door and jumped in. 'Thanks.'

Her name was Megan, and she was about fifteen, dressed in a skimpy Indian cotton sleeveless shift and black lace-up shoes and white socks. Dozens of cheap silver studs adorned her ears, and she wore several strings of tiny beads around her neck. Streaky fair hair hung over her face. The sun had turned her a dark gold. All her worldly goods were stashed in a canvas backpack with her name printed on it with black Textacolor. But for the bags under her eyes, the grubby hands with their bitten fingernails, the nose ring and the bluebird tattooed on her left upper arm, she could have been any suburban kid.

'Where are you heading?' asked Rachel.

'Hilltop.' It was a tiny settlement off the main highway about an hour's drive away.

'Visiting?'

'My grandmother lives there,' said the girl. Her tone warned Rachel not to pry.

There wasn't any need. Her story was written all over her: brought up by grandparents in the sticks, a runaway, coming home to see Gran, maybe to try to dry out, or to get away from trouble in Sydney.

'You shouldn't be hitchhiking,' said Rachel.

The girl shrugged. 'I'm broke. This is the only way I can get out here to see my Gran. She's got cancer.'

'I'm sorry,' said Rachel, feeling inadequate.

The girl didn't reply. Hundreds of people had told her they were sorry in her short life, and it hadn't made any difference.

'But you realise there's a murderer loose?' asked Rachel.

'Which one do you mean?'

'Lisa Broderick's killer.'

Megan stopped worrying a hangnail with her teeth. 'Oh, that one. I thought you might have been talking about the backpacker murderer.'

'Him, too.'

'I reckon I've already met him.'

The shock forced Rachel's foot down hard on the accelerator, and the car leapt forward. The girl laughed. 'And lived to tell the tale.'

She took out a cigarette, lit up, ostentatiously blew the smoke out the window, and held the cigarette in her left hand, waiting for Rachel to tell her to put it out. More interested in getting her story, Rachel refused to bite.

'You don't believe me, do you?' said Megan. She

took a long drag on her cigarette. 'He picked me up on the road to Canberra.'

It fitted the killer's MO, but the girl could know that from the television coverage of the serial murders. Nevertheless...

Knowing she now had Rachel's full attention, Megan became more animated. 'He had this van with curtains in the back. If I hadn't been so blasted that day, that would've tipped me off, and I wouldn't have got in. Anyway, everything's going fine, then he pulls off the highway into the national park. When I ask him what he's doing, he tells me he's promised to meet his mate at a picnic spot, to buy some dope. Then I hear this popping noise...'

A natural story-teller, she paused, letting the suspense build. 'He'd locked the bloody doors. I started to get the wind up then, I can tell you.' She took a long drag. 'But I kept hoping.'

She turned to Rachel: 'You know how it is.'

Sisters under the skin, that look said. There wasn't a woman alive who didn't know what it was like to be afraid of a man.

'He knew that place like the back of his hand, went up all these tracks—I'd never be able to find it again—and stopped in a sort of clearing. Told me to get out. He had a rifle.'

She trailed off, remembering perhaps, or making up the next episode. Rachel wondered if any of it was true.

Megan took up the tale again: 'He pointed the gun at me and told me to take my clothes off. Said he'd shoot me if I didn't. It didn't matter to him if I was dead or alive: it was just as good either way, he reckoned. I thought it was all over for me.'

It was bravado. Rachel imagined how the girl would have cried, begged for her life, unwittingly playing into the rapist's game, making it more fun, supplying the grist for his future fantasies. And nobody to hear or care: thousands of hectares of bushland, with only the sound of a plane arcing high above, or the distant whine of loggers' saws. A bird might call out, startled; small animals might rear up, frightened and wary for a moment, to return quickly to their own living and dying; but Megan's screams would go unheard by humans in the indifferent forest.

Rachel shuddered, and was thankful when Megan's voice jerked her back to the present. 'But my number wasn't up. I didn't die. I didn't even get raped. A couple of kids on trail bikes turned up. The creep jumped in his van and screamed off, and they gave me a lift back to their place.'

'What was he like?' asked Rachel.

'Greasy hair, beer gut, dirty jeans and a T-shirt. Blond hair long at the back, going bald at the front. Red face, piggy blue eyes. What else can I tell you?'

'Did you report it?'

'Never got round to it,' said the girl. What she meant was that the attempted rape of a tattooed street kid was too commonplace to attract any serious attention.

She's probably right, thought Rachel, newly sensitive to the priorities of certain elements in the police force.

'This was before all those tourists got murdered,' Megan went on. 'Nobody was interested. Hitchhikers get raped all the time.' She laughed. 'It's the price you pay for having fun.'

There didn't seem to be anything more to say. They travelled in silence for a time, then the girl, noticing the tape deck, opened the glove box to look for some music and caught sight of a police circular. 'You're a cop!' she said.

'Yes, but it's OK. Don't be frightened.'

'What are you, stupid? I'm not frightened of you!' said the girl. 'I just don't trust you lot, that's all.'

Rachel flushed, feeling foolish. She knew some people didn't want help from the police, weren't grateful for their attention, that most members of the public were ambivalent at best about the police, but the contempt of young girls was hard to swallow. 'Have I ever done anything to offend you?' she asked.

Rachel's tone of voice reached something in the girl, but though she coloured, she wasn't about to back down completely: 'Not yet,' she said.

After the initial surprise, Rachel found herself laughing. Some small breakthrough had been made, and the atmosphere in the car lightened.

Eventually the girl directed her off the new freeway into a small village that had once straddled the main highway. Even in the dark Rachel could sense the charm of Hilltop: weatherboard cottages with old-fashioned gardens that would bloom once more when the drought broke, a general store housing a post office and a bank agency, big pepper trees on the wide main street.

Somehow Hilltop hung on, its population ageing, its remaining kids bussed to school in a nearby town. Some day the hippies would discover it, buy up the cheap houses, open up craft shops and alternative medicine clinics and lure a few tourists off the freeway for perfumed candles and whole foods. In the meantime, the teenagers would go mad with boredom and leave for the big smoke.

They stopped in front of a dilapidated but neat cottage with a front garden full of neglected rose bushes. Though she'd brightened once they left the turn-off, Megan was unwilling to drop her air of bored sophistication. 'It's a dump isn't it?'

'Home's home,' said Rachel.

Megan shot her a searching look. 'Where are you headed?'

'Corella.'

'Business or pleasure?'

Rachel grimaced. 'I'm going to visit my parents' graves,' she said, not knowing why she was telling this street kid. Except that she felt the girl would understand.

As Megan got out of the car, she said: 'Look after yourself...Rachel.'

'You too.'

She's got a good little heart, Rachel thought, turning the car around and heading back to the freeway. I hope it doesn't bring her too much grief.

In her rear-vision mirror the woman saw the girl staring after the car. Then Megan heaved her backpack on to her thin shoulder, mounted the steps and was absorbed into the light, leaving Rachel alone with her ghosts.

17

We Hoped You'd Forget

She stopped for the night at a roadside motel. The local television station devoted almost all of its news program to the fires. Houses were burning near the national park on Sydney's north shore, new fires had broken out in the Blue Mountains, a state of emergency had been declared from the Queensland border to Coffs Harbour 1200 kilometres south. In a millisecond of footage from the southern suburbs, Rachel was almost certain she caught a glimpse of Mike's face in a group of volunteers, and her heart plummeted.

After picking at a huge country dinner of steak and vegetables and a glass of red wine in the motel's dining room, she retired early, only to spend a restless night, feverish dreams punctuated by the roar and rattle of an ancient air-conditioner. After an early breakfast, she set off for Corella, too restless to wait around. Though it was only seven-thirty, the sun was beating down relentlessly, the asphalt shimmering like pewter under the heat haze.

Returning to Corella and the past was like entering a familiar dream. The very smell of the country air triggered memories of her childhood, the wind carrying the scent of paddocks and eucalyptus overlaid with a tang of acrid smoke down from the purple hills and across the fields of high blond grass. Cicadas whined. Once she had to stop for two farmers, father and son by the look of them, moving a herd of complaining sheep across the road. Brick-red and sweaty astride tall horses, they tipped their hats solemnly, with the exquisite politeness of country people. Curious, they turned to watch her go.

She passed farms where dogs ran out to the road to announce her arrival with a fusillade of barks, and men on tractors looked up to see what the fuss was about. A bored policeman waiting in ambush behind bushes for speeding tourists recorded her passage. Passing a creek she mistook a clump of arum lilies for a flock of doves drinking. There was no sign of the parrots who'd given her home town their name, but a flock of grey, pink and white galahs gleaning in a field of wheat wheeled upwards, shrieking, at her arrival, hung suspended for a moment, then descended again, without breaking formation.

A Lion's Club sign told her she was entering Corella, a Tidy Town, population 8435. Corella itself was at once familiar and strange, like a hundred other country towns, real and fictional. To kill time and quench her curiosity, she took a tour of the town, passing the cemetery, an abattoir, several schools and churches, the train station with its ornate Victorian station house. Crossing the broad green river, low now in the drought, she dawdled through a manicured park and read the names on the war memorial, then took her courage in hand and found Corella North Primary School. It was here that her mother had taught Grades 2 and 3, and Alison Grade 1, and where Rachel, after much begging and pleading and hanging on the school fence, had been allowed to sit in on Alison Scott's class when she was only four. It was at this school that Claire Addison had taken Alison under her wing, and where little Rachel Addison had developed a passionate crush on her first-grade teacher. It was here that all their fates had been sealed.

In the middle of school holidays, the little school was deserted, glum-looking, lonely for the shouts and squeals of children. Rachel walked around the building and looked in the windows, identifying the cloakroom where she used to hang her blue raincoat with the hood, and her own classroom. She recalled its chalky, dusty smell and the strange, bread-and-buttery scent of children and cheese sandwiches and overripe bananas in school cases, Alison's faint scent of lily of the valley, and her mother's special smell, buried somewhere too deep to reach but too powerful to forget. And in the schoolyard the purple scent of jacarandas, the acrid tang of gum trees, the astringency of tall pines.

In the playground one of the swings creaked to and fro in a breeze, reminding her of a cold winter's day in another life, when she'd sat there swinging gently, pleasantly melancholic, listening to the wind moan in the power lines as she waited for her mother.

But time was wasting. Taking one last look at the school, Rachel drove up a hill to a lookout on the reservoir and watched the town come to life. Corella, from what she could see, was prosperous, clean and pleased with itself. On the surface, anyway.

She was back in the town centre by eight-thirty. The streets were beginning to stir. A few workers were buying breakfast from the milk bars and coffee shops, and the odd early shopper ambled by. Rachel found the police station in a recently restored historical precinct, crouched between the post office and the town hall, both ostentatious Victorian follies in gleaming sandstone.

While she was angling the car into a diagonal

parking space outside, two boisterous young officers bounded down the steps, leapt into a patrol car and took off. She'd have to go in there eventually, but her shallow breathing and sweaty palms warned her she wasn't ready to face Corella's finest just yet. Maybe a cup of coffee would help.

Broad awnings shaded the footpaths in the wide main street. Some of the original facades had been preserved, but modern banks in garish primary colours had muscled their way in among the restored Victorian buildings housing stock and land agents, drapery shops and chemists, ruining the symmetry of the street. There was even a branch of a major department store.

Repelled by the smell of fried food and rancid fat billowing from the doorway of a milk bar, Rachel explored until she found a coffee shop with an espresso machine, checked tablecloths and the regulation uncomfortable western-style chairs, at the entrance to a little mall. Choosing a table with a view of the street, she ordered a black coffee and a sticky bun. The waitress, a plump, bright-eyed teenager in a white blouse and black skirt, eyed her curiously. Though Rachel was plainly dressed—white cotton shirt and jeans, hair in a ponytail, no jewellery except for a watch and small gold ear studs—she was more sophisticated than the town women and most of the tourists who passed through on their way to and from Victoria.

285

'On holidays?' she asked, plonking down Rachel's order.

'Business,' said Rachel.

Unable to imagine what sort of business would bring someone like Rachel to Corella, the girl was struck dumb.

'Do you get many tourists here?' asked Rachel, taking pity.

'We used to get people driving through, and oldies with their caravans touring Australia, but the drought's killing off tourism just like it's killing off the stock.' She gestured at the empty room. 'Lots of farmers have gone belly-up already and the rest are hanging on by the skin of their teeth. Nobody's got money to waste in coffee shops. If it doesn't rain soon, we'll go broke.'

Rachel, who'd simply been passing the time of day, was impressed by the girl's seriousness. 'Were you born here?'

'Yes, but I don't reckon I'll die here. There isn't any work. When this place closes, I'll have to leave Corella and head for the city like everyone else. Melbourne, probably; Sydney's a bit too big for me.'

And too scary, thought Rachel. 'That's too bad.'

Emboldened by the sympathy, the girl asked, 'Are you from Sydney?'

'Yes,' said Rachel. 'But I was born here.'

The girl's eyes widened. She was preparing to

launch a dozen more questions when a middle-aged woman put her head around the kitchen door. 'Kim, the salads have to be made.'

Kim flushed, rolled her eyes, and withdrew.

The coffee was terrible, but the sugar in the nostalgic pink-iced bun was comforting. Rachel wished she smoked: it would give her something to do with her hands and an excuse to linger. Finally, she paid and walked the half-block back to the police station.

At the front desk, she introduced herself to the duty officer, showing him her ID. He was young and big, a footballer, probably, with fair hair and freckles.

'Sydney,' he said, appraising her. 'You trying to outrun the fires?'

Rachel smiled. 'Maybe.'

'Now you city folks know what we have to put up with out here all the time,' he said. 'We've had some big fires in this district, but the television stations are only interested in Sydney.'

So much for national solidarity, thought Rachel, amused. Oddly enough, his hostility had quietened her nerves.

'Thanks for the sympathy,' she said, earning herself a startled look. Smiling innocently, she asked if there was anybody on the Corella force who'd been there in 1970.

'Doing a history project?' he asked, still smarting.

287

'Researching an old crime.'

'Which one?'

'You're too young to remember,' she said. 'You were probably still in nappies.'

He blushed, then frowned. Picking up the phone, he dialled a number. 'Gerry Sullivan's our longest-serving officer. Been here fifteen years. Everyone else has been transferred or retired.'

While she waited for Gerry Sullivan, Rachel read the signs about firearms and drugs and missing children and wondered what it would be like keeping the peace in a place like this. Would you long for a violent crime to break the tedium of Saturday night pub brawls, speeding fines and cattle duffing? And if something terrible did happen, some unprecedented act of savagery, would you be able to handle it? What would it be like knowing the murderer could be a neighbour, somebody who attended your church, and whose kids went to school with yours, or someone you'd trained in gymnastics at the Police Boys' Club or thrown out of the swimming pool for rowdiness?

Her reverie was interrupted by a bulky middle-aged man with the country dweller's brick-red, corrugated skin. The sharp blue eyes summing Rachel up were surrounded by wrinkles earned by squinting into the violent outback light for forty-odd years. They shook hands, and Sullivan led her into his untidy cubbyhole of an office.

'You're a police officer?' he asked. He couldn't stop himself: she didn't look like any policewoman he'd ever seen.

'Yes. A psychologist.'

'Tell me, what exactly does a psychologist do in the police force?' His tone was neutral, but she detected a faint echo of the class and sex wars. He kept his opinions to himself, however; country cops mightn't hold with women with degrees horning in on their territory, but even out here they'd heard of the sex discrimination legislation.

'I'm with Homicide,' said Rachel. 'I do the same as everybody else on the team.'

Checkmate. Silently, they regarded each other across Gerry Sullivan's messy desk, the physical distance between them narrow, the historical and social gulfs wide and treacherous.

Sullivan cracked first. 'What are you working on?'

'Lisa Broderick's murder.'

The big league. It had hogged night-time television all over the state: now that he thought about it, her face did look familiar. 'Not making much progress, I hear.'

Rachel refused to be baited: 'You'd be surprised. It could break any minute.' That would give them something to talk about in the pubs and clubs tonight.

Realising he wasn't going to get a rise out of the city slicker, Sullivan decided to cooperate. 'So what can I do for you?'

'I'm looking for someone who might have been involved in a murder that took place here about twenty-four years ago.'

She watched him search his memory and come up blank. 'I was in Lismore then. It doesn't ring a bell with me.'

'It was the rape and murder of a young schoolteacher in a farmhouse about ten miles out of town.'

'What's your interest?'

'It's personal,' said Rachel. The policeman waited, but she didn't elaborate. Their eyes met and his veered away. 'You could try Russ Morgan. Nothing's happened in this area in the past forty years that he doesn't know about. He's retired now, but his memory's fine. He'll be glad of the company. I hope you've got all day, though: Russ can talk the leg off a chair.'

After he'd cleared it with Morgan and given Rachel directions, Sullivan showed her out, wondering what it was all about. Not to worry: a couple of beers would prise it out of old Russ at the Returned Servicemen's Club before the weekend was out. Or so he thought. Gerry Sullivan was only one of the Corella townsfolk who'd misjudged Russ Morgan.

The old cop lived in a run-down weatherboard house on the outskirts of town. The front gate, which was held up by a piece of rope, complained so loudly when Rachel tried to open it that she ended up climbing over. A few dahlias and woody looking roses struggled on in the overgrown garden, losing the battle against thistles, couch grass and the long dry. As Rachel mounted the front steps on to the porch, an old yellow Labrador waddled out of the house, gave one loud, rapturous bark, wagged its fat rump in greeting, and slobbered on her knee.

Alerted by the dog, an old man appeared. He was strong-looking still, though a little stooped now, and his reddish hair had thinned and turned the colour of nicotine. The hazel eyes that appraised his visitor were sharp and clear.

He stuck out a gnarled hand. 'You must be the lady copper from Sydney.'

'Rachel Addison, and you'd be Russ Morgan.'

'The one and only. Let's get inside out of this bloody heat.'

Shoving the dog out of the way with his boot, he led her down a gloomy hallway into a kitchen that hadn't been redecorated since the early sixties, and nodded towards a chair. Rachel sat down and surveyed the room. Linoleum flooring in a red and cream fake marble effect, cream wooden kitchen cupboards with red plastic handles, an old Kooka gas stove, an ancient cream fridge. The table and matching chairs, with their much-mended plastic seats, were red and white laminex with chrome legs. A Holland blind was drawn against the glare.

Following her gaze, the old man said: 'I'm a widower. The wife died about ten years ago. Cancer.'

The ghosts of a million greasy meals haunted the room, but he was still trying. The floor was clean, and the faint smell of pine-scented disinfectant was detectable through the fat, the dust and the mould. It was a time capsule. All that was missing was a flypaper hanging from the ceiling festooned with dead insects.

The thump of a mug on the table recalled Rachel to the nineties. Russ Morgan filled it from an old brown teapot.

'Milk?'

'No thanks, but I think I'll have some sugar,' said Rachel, guessing the tea would be bitter and stewed.

After he'd added milk and two sugars and stirred his tea thirty or forty times, Morgan said: 'Gerry Sullivan said something about an old case.'

'Alison Scott's murder,' said Rachel. 'You were here when it happened, I believe…'

Russ Morgan stopped stirring and gave Rachel a long, appraising look. Before she had arrived, he'd decided he wouldn't give anything away until he was sure, but as soon as he'd clapped eyes on her, on the heart-shaped face, the intent green gaze, he'd known.

'Yeah, I worked on it. I'll never forget it. What do you want to know?'

'I know who she was, and what happened…The bare bones, anyway. I want the details, the colour.'

'Colour,' he said, grimacing. 'There was plenty of that. You know she was a schoolteacher?'

Rachel nodded.

He gazed off into the middle distance. 'This was her first posting. She started out living at one of the pubs like they all do, but then she heard about this farmhouse on the river road, and moved out there. Wouldn't be talked out of it. She was a strange one, said she wouldn't be lonely, didn't seem to be afraid to live alone. She bought a dog, though. Maybe she thought that would protect her…'

'What happened to the dog?' interrupted Rachel.

'They found it later, strangled with a piece of rope. Somebody had thrown it a hunk of meat and ambushed it.'

'Bilbo,' said Rachel. She had no idea where it had come from. 'Sorry, please go on.'

'Alison Scott was reading and listening to music on the night she was murdered. The book was on the floor beside a chair, the reading lamp was on, and we found the record still going round on the turntable. The body was just inside the living-room door, so she must have got up and walked to the doorway to have a look down the passage to the back door. He jumped her, bashed her in the head with his fists, knocked her out, dragged her back into the living room, raped her, then shot her in the head. Used a shotgun to make sure. There was blood everywhere, brains, too: on the carpet, the walls. It was a slaughterhouse.'

He looked at Rachel, who'd gone pale, but was determined to continue. 'What else?'

'There's nothing else.'

They stared at each other like a pair of poker players. Rachel caved in. 'Witnesses. Were there any witnesses?'

'No. It's miles from anywhere out there. No neighbours.'

Rachel realised what the old man was up to, but she wasn't ready to reveal her hand. It might put ideas in his head, and she wanted the truth. 'Was there anything that didn't fit? Something that seemed strange to you?'

Having waited over twenty years for this moment, the policeman was determined to extract every ounce of drama out of his revelations. 'Well, the tip-off was strange.' He paused, and Rachel had to resist the impulse to jump up and shake the story out of him. 'Somebody rang us and said there'd been a murder.'

'Somebody?'

'A woman.'

Of course, it would have to be a woman. 'Did you recognise her voice?'

'No, she sort of whispered. She didn't leave her name.'

'Didn't you find that unusual?'

'Yeah, but it was pretty obvious why afterwards. It took me a while to work out, but I finally twigged.'

He poured himself another cup of tea and marvelled at the woman's patience and self-control. He wouldn't want to be on the wrong side of the desk from her. 'You see, I think there was someone there that night besides Alison Scott and the murderer.'

In the silence that followed, Rachel could hear the ticking of a grandfather clock somewhere deep in the house. The dog suddenly reared up and snapped at a fly, making her jump. Morgan smiled. 'A child, I think,' he said.

Adrenalin surged through Rachel's veins and set her tingling: her heart raced. Stress? Anticipation? Dread? 'What makes you think that?'

'Three things. First, Alison's bed was rumpled, but she was still up and dressed when the assailant got in; second, there was a toy giraffe behind the couch in the living room, and third…'

He paused, wondering where his wife might have put the child's toy; he hadn't seen it in years. 'Why don't you throw that thing out?' she'd said. 'But what if she comes back for it one day?' he'd answered. Hands on hips, his wife had clucked and called him a sentimental old fool, but she'd been smiling. He missed her every day.

He looked up to find Rachel gazing at him expectantly: 'Third,' she prompted.

'Oh, yeah. This bit's the scary part. There was a pool of piddle in the hallway near the front door. I didn't see it at first, because it was behind the raincoats and the gumboots.' The clock ticked into the silence. 'As if somebody had hidden there. Somebody who was frightened enough to wet herself.'

Herself, thought Rachel. Of course he knows. He's always known. Just like he knew who made the call.

Now that they both knew, the tension ebbed. Russ Morgan said: 'You're the dead spit of your mother. The hair's a different colour, but the eyes are the same.'

'My father couldn't call because you would have recognised the American accent,' said Rachel, relieved that they'd stopped playing cat and mouse.

'Yeah. It was obvious once I thought it through, but by then it was too late.'

'They were both dead.'

He nodded. 'But you were alive. There didn't seem much point putting you through all that grief, not after the trouble they'd taken to keep you out of it. You were too young to be a credible witness, anyway.'

He'd been watching her carefully, gauging how she was taking it, and decided she was ready to talk about that night. 'What do you remember?'

Rachel told him what she'd pieced together from the dreams, the memories, the hypnotic trance: 'I was half-asleep in her bed. I could hear the music...Then I must have dropped off, because something woke me with a fright. It was Alison, screaming. I climbed out of bed.'

A wave of nausea, exacerbated by the heat, the closeness of the room, the smell of the dog, rose up in Rachel. For a moment she thought she might faint. Morgan moved towards her, but she put out her hand to stop him. 'I'm all right.'

The old man poured her a glass of cold water out of the fridge, and she drank some before going on. 'From the bedroom door I could see straight into the living room. There was a strange man on top of Alison. I knew he was hurting her, because she was moaning "Help me. Please God, help me." She was looking straight at me, but she probably couldn't see me. He'd smashed her glasses.

'I tried to scream out, or run to help her, but I was paralysed; it was like in one of those dreams where your feet are stuck in quicksand and you try to scream but nothing comes out. But I must have squeaked or disturbed him somehow, because he looked up and saw me. I'll never forget that face.'

She stopped, realising what she'd said. She had forgotten that face; she had even forgotten Alison.

'He didn't come after me right away because his trousers were down around his ankles—he was raping her, of course, though I was too young to know that—but the look he gave me scared me so badly I ran and hid behind the coats.

'When he'd finished with Alison, he started searching the house, looking for me. I could hear him moving away and coming closer. Then the footsteps came into the hallway, and stopped. I held my breath and tried to hide, to flatten myself against the wall, to disappear, but after a time I couldn't stand the suspense. I peeked out. He was silhouetted against the light from the living room, a giant. He started to move towards my hiding place, and a wave of something vile reached me.' Rachel shuddered. 'It was him; he stank like some animal that's been hibernating in a cave.'

Russ Morgan started, sat up straight, opened his mouth, then shut it again.

Rachel was breathing shallowly, as if the smell were in this room. 'That's when I wet myself,' she said. 'That was the puddle you found.'

The policeman was incredulous. 'He was that close and he didn't find you?'

'Oh, I think he knew where I was. He was probably enjoying the hunt, spinning it out, getting off on my terror. But when he was almost on top of me, the phone rang. You remember those shrill, loud old phones? It stopped him in his tracks. He hesitated, then turned and went back into the living room. The phone rang and rang. I heard a loud noise. Then I heard him leave.'

Russ Morgan took over. 'If he'd been watching Alison's place, and he must have been, he would have known you were there. So he would have figured it was your parents, checking on the baby-sitter. He knew they'd panic and come rushing out there if she didn't answer. He couldn't afford to stick around, and he couldn't let her regain consciousness and answer the phone.'

Rachel had worked this out for herself, but here, finally, was the proof she'd craved. Russ Morgan had been there; he knew it was real, not some morbid fantasy. Thank God I found him, she thought.

'Were you still hiding when your parents arrived?' he asked.

'No. I don't know how long I stayed behind the coats...I suppose I was waiting for Alison to come and get me. When I couldn't stand the tension any more, I crept out. I had to know if she was all right. I idolised Alison. I loved her funny glasses and her music and her seriousness. She must have been a gifted teacher.'

'Pretty girl, too,' said Morgan. 'All that lovely red hair.'

A bee appeared from nowhere and buzzed around Morgan's head. He got up, opened the screen door and shooed it out with a newspaper, then closed the door again and sat down. It was an oddly gentle gesture.

He's a good man, thought Rachel. I was lucky. Somebody like that insensitive ox Gerry Sullivan could have been on duty that night. God knows what would have happened to me then.

'So you found the body,' said Russ Morgan.

Rachel shuddered. 'Yes. I got blood all over me. Then the screen goes blank. I don't know what happened after that. This part might never come back.'

The old policeman took up the story. 'When Alison didn't answer the phone, your parents went racing out there and found her dead and you covered in blood and got you the hell out of there. Then your mother called me.'

'I remember a hospital...' said Rachel.

'A friend of your father's, Fred Hollis, was an

RMO at the hospital. Your parents took you in and got Hollis to have a look at you and keep you under observation overnight. It was all done on the QT, mind you. No records.'

'I don't know if it's a memory or something I've imagined,' said Rachel. 'But there's something very frightening about that night in the hospital. Did my parents leave me there alone by any chance?'

When Russ Morgan shifted uncomfortably in his seat, Rachel knew she was about to hear something he'd rather not say. 'Your father had been hitting the grog that night. He wasn't in any fit state to handle an emergency. When he started playing up at the hospital, the staff complained, and Hollis had to throw him out. He was afraid someone would call the police.'

Rachel had a sudden flash of her mother's face, turning to look at her before she left the hospital room. Claire had been weeping. 'And they had the accident on the way home from the hospital?'

He nodded.

'Where were you while all this was going on?' asked Rachel.

'Out at the farmhouse. I was in a bit of a dilemma, you realise. When I found the puddle, I figured a kid had been there, but there was no sign of her and no body. But it was pretty obvious what had happened when your mother rang. If I hadn't received that call, I would have assumed the killer

301

had taken the child.' He paused. 'If your parents had taken you home instead of going to the hospital, I might never have known for sure it was you.'

'And they'd be still alive,' said Rachel.

He shrugged. There was no point second-guessing fate.

'The next thing I remember was being taken to Sydney by my aunt,' said Rachel. 'How did that happen?'

'When your parents were killed in the head-on, Fred Hollis called me in. He didn't have much choice. You were in a bad way emotionally, but he said you hadn't been physically damaged. I went out to your folks' house and looked through their records and found your aunt's address and called her. We were out of the game then.' He opened his hands. 'After that, it's your story.'

Rachel stared at the old man. 'You've kept this story a secret for twenty-four years...Didn't you ever want to tell someone?'

The old man looked uncomfortable. 'I told my wife, but she was used to keeping secrets. And of course, I talked it through with Fred Hollis. We decided it was best if nobody ever knew you'd been there. If we'd talked, the media would have had a field day. You'd been through enough. Besides, you were the only witness to Alison Scott's murder, and the killer was still on the loose.

302

Still is, for that matter. We thought you'd be safer away from here.'

I probably was safe until Lisa Broderick was murdered, thought Rachel. Until my name and face got plastered all over national television for weeks, anyway.

Rachel felt cold, suddenly, in the stuffy kitchen. If Alison Scott's murderer had known the name of the little girl she'd been baby-sitting that night, he could well have recognised her. The New South Wales Police Force might have handed her to him on a platter.

With a shock Rachel realised she hadn't kept her eye out for a tail on this trip: she'd let her personal needs override her professional training.

Russ Morgan had been watching her face. It occurred to him that she'd picked his brains but hadn't given away much herself. He hoped she knew what she was doing. But character was destiny, and the little girl who'd been brave or foolhardy enough to emerge from her hiding place to see if her friend was all right was probably still taking too many risks. Like becoming a cop.

'Do you think we did the right thing?' he asked.

How many hours had he spent worrying about that decision over the years? she wondered. There wasn't any point blaming the policeman and the doctor for what had happened later, though: she had been Louise's responsibility, not theirs. But that was another story. 'I'm sure you did what you thought was best, Russ,' she said.

The silence stretched. Then Russ Morgan said, 'You were just a baby. We hoped you'd forget.'

18

One Wilful, Childish Act

The Corella hospital had been privatised several years ago, and Fred Hollis was now the medical superintendent. He'd agreed immediately when his old friend rang with Rachel's request to visit the place where she'd last seen her parents. He'd been half-expecting this call for years, and was intrigued by the prospect of seeing how Claire and Tom Addison's daughter had turned out.

On the way, Rachel quizzed Morgan about her father, and learned that he had made a good living crop-dusting. It was a dangerous job, but Tom had been an excellent pilot, and fearless, Morgan said. A bit of a daredevil, too: he'd caused a scandal once by buzzing the playground of Claire's school and sending the kids mad with excitement.

'Russ, how did an American find his way to Corella?' she asked.

The old man was surprised. 'Didn't your aunt tell you anything about him?'

'Not much. She talked about my mother occasionally, always with regret; she never got over her little sister dying so young. I think she blamed Tom for everything. I knew he was an American, and I always wondered if I had relatives in the States, but if Louise ever contacted them, she didn't let on. Maybe she thought they'd try to take me away. Without coming right out and saying it, she made it perfectly clear that I wasn't to ask about anything that happened before I went to live with her. It became a sort of loyalty test. She must have thought it would make me forget about the murder.' Rachel took her eyes off the road and looked at Russ Morgan. 'I assume she knew.'

'Fred and I told her what we suspected and left the rest up to her. There wasn't much else we could do: she was your next of kin. I can remember thinking it was a lot to dump on a single woman.'

'Me, you mean?'

Morgan was offended. 'The responsibility, the decision about what to tell you.'

'I'm sorry. I suppose everybody thought they knew what they were doing.'

'And you don't?'

'No.'

'You're your father's daughter, that's for sure,'

he muttered. It wasn't a compliment.

'Did you know him personally?'

'I knew everybody; it was my job. We didn't socialise, but we got along all right, apart from the occasional run-in.'

'What do you mean, "run-in"?'

'He was no saint, your old man. The local lads used to torment him because he was a Yank, of course, but he knew how to handle himself. I never had to lock him up, but I read the riot act on a couple of occasions. From a few hints he dropped, I worked out that he'd been in Vietnam with the US Air Force. These days they'd probably say he was suffering from post-traumatic stress, or some syndrome or other, but back then we just put it down to a wild streak.'

'How did my mother get mixed up with him?'

'He was passing through and his car broke down. God knows what he was doing in this part of the country; looking for a place to grow dope, probably.' He chanced a look at Rachel, but she didn't bite. 'He was driving one of those ridiculous Italian sports cars that didn't last five minutes on the roads we had back then. He hit one of our potholes and wrecked the transmission. The local garage had to send to Sydney for parts. While he was cooling his heels in Corella, he went to a dance and from what I heard it was love at first sight. Claire was the best-looking woman in the district, but she was off-limits to us yokels: polite, but very cool. We expected her to go back to the city as soon as she'd finished her tour of duty.'

'But what was Tom like?' Rachel persisted.

The old policeman shrugged. 'Who knows? He was charming—the women loved him—but you couldn't get close to him. Maybe your mother got through. He never even said where he was from in the States, but the accent sounded like Texas to me.'

'Who were his friends besides this doctor?'

'Charlie Rusk, he runs a big property and owned the crop-dusting fleet, and there was a solicitor, Frank somebody or other, but he's long gone. They were serious party animals, that lot. I don't think your mother liked any of them much, but she went along rather than let him out of her sight. They were all at Frank's house with their wives the night of the murder. Charlie Rusk told me later your mother had intended taking you along, but you put on a turn because you wanted to go stay with Alison. She used to baby-sit you quite often, apparently.'

Rachel was stunned. One wilful, childish act had changed her whole life.

Catching the expression on her face, the old man cursed himself for letting his tongue run away with him. Now the girl would blame herself for everything that happened that night.

'Tell me about Alison,' said Rachel, recovering.

'She came from one of the coastal towns, Taree, I think. In those days the government used to send scholarship students to the bush to work out their bond, and Alison ended up in Corella at your mother's school. She was pretty green, but a lovely kid; took quite a shine to Claire. Hero-worship, I suppose.'

She hadn't even started to live, thought Rachel. She imagined her parents that night, rushing out to the farm in their ridiculous car, finding Alison slaughtered and herself—in what state? Mute with shock by that time, probably. While her father raged through the house looking for the killer, her mother would have tried to soothe the child. Then they would have had to decide what to do.

'Do you ever feel fortunate, Russ?'

'All the time, mate.'

They thought their own thoughts, then Rachel said: 'Who did it?'

'We never found the killer.'

'That's not what I asked.'

He decided to tell her what he knew. It wasn't as if she could do anything stupid: Jenkins was long gone. 'There was a farmhand working on a property about twenty miles away. Gordon Jenkins, his name was. We got a call from the owner's wife one night, said their farmhand was beating his wife, said she couldn't stand the screaming a minute longer.

'I'll never forget that house. Filthy, it was. The wife had bruises every colour of the rainbow...She was just a girl really, but old looking, like a hill-billy. She'd probably been pretty once, in a rabbity sort of way. There were two dirty, snotty-nosed kids: one was a little girl, about five, too quiet— probably got her fair share of the strap—and a baby with a shitty nappy hanging down round its knees. Jesus. I reckon their mother was so far gone she didn't care any more.

'Jenkins was a surly, sinister brute. These days they'd say he had an attitude. While my partner was trying to get him to talk, I had a look around. He had a couple of shotguns on the wall. You didn't need a gun permit in those days, otherwise I would have run him in. But there was something else...Look out!'

But Rachel had already noticed the dusty farm truck bearing down on them from a side street. She measured the distances with her eye, decided she didn't have room to brake without a dangerous skid, and put her foot down. They flew past with centimetres to spare.

Morgan yelled: 'Christ!' and turned to see the farmer leaning out his truck window shaking his fist at them, despite the fact he'd been in the wrong.

Accustomed to the anarchic Sydney traffic, Rachel had scarcely registered the incident. She gave Russ time to regain his composure, then said: 'You were telling me about Gordon Jenkins.'

'Right. When Alison was murdered, we questioned every male within cooee with the slightest blot on his copybook. Bashers, flashers, brawlers, dirty old men, the lot. Always start close to home, I say. I questioned Jenkins myself. He didn't even pretend to give a damn about the murder, just denied all knowledge. Of course his wife swore he was home with her and the kids that night, but I had a poke around, anyway. One of the shotguns was gone.'

'Did you know about Lorraine Stanton's murder, Russ?'

'In Swan Hill? Of course. It was close enough to frighten all the women in this area out of their wits.'

'Did you connect it with Alison's murder?'

'The Victoria Police handled it,' said Russ. 'They were convinced her boyfriend did it, but they never got enough evidence to try him.'

'Similar MO,' said Rachel. 'And Lorraine Stanton was a redhead.'

'You think Jenkins might have done it? A serial killer, here in Corella?' His tone accused her of watching too many American movies.

'We'll probably never know now,' said Rachel.

'The states kept their own records in those days, so we wouldn't have had access to the details of the Stanton murder, and they wouldn't have been thinking about serial killers anyway. Nobody really knew anything about them in those days. If it happened now, the proximity of the murders, the red hair and the age of the victims would ring an alarm, and people would start comparing the forensic evidence.'

'It's all academic, anyhow,' said Morgan. 'Jenkins disappeared years ago.'

'What did he look like?'

'Big bastard, dark.'

'Do you have a photo?'

'No. And there wasn't a single picture of him at his house, which is pretty strange, when you think about it. Most people have a wedding photo at least.'

He probably never married her, thought Rachel. 'What did you do about his wife and kids?'

'I called the social services after we got through with him, but by the time anybody got out there, they'd up and left. And nobody knew where they'd gone.'

A few minutes later they pulled into the hospital parking lot. The hospital was a converted country mansion with extensions tacked on higgledy-piggledy as need arose, reminding Rachel of an

elegant woman dressed in charity handouts. Fortunately, the grove of trees the original owner had
planted a hundred years before had survived the
architectural vandalism, saving the building from
complete shame.

Dr Fred Hollis had grabbed the best room in the
old house for his office. Looking out over huge fig
trees, across the town to the river, and beyond to
the rolling plains, it was an open-ended view, full
of possibility. And longing, perhaps.

The man himself was slight, dapper, grey and
professionally polished, but on this occasion,
nervous. He and Rachel sized each other up, and
the doctor gave his verdict: 'The image of your
mother.'

'You knew her well?'

'I was probably closer to your father, to Tom;
but yes, I knew her. We were part of the same
social group, played tennis, had each other over
for dinner, that sort of thing. You have to make
your own fun in small towns.'

He gestured towards a couch facing the view,
and they sat down.

'You know why I'm here, don't you?' asked
Rachel.

The doctor glanced at Russ Morgan. 'Russ said
you were trying to find out what happened the
night Alison Scott was murdered.'

Rachel nodded. 'The silence has been poisoning

my life, doctor. I've been working on the investigation into the murder of Lisa Broderick in Sydney...'

'Yes, we saw you on television,' said Hollis.

'It was Lisa Broderick's murder that started all this,' said Rachel. 'Something about it triggered an emotional crisis in me. I started having nightmares about a man stalking me, and then I remembered Alison's name. But it was an incident early in the case, in St Bartholomew's, where Lisa Broderick worked, that led me back to Corella, to this hospital. I need to know what happened here the night of the murder.'

Fred Hollis went to the window and stared out along the river road. 'I don't quite know what to tell you.'

'Anything will do. I'll know what's important.'

'We were all at Frank Lomax's house that night, having dinner. It got pretty raucous because Frank had just been promoted. The men had been drinking heavily. Your mother—she was stone-cold sober—left the room to call her babysitter, Alison Scott, the little teacher. When she came back into the room, she was as pale as a ghost. I remember she said: "Something's wrong at the farm, Tom. The phone isn't answering. I let it ring and ring. This isn't like Alison."

'Your father jumped up and they left. It stirred us up. We weren't quite sure whether to call the police or what. In the end we decided Tom could look after himself, and went on with the dinner. The party broke up early, though. Everyone was jittery.

'I'd just walked in the door of my house when the phone rang. It was Grace, the sister in charge of casualty at the hospital. Tom and Claire were there with you, wrapped in a blanket. They said you'd been hurt, and wouldn't let anyone but me look at you. I rushed down and got you into an examining room. Tom was pretty agitated, and started making a ruckus. I think when he saw you with your big frightened eyes sitting there covered in Alison's blood, he realised what could have happened, and lost it. The alcohol didn't help. Your mother was shocked but staying calm for your sake, and I was able to get the story out of her.

'I told her you weren't physically hurt, but that you should be kept in hospital overnight for observation. She wanted to stay with you, but Grace was getting very twitchy because of the noise. I told Claire to take Tom home, that I'd look after you.'

The doctor held out his hands in a gesture of conciliation. 'I know it wasn't perfect—your mother should have been there—but at least you knew me...' He trailed off. 'We're much more careful about separating children from their mothers, these days...'

'So my mother was driving?' Rachel interrupted.

'Oh, yes. Your father wasn't fit to drive. I saw her take the keys from him.'

'So the accident was my mother's fault?'

'Where did you get that idea? A car full of drunk teenagers took a bend too fast and ran into them head-on. There wasn't a thing Claire could do about it.'

Rachel's voice wobbled: 'So when I woke up I was an orphan.'

She isn't as tough as she pretends, thought Russ Morgan.

The doctor grimaced. 'It was the worst night of my life. I've never faced anything harder. It was bedlam when the ambulances arrived. There were five kids in the car, and three of them died. Tom was DOA, and Claire didn't last the night. We had police, paramedics, families, the media milling about. And all this on the same night as the murder. I'll never forget it, and neither will the town.'

A scene from hell, thought Rachel. And I was in the middle of it. No wonder I have a phobia about hospitals.

'When Claire died, I had a talk to Russ, here,' said the doctor. 'He'd guessed you'd been at the farm and had come into the hospital just before they brought the accident victims in. We had a confab and tried to figure out what to

316

do about you. In the end Russ went out to the house and found your aunt's phone number. We thought it best to get you out of here as quickly as possible.'

'What state was I in?'

'Shocked, grief-stricken, scared. We couldn't get a word out of you. I tried to find out what you knew, but you wouldn't talk to me. When your aunt turned up I told her to get you some professional help. I don't know if she ever did.'

'No. I think she decided that a quiet life would heal me. I got some help myself later on...And I became a psychologist.'

'Physician heal thyself,' said the doctor.

'If only,' said Rachel. 'Dr Hollis, there's just one more favour...'

'Anything. And do call me Fred.'

Rachel nodded. 'It's going to sound weird, but I want to see the room I was in.'

'Closure?' asked the doctor, who kept up with the psychology journals.

Rachel smiled: 'Something like that.' More like a compulsion, she thought.

Leaving Russ Morgan in his office, Fred Hollis led Rachel along the hall to one of the examining rooms. The little hospital was pleasant inside, sunny and bright, entirely different from the Dickensian St Bartholomew's where Lisa Broderick had worked. Everybody who passed said hello to their boss. He seemed genuinely well liked. Rachel liked him.

He deposited her in a narrow cubicle in casualty. 'If I'd put you into a ward, it would have left a record,' he explained. 'Then the whole town would have known you were at the murder scene.' He paused. 'Russ and I thought the notoriety would ruin your life.'

Rachel touched his hand. 'I understand. And I'm grateful. Thank you.'

He smiled uncertainly and withdrew, leaving the door ajar.

Rachel sat on the side of the bed and tried to recall being here. It was no good: she had no conscious memory of the room. All that had survived was a deep, atavistic fear. She knew she should go back to Hollis' office, but she stayed on, her mind working overtime, trying to process all she'd heard today.

She was interrupted by the squeak of a trolley outside in the hallway, and looked up. The door opened, and an orderly, a dark-haired, middle-aged man, poked his head in, jumped slightly to see her there, smiled and withdrew. It was then that Rachel knew for sure.

She hurried back to Hollis' office. Head to head, the men looked up as she burst in. 'Russ, you were telling me something about Gordon Jenkins when that truck nearly collected us. Can you remember what it was?'

The tension in her body told him it was important. 'I was about to tell you there had been two bad rapes in the Riverina while Jenkins was living here. But because they happened across the border, the Victoria Police investigated them. They didn't get much of a description from the women, but both of them mentioned the way the bloke stank. After that we called him Stinky.'

He shook his head, as if trying to clear the reek of the murderer out of his nostrils and his memory. 'I noticed Jenkins' BO when I questioned him, but lots of labourers are on the nose, and I didn't make the connection. The murder had driven the rapes clean out of my head, I suppose. It wasn't till about a week later, when someone mentioned the rapes, that I put two and two together. By that time Jenkins had cleared out. I tried to find him, but it was like he'd gone up in smoke. Changed his name, obviously. It was easy to do in those days.

'I'm not proud of missing it. There's no excuse. I buggered it up, and I've spent years wondering if it would come back to haunt me.' He paused, and his voice hardened: 'He wouldn't get by me a second time.'

His face told her what the admission had cost. There was nothing for her to say: every cop had to live with the possibility of making a mistake that cost lives.

When he realised she wasn't going to comment, Hollis looked relieved and said: 'What's all this about, anyway?'

'I think the man who killed Lisa Broderick is the man who killed Alison Scott and tried to kill me. Neville Brady.'

'How do you...'

Rachel cut in. 'Also known as Gordon Jenkins. I don't think it was just the hospital that spooked me at St Bart's that day; it was the janitor as well. When he brushed past me to open the door of the conference room, I recognised him somehow—by his smell, most likely. I'm almost certain now he was the man who murdered Alison and tried to kill me. It frightened me so badly I fainted, but when I woke up, it was gone again. I didn't remember what had done it.'

19

It Was Happening Again

Rachel made a detour to drop Russ Morgan off at his place before she set out to visit her parents' house and Alison's farm on the river road. The old policeman had been keen to go along, but Rachel needed to confront her ghosts alone. Before he got out of the car, she said: 'Did I go to my parents' funeral?'

'Yes. I didn't think it was such a good idea, but Fred Hollis and your aunt said it would be better for you in the long run; something about helping you understand they were dead, that they didn't just run off and leave you. You were at Alison's funeral, too.'

'Was there a children's choir?' asked Rachel.

She's a strange one, he thought, wondering where this was leading. 'Yeah. The kids from Corella North sang at both of them. It was hard on the poor little buggers, but they wanted to do it. A huge turnout, it was. And you'll never guess who showed up...'

'Gordon Jenkins.'

'Yep. Large as life.'

'Coming along to gloat,' said Rachel.

'Probably, but he had a perfect excuse to be there. His little girl was in Alison's first grade class...'

So that's where he'd staked her out, Rachel thought. In the schoolyard of Corella North Public School. If my mother had been redheaded, he might have chosen her.

'Dawn Jenkins,' Morgan was saying. 'Do you remember her?'

Rachel shook her head, wondering how many more shocks awaited her in Corella. Suddenly she wanted to be away. Not knowing if she'd see him again before she left the town, she said goodbye to the old man and thanked him.

'Are you going back now?'

Rachel shrugged. 'Soon, after I have a look around.'

Their eyes locked, and Rachel's expression warned him not to interfere. 'Be careful,' was all he said.

As he was walking up his front path, he heard his name and looked around. 'If you happen to know where my giraffe is, I wouldn't mind having it back,' she said, and drove off before he could respond. Full of surprises, she was.

Before she faced down the past on the river road, Rachel had an appointment with Claire and Tom Addison. They were buried in the old town cemetery, among the last-known addresses of pioneers, Victorian city fathers, farmers, and all the anonymous folk who live and die in small towns and leave nothing except their names. Two simple headstones and a pile of bones were all that remained. And herself.

Standing beside their graves, she opened her bag and took out a photograph of the Addison family—Claire, Tom and the little girl—squinting into the sun on a day just like this, in this town. In the long grass in the sunlight, bareheaded, with the cicadas sawing away, Rachel passed into a waking dream and saw, or thought she saw, remembered, or thought she remembered, the man and woman taking the little girl's hand and swinging her high in the air.

The drone of a mower recalled her, and she made her way back to the car, thinking now of her aunt, and what she'd walked into when she rushed to Corella to bury her sister and brother-in-law and rescue her niece. Growing up, Rachel had taken Louise's guardianship for granted: she lived with her aunt, and it had always been that way. Now she knew what it must have cost. But her aunt's decision to bury Rachel's history with her parents, though understandable, had been wrong; the secret had anchored them both to the past. The adult Rachel knew Louise should have given her the chance to grieve and recover, to forgive herself.

The taste of salt surprised Rachel. Before all this had happened, she'd never been able to cry: now she wondered if she'd ever stop.

In good times, the road to the old Addison house, with graceful houses on big lots on the town side of the river and farms on the other, would be picturesque, but the drought had turned the river into a muddy, sluggish stream, and the fields were parched. On the way Rachel passed a car ferry, and farther on, a pub with a big verandah, ancient shady trees and views along the river to the town. She promised herself she'd stop in for a drink on the way back.

With one eye on the road, Rachel thought about what Russ Morgan and Fred Hollis had told her. They'd risked their careers to protect their friends' child from police questioning, media hysteria and the idle, destructive curiosity of the public, but their good intentions had gone awry. It was no use blaming them: they weren't to know Louise was no better equipped to deal with the aftermath of tragedy than they were. Faced with her young self today, Rachel would organise grief counselling and monitor the child closely for symptoms of post-traumatic stress, but those were simpler times, simpler people.

At least the visit had cleared up the mystery of the fiasco at St Bart's Hospital...was it only three weeks ago? From this distance it seemed like another life and another time. She was sure now that Lisa Broderick's murder, the atmosphere in St Bart's and the deep, subterranean shock of meeting Alison's murderer face to face had forced her sense of abandonment and grief to the surface. Though it didn't solve anything, was only the beginning, it was a relief to be able to name the emotions that had crippled her for so long.

Especially the guilt. Rachel herself had counselled the mother of a four-year-old who'd burned herself badly playing with matches: as they'd taken the little girl away in an ambulance, she had begged her mother for forgiveness. At the same age, Rachel would have been quite capable of understanding her role in the chain of events that changed all their lives. If she hadn't thrown a tantrum and forced her mother's hand, she wouldn't have been at the farm, she wouldn't have ended up in hospital, and her parents wouldn't have been on the wrong road at the wrong time. They'd still be alive.

Irrational though it may have been, she'd blamed herself. It was guilt that had made her collude with Louise in a denial of the past, and guilt that had turned her into a good girl, forever trying to redeem herself.

The biggest bombshell had been the realisation that Gordon Jenkins' trail led all the way from Corella to Crossley Station and perhaps into her own bedroom. Had he realised the police officer on the Broderick case had been the child he'd terrorised at the lonely farmhouse in Corella a quarter of a century ago, or was she just another redhead to him?

The former Addison house was a white bungalow on a couple of acres of land next to a prosperous, well-kept farm. It was meticulously maintained, the owners somehow managing to keep a riotous garden alive despite the drought. The air was full of the scent of grass and flowers, with a pungent overlay of horse manure. A middle-aged woman answered the doorbell, smiled and waited. No city folks' fear or aggression here.

Rachel introduced herself, explained her mission. The woman, whose name was Grace Hart, immediately asked her in, sat her down in a huge plush velvet armchair with crocheted arm rests, and made a pot of tea. Grace Hart's tea-set was Royal Albert, patterned with red-black roses: 'My mother's,' she told Rachel. The room, which was cool and gloomy, shaded from the outside glare by blinds and lace curtains, exhaled lemon furniture polish, pot-pourri and the aroma of baking.

'I just heard on the radio that they've got the fires under control at last,' said Grace Hart, pouring Darjeeling tea through a silver strainer.

A weight dropped from Rachel's shoulders: now she could stop worrying about Mike.

The two women swapped bushfire stories, then, proffering a plate of home-made cupcakes with passionfruit icing, Grace Hart said: 'I remember your people. That pretty schoolteacher and the American pilot. They were quite a dashing couple...' She stopped, embarrassed, remembering what had happened to them.

'Please, it's all right,' said Rachel. 'It was a long time ago.' Yesterday.

'That was a bad year,' said the woman. 'The schoolteacher murdered and then your parents and those teenagers killed in that terrible accident. I was nursing at the hospital then; I was working in casualty that night and saw them all come in...'

This is the Grace who called Fred Hollis that night, thought Rachel. Does she know the whole story or not?

'All those funerals,' continued the woman. 'The kids from the primary school were heartbroken, sobbed their hearts out in the church at your mother's funeral. And at Alison's, of course. She didn't seem much older than some of them.

'These days they'd get counselling, but back then everybody tried to put it behind them. Thought it would go away if you didn't talk about it. Nothing ever goes away, of course; nobody ever really gets over anything.' The gaze from the agate-coloured eyes was sympathetic but shrewd. 'I suppose you know that. And they never did catch the man who killed Alison. It's all water under the bridge now.'

Not quite, thought Rachel.

'But I'm chattering away. I don't get many visitors out here. Would you like to take a look around? I'll be in the kitchen if you want me.'

Suddenly apprehensive, Rachel toured the house. It seemed much smaller than her fragmentary memories of it. To her surprise, she immediately recognised one of the bedrooms as her own by the scent of honeysuckle through the open window. As she stood looking out into the backyard, a sharp image of the toy giraffe flashed into her mind. Her father had bought it for her. Tom. The thought made her sad, but sadness was an improvement. Maybe when all this was over she could enjoy the luxury of simple grief.

Nothing else in the house was familiar, so she thanked Grace Hart and left. Watching from the window, Grace saw Rachel turn left, and realised that she must be going to visit the old farmhouse where the little teacher had been murdered. It wasn't safe out there now that a biker had moved in. Sometimes, in the middle of the night, she heard the roar of motorbikes speeding along the river road. Suddenly uneasy, she picked up the phone.

The river road was strangely deserted, a dreamscape with no soundtrack. In the past hour Rachel had seen only one other car, which had overtaken her when she'd pulled into Mrs Hart's house. The only other habitation between Rachel's childhood home and Alison's farm was a derelict-looking shack that seemed to have been taken over by hippies, judging by the sarongs and tattered jeans on the line. Someone was home: the front door was open, and a car was parked in the yard.

The tension increased as she moved closer to her goal. Wondering if she should have let Russ Morgan come along for moral support, she rehearsed what she'd tell the new owners. They might not take kindly to a stranger stirring up their household ghosts.

Alison's place was the end of the line; beyond it lay fields, scrubby bush and the river. Outside, old machinery lay rusting in the weather, along with an ancient red truck with no wheels. There were traces of a flower garden in front and a patch of vegetable gone to seed at the side of the house, but thistles and nettles were taking over.

It was eerily quiet, and the heat struck like a hammer. The smell of eucalyptus, dry grass and dust was hypnotic. Rachel parked the car, got out and looked around. She called out, but there was no sign of life and no movement from the house or the shed at the back. Like most women, Rachel seldom moved anywhere without her handbag, but because of the heat and the weight of her gun and mobile phone, she considered locking it in the car. At the last minute the small, undeniable voice of caution told her to take it with her.

The front door refused to open when she tried the handle, but the back door was not locked. Hesitant now, Rachel eased herself into the kitchen of the house, leaving the back door open for a quick retreat. Despite the squalor, someone had been using the kitchen: there were two cups on the draining board, and on the old pine table a jar of instant coffee and a jam jar half-full of white sugar. Beer cans spilled out of a rubbish bin. Squatters probably. She hoped they wouldn't walk in and catch her trespassing.

Moving through the house, she found a bedroom containing an iron bedstead with a stained mattress, a grubby Indian cotton bedspread and pillow. Beside the bed lay a pile of clothes and a tattered Stephen King paperback. Backing out of the room, she stepped on a framed religious text and the glass shattered underfoot, making her jump guiltily.

In the hallway, the bare boards creaked as she made her way to what used to be Alison's bedroom. It had been the best room in the house, with a bay window with a padded window seat and a view of the river screened by weeping willows. She crossed to the window. The backyard was overgrown with brittle, yellow, knee-high grass, but the willows, with their deep thirsty roots, were clinging to life on the muddy riverbank.

The room was empty, but Rachel's memory furnished it with Alison's possessions. Against one wall stood Alison's precious brass bed with flower-patterned china knobs and a cover crocheted by her grandmother. A huge, frightening wardrobe of dark polished wood loomed against another: before she'd gone to bed that night, she'd made Alison open it to prove their were no creatures lurking inside. And over there was an old-fashioned dressing-table with an oval mirror, hats and beads hanging from its posts. Alison's rocking chair, with a colourful Afghan rug thrown over its back crouched near the window: she'd sat there in the half-dark on that twilit night reading Rachel a bedtime story. Concentrating hard, Rachel conjured up a little girl in a red dress from the cover of the book.

Something strange was happening to time: it had become elastic, hallucinatory, giving Rachel the sensation of moving under water. She was simultaneously in an abandoned, empty house and in Alison's home the night of the murder. She could even hear Alison's favourite music.

It occurred to Rachel that old people must experience the world this way, with layer upon layer of memory superimposed like the rings in a tree or a rock; living in parallel time zones; discerning young faces under the old; communing with the long-dead. Her breath, which she'd been holding against the dust, exploded in a sigh.

The living room waited across the hall. There the unquiet ghosts dwelt: Alison's ghost, the ghost of her childhood and the ghost of the monster, the man who smelt like death. Feet like lead, she approached.

The room was empty, its faded wallpaper peeling in loops; the carpet, which had once been fawn, was now a crazy quilt of stains and cigarette burns. A tattered Holland blind excluded the worst of the midday glare and turned the light inside the room into liquid amber. An empty stage set. Rachel halted at the door and gazed in.

The walls drew her eyes, but they'd been papered over since her time, leaving no trace of blood, not even the faintest stain, but under the grime on the carpet, faded patches showed, where someone had scrubbed out the bloodstains.

Then the scene changed, and Rachel was back in that night. Against the wall on her right was the armchair where Alison had been sitting, reading under a lamp, and to her right the stereo with the record turning, turning...And here, just inside the door, was the place where she had stumbled over the body, its head a chaos of blood and brain tissue.

Shotgun blast at close range, thought the adult Rachel, the police officer.

The child continued her rendezvous with the past. On the floor beside Alison's body lay her spectacles, covered in blood, the glass smashed. Snapping out of the trance, Rachel rushed for the bathroom, knowing instinctively where it was, dropped her bag on the floor and retched into the stained, reeking lavatory bowl. Recovering, she washed her hands and cleaned out her mouth under a rusty trickle from the basin tap.

Shaken, she returned to the hallway to look for her hiding place. Alison's old raincoat, a wool coat and ancient hooded parka had hung there, and muddy gumboots, walking shoes and a pair of knee-high leather boots had been aligned in military precision on a folded newspaper underneath. Even now she could recapture the smell—plastic and mould, rubber and leather, shoe polish and dust. The scent of Alison on the coats. Later, the spoor of the predator and her own acrid urine.

The ruby glass in the front door had been broken since that night and boarded up, throwing the hallway just inside the entrance into deep shadow. Rachel could just make out the coat hooks. They were empty now. Leaning against the wall, she relived her claustrophobic fear as the beast had lumbered around the house looking for her, and the sheer terror as he had approached her hiding place.

As if her own nightmare had suddenly come to life, the floorboards in the kitchen creaked. Dread took Rachel's breath away. It's just a squatter, she told herself, but the spell of the past bound her still, and she couldn't bring herself to move or to call out. The front door, the only escape from the intruder, was locked. She was trapped: it was happening again.

Back to the wall, taut with tension, she listened as the back door slammed shut and heavy footsteps crossed the kitchen and entered the dining room. Then they stopped. Rachel tried not to breathe. Perhaps he doesn't know I'm here, she prayed. But her car was parked outside: of course he knew. She reached for her bag and gun and realised with a spurt of panic that she'd left it in the bathroom.

To get to the bedrooms, the man would have to enter the hallway. And then he'd see her.

The footsteps resumed. He left the living room, entered the hall, and sensing a human presence, turned. She saw him first: his eyes hadn't yet adjusted to the gloom. Silhouetted against the light from the back of the house, he looked enormous and menacing. She couldn't see his face, but she could smell him. Stinky. Gordon Jenkins. Neville Brady. The trinity. This was the reek that had made Rachel faint at St Bartholomew's, when he'd been so close she could see the pores in his greasy skin. This is what had triggered her journey into the past.

Hunter and prey, their eyes locked. It was the oldest relationship in the world. He was savouring her fear, in no hurry, his double-barrelled shotgun pointed nonchalantly at the floor. He had her cornered. He had all the time in the world.

Brady must have followed her all the way from Sydney, she realised, but she'd been too preoccupied to notice. It would have been his car that had passed her back at Grace Hart's: he'd hidden it somewhere—in the shed, probably—and waited.

This was the time to fight, but Neville Brady's desire to annihilate her was almost irresistible. Rachel knew now she'd spent her life waiting for this man to find and kill her the way he'd killed Alison Scott. Without speaking, he gestured with the gun, and she understood that she was to pass him and go into the living room. The prospect of entering the killing field made her weak with dread, but she obeyed. Anything to gain time.

Passing him, she gagged and shied, noticing the sheathed knife on his belt, the knife that had hacked the life out of Lisa Broderick. He prodded her impatiently with the barrel of the shotgun. Then they faced each other in the room where he'd slaughtered Alison Scott, and he smiled. It was a terrible smile, exultant. She couldn't seem to look away. Faced with death, she was paralysed.

She'd never know how long he'd held her with his butcher's eyes, but suddenly the roar of a powerful motorbike rent the silence. Brady's smile faltered, and for the first time he seemed uncertain. The display of weakness snapped Rachel out of her torpor. Brady was a brute without a conscience, but he was human, too: he could make mistakes. He'd had it too easy in the past, had chosen easy game, but he'd underestimated Rachel Addison: she was not going to bare her neck. She was fully alert now, waiting.

Brady pointed the gun at her head and said: 'Keep your mouth shut or I'll kill you.' His voice was flat, unemotional, perfectly persuasive.

Outside, the motorbike roared around to the back of the house and the rider cut the engine. 'Hello?' he called.

He's seen my car, thought Rachel, hoping

against hope the presence of strangers would make him tread warily.

There was silence for a moment—as the biker checked out the car, no doubt—then the back door opened and footsteps sounded in the kitchen. Brady, who'd been listening intently, smiled and motioned Rachel out of the way with his gun to get a clean line of fire.

He's going to shoot him in cold blood, thought Rachel. Her bowels churned. If Brady was getting rid of the witness, it was proof he intended to kill her. Knowing she had nothing to lose, she decided to try to save the stranger. Too many people had died already. 'Run for your life!' she shouted.

Brady made a lunge at Rachel as if to shut her up, but she jumped backwards. As Brady hesitated, Rachel tried to anticipate his moves. With two shots before he needed to reload, he could dispatch them both in less than a minute. But was that what he wanted? She thought not. Having witnessed Brady's handiwork, thought long and deeply about the impulses that drove him, Rachel believed she understood him as well as any normal human being could understand a killer. She was certain he'd want to kill her slowly, savouring her fear and pain, prolonging his own pleasure; he'd go after the squatter first. It would give her only a split second to act, but it might be enough.

Betting her life on her instincts and training, she tensed, ready to hit the ground, run, fight: whatever it took to survive.

She analysed the terrain. The front door was locked; she'd never be able to get to the bathroom and her gun without being shot or caught; and Brady was blocking the back exit. There was a clear run to the window, though.

In the meantime, in the farmhouse, it was as if time had stopped: in the kitchen the squatter still dithered; in the living room Brady still waited.

Then the squatter made his decision, and as Rachel watched, helpless, a face appeared in the doorway, the face of a nondescript, fair youth, almost a boy still. When the youth saw the black, empty eyes of Brady's shotgun pointing at him, his own small blue eyes widened in disbelief and skittered to Rachel in mute appeal. Then the gun thundered and his chest exploded; there was one last terrible gurgling moan from the man, and the room filled up with the acrid smell of the shot and the reek of death.

The reality was worse than all her imaginings. Sickened, horrified, Rachel fought the urge to throw herself on the floor, scream, beg for mercy. It was then Brady made his mistake. Gun raised, he moved towards the squatter to make sure, forgetting Rachel for a moment. Arms raised to protect her face, Rachel threw herself at the window, and was gone in a crashing and splintering of glass.

Bleeding but not badly hurt, she scrambled to her feet and took off around the house. There was no use trying to get to her car: he could see it from the window: she'd be dead before she got the engine started. Her only chance was to reach the bush and try to make her way back along the river road towards town and safety. The spindly gum trees wouldn't be much cover, but she was younger, fitter and faster than Brady and should be able to stay out of range of his shotgun.

Stumbling at the sound of a blast, she risked a look back. Brady had shot out the front tyre of her car. Half-sobbing, she cursed herself for her pride. Why hadn't she promised Russ Morgan she'd drop in before she left town? He would have raised the alarm if she hadn't turned up, or at least come looking for her.

By now she'd run flat out for fifteen minutes in the dense afternoon heat, and was tiring. She was parched, her arms were bleeding steadily, and insect bites and scratches covered every inch of bare skin. Soon her fair skin would begin to blister. Finally, figuring that she'd hear him if he got close, she slowed to a trot. When the panic receded a little, and she was more rational, she realised she was running from her own imagination, that there was nobody following her. Brady was simply letting her run herself into exhaustion. He'd assume she would flee to the hippie house or to Grace Hart's for help: all he had to do was drive there and wait or cruise the river road until she broke cover. It was then, as she realised there was no asylum anywhere on the river road, that Rachel came close to giving up.

Hunkering down in some shade, she tried to psych herself up and think strategically. She closed her eyes, then jerked them open as the biker's heart exploded again in her mind's eye. Breathing deeply, she tried to calm herself. The road was the quickest route to safety, but the most dangerous. She couldn't run on the bitumen for fear of discovery, but had to stay close, in case she got lost. And though the bush gave her cover, it was inhospitable, full of insects, thorns, potholes, hanging branches. She longed for a real rest, but the prospect of being caught out here at night with Brady on her trail drove her onwards.

Some time later, it might have been five minutes or fifteen—Rachel was past knowing—she picked up the sound of a car approaching. Stopping, she listened hard: it was coming from the direction of town, so it was unlikely to be the killer. Frantic with hope, she ran to the side of the road, hanging back in the undergrowth in case he turned up.

When the car got close enough for her to see, she realised that the driver was Fred Hollis, with

Russ Morgan in the passenger seat. Screaming for help, she scrambled though the shrubbery and burst on to the roadway to flag them down. The car slowed, then skidded to a halt as they recognised her, and the two men jumped out. Weak with relief, Rachel ran towards them. In the confusion, none of them heard Brady's car until it rounded the bend and was almost upon them.

'Get down, it's Brady!' warned Rachel, racing for cover behind Fred Hollis's car. 'He's just killed a man!'

As Rachel had expected, Brady was driving slowly, scanning the verges. At the last minute, surprised by the sight of a stationary car, he lifted his foot from the accelerator. As if in slow motion, Rachel saw Russ Morgan raise his hunting rifle and fire. Neville Brady's head snapped back, then lolled forward, and his car ran off the road and smashed into a tree. There was the pungent smell of oil and spilled petrol, and silence descended once more on the river road.

The former policeman and the doctor glanced at Rachel and saw she was safe, then walked across the road to the car and peered in. Fred Hollis felt the man's neck for a pulse and shook his head: the driver was dead.

'It's Gordon Jenkins,' said Russ Morgan.

'He shouldn't have tried to run us down,' said Hollis, and the two men exchanged a long look.

The official version was now in place.

Rachel remained rooted to the spot, torn between relief and rage. History seemed destined to repeat itself forever. Once again they had stepped in to save her, good people convinced they were doing the right thing. For them, and for Neville Brady, the case that had begun in Corella almost a quarter of a century ago was closed, but for Rachel, Brady's death was simply another milestone on a long journey.

What this ending had denied her, she would later come to understand, was the catharsis of judgment and punishment, the rituals of retribution. These were necessary, she recognised, not only for the sake of society and the murdered girls' families, but for her own peace of mind. In the glare of public scrutiny, Brady would have ceased to be a terrifying phantom and been exposed as the stunted, warped and foul-smelling human being he had been all along.

Then, perhaps, she could have stopped dreaming about him.